Kayden: The Past

By Chelle Bliss

Chelle Bliss

Dedication

To my grandparents ~
thank you for always being there for me and showing me love. I adore you both, but sadly this is the only page you can read.

To my brother ~
I love you. Thank you for your love, support, and never reading the books I've written.
I'm proud of the man you've become.

Acknowledgements

Thank you to Brenda Wright and Rebecca Barney for making my book as close to perfect as possible. Without you two lovely ladies I'd be lost. Brenda, thank you for listening to my rants throughout my writing process and cheering me on when I felt lost. Rebecca, thank you for swooping in at the last minute and helping finalize Kayden, you're invaluable.

To my beta readers: Mandee Migliaccio, Deb Schultz of Rough Draft Book Blog, Kathy Coopmans of Panty Dropping Book Blog, Amanda Lanclos of Crazy Cajun Book Addicts, Skye Callahn, Christina Omar, Kelly Adkins, Maria Reyes, Stephanie Byrd, Amanda Davis, Wendy Shatwell of Bare Naked Words, Ronda Brimeyer, Shannon Ryan, Tonya Clark, Tonya Mabe, Krystyn Katsibubas, Nikita Alexis, Stephanie Powell, Erika Lynn, Verna McQueen of Verna Loves Books, Brenda Wright and Angie Johnson of Twinsie Talk Book Reviews, Tina Mason, Tracy McKay of Books, Coffee, and Wine, Melanie Lowery of Sassy Mum Book Blog, Joann Hohl of The Book Junkie, MaryAnn Litton from MA Book Review, Shannon White, Kathy Lee-Herbst of Abibliophobia, and Rachelle Marie -- without you ladies I'd go crazy and would've chewed my fingernails off.

To my readers, thank you for all your kind words and messages. I love each and every one of you. You're friendship and support has meant the world to me. Thank you for giving me the courage to continue writing and for wanting to know more about Kayden. I hope he lives up to your dreams.

To my friend and writing buddy, Skye Callahan, thank you for keeping me on track and always being there to sprint. I couldn't have stayed on track without you. I'm honored to call you a friend.

Thank you to Rachel Brookes for saving me at the final minute with my edits. You're help solving the mysterious track issue in Word stopped me from having a meltdown.

Thank you to Joni Payne and Melissa Gill of Feisty Girls Book Blog for organizing my release blitz and first blog tour for Kayden. To Ing Cruz of As The Pages Turn, the one that gives a gentle fuck you, thank you for our 'chats' and planning a Kayden tour for me. I adore the hell out of you. Angie Stanton-Johnson and Brenda Wright of Twinsie Talk Book Blog for also organizing a tour and just being kick ass girls.

Last, but not least, to my girls - Tara and Dawn of Sizzling Pages and the amazing Kelly Adkins. Thank you for all your Voxer messages and making me laugh each day. You're some sassy bitches and I love you for it - Vaginas United.

Kayden: The Past

Kayden: The Past Copyright © 2013 Chelle Bliss
Published by Chelle Bliss

All rights reserved. No part of this book may be reproduced or transmitted in any form, including electronic or mechanical, without written permission from the publisher, except in the case of brief quotations embodied in critical articles or reviews.

This is a work of fiction. Names, characters, businesses, places, events, and incidents are either the products of the author's imagination or used in a fictitious manner. Any resemblance to actual persons, living or dead, or actual events is purely coincidental. This book is licensed for your personal enjoyment only.

This book may not be re-sold or given away to other people. If you would like to share this book with another person, please purchase an additional copy for each person you share it with. If you are reading this book and did not purchase it, or it was not purchased for your use only, then you should return it to the seller and purchase your own copy. Thank you for respecting the author's work.

Published: Chelle Bliss 2nd January 2014:
authorchellebliss@gmail.com
Editing: Brenda Wright
Proof-reader: Rebecca Barney
Cover Design © Stephanie Mooney
Formatting by: Brenda Wright
Chapter Headers & Other Graphics:
Canstock: http://www.canstockphoto.com/

This book is intended for a mature audience.

Prologue

Why?

I was an addict.

Sophia didn't know this about me when we met – when I stole her heart.

I struggle every day with my sobriety, and Sophia is my compass. She's what keeps me grounded and always points me in the right direction. She doesn't nag or yell but smothers me in her love and understanding.

Sophia asked to hear my story, my past. She wanted to know everything about me…what led me to her. I gave her a condensed version – one that is closer to PG-13 compared to the NC-17 reality that I lived. No matter how much the person you love the most, the one who is the center of your universe asks about your past, you never give the full truth. I never want Sophia to compare herself to any of the women or experiences that I've had before her. Sophia is perfection in my eyes. No one could ever compare to her.

Kayden: The Past

I'd like to say my life began again when I met Sophia, that I was given a clean slate. Sophia met me at the point in my life where I had given up on love. My life consisted of work and pleasure – pleasure from the unattached sexual relationships and the booze that had filled my nights.

When my life spiraled out of control, Sophia caught me in her web of security and love. She is my savior, the only thing that is true in my life. She can't know my entire story. Who would want to know the true story of the love of their life, the father of their child?

The thought of Sophia being with another man makes my skin crawl and pisses me off. She's mine, and I'd like to think that I've been the only man in her life and the first one to taste her, but I know I'm lying to myself. Ignorance is bliss, and I'd rather stay in the dark.

After our child was born, I thought it was necessary to get help to control my drinking. I needed to make sure I never walked down the path of self-destruction again. I had too much to lose. For the first time in my life, there was something more important than myself or even Sophia. There's a tiny little life that depends on me and needs my love and adoration.

I didn't want to go to group counseling – I've done that before, and it sucked; it wasn't more than a temporary fix. I needed something to get to the root of my addiction and allow me to find other ways to cope with the pressures in life besides at the bottom of a bottle. The counselor told me to write down the major events in my life – the ones that caused my drinking to go out of control or drove me to drink. He said I needed to understand the cycle. What came first – the booze or the problems? He asked me to write a journal about my life. Everyone who I could remember that triggered my drinking, use of drugs, and events that were caused by my addiction that had an impact on my life. I didn't see the use in writing it for someone else to read and analyze, but he said I would understand it in time.

Where do I start the tangled mess that was my life? Do I start with my first taste of booze, the first sniff of coke, or the crazy bitches I've experienced? There will be bits that I leave out; things I don't want the world to know. I've included the ones that show what has molded me into the man I am today. The ones that will fill in the gaps on my troubled journey that Sophia and I overcame and show the depths of my depravity and addiction before Sophia walked into my life and turned my world upside down.

I'll start at the beginning, what led me off the path of righteousness through my moment of self-destruction and finally salvation in the arms of a loving woman too good to be mine.

Chapter 1

High School ~ Mindy

My high school years started with a bang. I had my first drink before the start of my freshman year. My friends and I stole a bottle of Black Bull Whiskey from my parents and sat behind the garage gulping it down as quickly as possible. It was dusk, and lightning bugs were dotting the air in the large wooded backyard. We sat in a circle passing the bottle around, taking swigs, and trying not to cough from the burning in our throats.

The taste was strong, but the feeling it gave me was unforgettable. The lightheaded loopy feeling that was followed by uncontrollable laughter is a memory that will forever be burned in my mind. Our fun was interrupted by my mother's voice. "Kayden Michaels, get in here, now." Her usage of my full name made all the hairs on my body stand up.

Everyone scattered running back to their homes, leaving me to take the fall. I grabbed the bottle off the ground and walked towards the garbage cans hoping to discard the evidence. As my hand touched the lid, my mother's fingers closed over my hand.

"What the hell are you doing?" she asked.

I stood there for a moment stuttering, trying to come up with a good excuse. My mind went blank as I looked in her eyes. She caught me red handed-without a viable excuse or plausible deniability. I gave her an innocent smile, "I'm sorry, mom." I had nothing else to say.

"Did you take that from the house?"

"I didn't think you'd notice," I said without thinking.

Her face grew red; the anger oozed off her skin like perspiration. "In the house, now," she spat. My feet felt heavy, and my head swam with all of the ways I'd be punished. "Throw the bottle out first."

I did as told, knowing I would have to be smarter in the future.

That night I was lectured for hours and hours. When my father came home, all hell broke loose. I got the belt that night along with being grounded for two weeks. Thankfully I still had a month left before school started; plenty of time to still have some fun and experience new things.

I bided my time and planned with my friends over the phone for the remaining days of summer vacation. I had a large group of friends, boys who had my back, except the moment my mom came screaming out of the house. We grew up in the same neighborhood spread out across a couple streets and we were thick as thieves. We built forts together as children, and now, our creativity was becoming a little more… delinquent. My boys were Ron, Scott, Freddie, and Tiny. There were more, but we were the core five.

Kayden: The Past

The five who were inseparable through grade school, but life changes and friends often fade away.

Scott was my best friend; he and I used to have sleep overs when we were kids. We loved Batman and all things super hero related, but our interests changed as we grew. Scott's sister, Mindy, was hot as fuck. I used to go over there just to catch a glimpse of her, but she was a rotten bitch. She hated Scott and by relation, me. She always treated us like shit, but she still gave me a boner.

They planned a party for my release from the Michaels' Prison Facility. Scott's parents were going to be out of town, and luckily for us, it coincided with my freedom. The party wasn't really for me, but I liked that they waited until the end of my solitary confinement to throw the damn thing. I would have climbed the fucking walls knowing they were partying their asses off while I sat in my bedroom and played Pong.

I put on my best pair of Z. Cavariccis with a black silk shirt and misted myself with Drakkar. I checked my hair making sure every hair was perfect. My brown hair was short in the front and long in the back; mullets were hot – who the fuck ever picked that hairstyle should be fucking shot. My face, thankfully, was pimple-free unlike some of the kids at school. My eyes were always my best feature – they were jade green, but changed depending on my clothes. The black shirt I picked helped my eyes stand out against my tanned skin.

"Where you going, Kayden?" I heard my father say from the living room as my hand touched the door knob.

"The guys and I are going roller skating, it's a late skate," I replied, closing my eyes waiting for a response. I needed a reason why I was dressed up. Going to hang with the boys or play sports wouldn't match my clothing. We always went to the rink, and I knew my father wouldn't question me any further.

"Midnight, Kayden. Don't be late or you'll get another week." I knew it was pointless to argue.

"Okay," I said as I opened the door and closed it behind me. I felt like I broke free from a long term jail sentence. Two weeks in the scheme of life is nothing, but when you've only lived about six hundred weeks total – it's an eternity.

I inhaled the warm sticky air, pulling it into my lungs, and felt the gentle breeze on my skin. The weather would be changing soon, and the Ohio winter would grip us causing everyone to go into hibernation.

The gang assembled on the street corner waiting for me. Scotty lived a couple of streets over, and we travelled on foot together through the fields and cut through the backyards. The light of the house came into view through the trees and the music was a whisper in the air as we drew closer. We moved quicker not wanting to waste another minute.

I reached the door first, and it moved slightly with each beat of the bass. The sound of "Walk This Way" blared as I opened the front door and stepped inside. There were people everywhere, filling the stairway and all the rooms. We squeezed through the crowd to find Scott.

He was in the kitchen filling up glasses from a keg and handing them out with a smile on his face. We wrestled together in middle school and spent the summer working out together to get ready for the upcoming season.

Scott spotted us across the room. "Come on over here guys, grab a drink," he said.

We grabbed our red plastic cups and made our way into the living room. There were so many girls; I

Kayden: The Past

didn't know where to look first. I bumped into Mindy when I wasn't paying attention, spilling my drink on her top. She shrieked when the cold liquid soaked her top, outlining her breasts.

"Damn, I'm so sorry, Mindy," I said.

"Jackass," she said as she walked away, she may have called me a jackass, but at least she acknowledged my existence.

The rest of the night I spent flirting with other girls and made out with one, but I pictured Mindy in my mind the entire time.

I didn't drink too much; I couldn't afford more time in the MPF. I left the party in time to return home by midnight and avoid any grilling or possibility of the smell of beer on my breath being discovered by my dad.

The house was dark when I walked inside; my parents were in their bedroom watching Johnny Carson and waiting to see if I made it home by midnight. I knocked on their door "I'm home, night."

"Night, Kayden," my mom said. She didn't have to tell me, but I knew she was thankful that I wasn't late. She didn't want to hear my dad's shit about my behavior lately. Crawling in bed, I grabbed my Walkman off the nightstand and pressed the play button. I lay in the darkness listening to "Livin' on a Prayer" by Bon Jovi and thought about Mindy's tits glistening through her wet t-shirt.

High school helped develop my love of women and alcohol. I wrestled and made the varsity team my sophomore year. I worked out like a man driven with a purpose—I wanted to be the leanest and most muscular guy on the mat. Being a member of the team made girls notice me more than they did previously. The singlet, the little tight uniform, I wore helped show off my manhood. I was a beast on the mat; my opponents knew I would take them down, but that never stopped them from trying. No one was faster or stronger in my weight class. I was the champ.

Sophomore and junior year, I found myself in trouble with the law more than once. We did dumb ass things that we thought were funny and harmless, but my parents didn't see it that way. My first run in with the law came at the hands of my friends. A dare is something I could never ignore – no stupid teenage boy ever backs down no matter how stupid or risky.

We were walking back from a party across town when Freddie turns around, "I dare one of you to walk your drunken ass into the police station and ask them a random question."

The alcohol in my body must have altered my thinking because I took that challenge and didn't think twice. "I'll fucking do it," I said as everyone came to a complete stop.

"You're fucking crazy," Tiny said. "You're gonna get arrested."

"I'm too smart to get caught; I'll take the dare. You guys are pussies."

I walked toward the police station door with wobbly legs and tried to figure out what I'd ask. My palms grew sweatier with every step. I squinted when the light streaming through the door shone on my face. I grabbed the handle, took a deep breath, and pulled it open with authority.

A man sat behind the front desk and looked up when he heard the door close behind me. "Can I help

Kayden: The Past

you, son?" he eyed me suspiciously. The town was so small and devoid of action that running a stop sign was a major offense and gossip worthy.

I leaned on the desk steadying myself, "What time is curfew?" I'd like to think that I was wittier than that or had some great line, but I drew a blank and concentrated more on not puking than the actual words falling from my lips.

"Have you been drinking?" he asked.

"No, sir. I just want-tid-to make sure I'm not out past curfew," I said and belched. *Fuck, what an idiot.*

"It's already past curfew, and you've obviously been drinking. I can smell the beer on your breath." He stood up and walked around the desk and stood right in front of me. I didn't make a move to leave, just stood there like my feet were super glued to the floor. "You're not going anywhere, son. Come with me and we'll decide what to do with you."

"Do with me?" I asked.

"Yes, I'll let my superior decide if we're going to arrest you or just call your parents to pick you up." Neither option was good. I was going to be in deep shit no matter the decision.

I followed him into an office and sat there. I knew the guys had split by now knowing nothing good came out of their little dare and my stupid ass needed to always be the one with the biggest balls. I sat there for what felt like eternity before the door to the office swung open, and my dad stood in the doorway looking like he had murder on his mind.

"Let's go, Kayden."

"Is that all you're going to say?" I asked.

"I have no words right now. Get your ass up."

I stood up and my stomach felt like someone was doing cartwheels inside. I always hated when my dad was pissed off, especially when he had no words to express his feelings. I followed him to the car with my eyes staring at the ground. I climbed into my dad's orange Chevy Vega and closed the door softly. I wanted to disappear. I stared out the window as he pulled out of the parking lot.

I closed my eyes, the motion of the car causing my eyes to hurt and my stomach to gurgle. A sharp pain woke me from my slumber as my face hit the car window. My dad had slammed his fist into my face; cold cocked me while I wasn't looking. "You're a stupid fucker, Kayden," his fist hit me again, "What the fuck were you thinking?"

The pain drew me out of the alcohol haze and I could feel my blood almost begin to boil. "Don't you dare fucking hit me, again," I said.

"What are you going to do about it?" his fist started to move in my direction, and I moved avoiding another blow.

"I don't know if you noticed, Dad… but I'm bigger than you now. Don't push me," I said staring at him in the eyes.

"Are you threatening me?"

"No. I'm just telling you I won't take your shit anymore. I'm not that scared little kid who will hide under the covers. If you want to hit me, at least do it like a man. Don't hit me when I'm not looking."

"I brought you into this world, and I'll take you out," he said with a look of such hatred, unlike anything I had ever seen before.

"I'll go out bringing you down with me, remember that." The car stopped, and I climbed out, preferring walking home to being in the car with that

Kayden: The Past

bastard any longer. I was so angry with him; it took everything I had not to physically fight back in that moment. I knew I had to get away from him and give us both time to cool off. I walked to Scott's house and found refuge on his floor for the evening. Tomorrow I'd face the music, and I prayed that neither one of us would speak of that moment again.

I studied hard and wanted to give myself every opportunity to a college scholarship, but my senior year everything started to fall apart. In October, my parents sat me down and told me the worst news a kid could ever hear; they were getting divorced. Everything fell apart quickly after that 'talk'.

My dad moved out, and my mom immersed herself in her work. Money became something just out of reach, and we never had enough. Dad didn't contribute his share to household expenses or help out with my team costs. Wrestling, besides girls, was my one true love. I watched it and studied it like an obsessed fan. Without money, I couldn't continue to play. My mom apologized over and over again, and I knew she meant it, but my dad, the one person I thought would understand my love of the sport, didn't seem to give a fuck.

I quit the wrestling team half way through the season, right after my eighteenth birthday. I know it pissed off my teammates and my coach, but we didn't have extra money to pay the team fees and barely paid the household bills each month. It ripped my heart out; my one true reason to do well and achieve in school had vanished. Not only did my family disintegrate, but so did my only way to attend college and the reason I stayed out of trouble.

I started working to fill the void after school and help my mom pay the bills. My life became something entirely not my own. I needed to escape my new reality. I found other things to occupy my time. They were the only things that made me forget the bullshit that filled my life.

A friend, who will remain nameless, gave me my first taste of cocaine towards the end of senior year. A small bump, but it rocked my world. I'm not condoning drugs, but the rush it gave me is unlike anything I've ever experienced and spent the rest of my life chasing. I knew it was something I couldn't do again, at least not anytime soon. I needed to stay on track and graduate from high school.

I worked at night and tried to stay awake during the day in class. I wasn't always successful keeping my eyes open; the boredom of hearing a teacher give a monotone lecture was better than any sleeping pill I've taken in my life. I wanted to kiss the ground and thank my lucky stars the day senior exams rolled around. I had made it and done well enough that no matter my exam scores, I'd receive my diploma.

My mom had a new boyfriend, Joe, and he occupied her free time by the time graduation day arrived. I was nearly blind from my mother snapping so many pictures; she wanted to capture every moment of her oldest child graduating from high school, an event she never experienced for herself.

My mom found out she was pregnant with me at the beginning of her senior year, and she dropped out to raise me and work full-time. I have a younger brother and sister, but we were never really close. The age gap was too great, and we were nothing alike. They were close, but I was the outsider.

"Is dad coming today?" I asked as she placed the small pink camera in her purse.

Kayden: The Past

"I don't know, baby. I haven't spoken to him in a long time. I sent him the invitation; the rest is up to him," she said before kissing me on the cheek. I knew with her words that he wouldn't be there. He barely even acknowledged my existence since he left months ago.

As I walked down the aisle, I looked through the crowd trying to find him, but he wasn't there. I don't know why I even fucking bothered; I knew the bastard wouldn't be there. Besides the money he made, he wasn't missed in the house. He was a miserable bastard and not very loving. Things had been calmer, and my mom and I got along better without his sorry ass around. I sat there stewing about my feelings, or lack thereof, for my father while everyone gave speeches that I had tuned out.

The kid next to me stood up, and it was my queue that I'd be next. My moment had finally arrived; high school official ended the second I walked across the stage and shook the hand of the principal. I could hear the cheers from the crowd and the hoots of my mom from a distance.

There would be no graduation party filled with family afterward. My mom had to work, and there wasn't extra cash to pay for a party. I understood and had enough to do that evening to fill the time and celebrate. Scott's family was throwing a party, followed by a party for all his friends, without the older crowd to bring us down.

My friends and I gathered in front of the school after throwing our caps in the air. Our parents took pictures of us as a group; none of us knew how close we'd be after high school. They were going off to college all over the country while I'd stay home to work and figure out my future. We still had the summer to party and hangout, but I knew shit would change soon enough, and I'd be left behind.

I had a mission for the evening of graduation—Mindy. I've liked her for years, and she hardly noticed me, but tonight that would change. She left for college two years ago, and I've changed and grown into a man during her absence. She'd be mine tonight... paybacks are a bitch.

I strolled into Scott's backyard shortly after nine, and the party was already in full-swing. The family had cleared out; a bonfire was roaring in the middle of the yard, and people were everywhere. I found Scott in his usual spot, dispensing drinks.

"Dude, can you believe it's all fucking over?" he asked handing me a drink.

"I thought this day would never come." I sipped the beer letting it run down my throat. "The last couple of months fucking sucked. I'm ready for whatever's next," I said.

"I can't wait to get out of this shit hole town and head off to Chicago for school. I can't believe I got into Northwestern," he said with a smile.

"I'm happy for you. Maybe I'll come out and see you sometime. It's going to be weird without you here, though," I said my smile dropping with the thought.

"I'm sorry, Kayden. I keep forgetting you're not going off to school like the rest of us. What happened to you is not right, dude, just not fucking right. You would have been offered a full scholarship," he said with a sincere look on his face. Scott's my best friend and I'd be forgotten and replaced within months of his departure.

"Scott, don't be sad for me. I'll make it and figure shit out," I said slapping him on the back. "This is a night of celebration, and I see your sister is here." I motioned with my head in her direction.

Kayden: The Past

"Yeah, but she's still the same miserable bitch she's always been," he said with a sour look.

"Well at least you're not going to the same school, you'll rarely see her."

"You got that shit right. She'll get hers, that nasty bitch," he said taking a swig of the beer he'd been fidgeting with during our conversation. Scott and Mindy always had a tumultuous relationship. She treated him like shit since he was little. She never got over the fact that their parents fawned over Scott; he was the golden child, the one who would carry on the family name. He was lavished with love and affection, and Mindy became more miserable over time. Scott never felt her absence when she left for college.

I casually walked towards Mindy; she sat on a log near the fire talking with friends and laughing. I kept my eyes on her waiting for her to notice me. I knew she would notice me, but maybe not recognize me, at first. Her eyes zeroed in and locked on me when I was within ten feet of her.

"Hey," she said with her mouth hanging open in shock.

"Hi... Mindy, right?" I said. I didn't want to give her the satisfaction of knowing her name. She looked over my entire body slowly eyeing me with her mouth still open.

"Kayden?" she asked in a voice that showed her disbelief.

"Yes," I said giving her a devilish smile and winking at her. My one and only target tonight was her. She'd get what I wanted to give, but it was more about taking it from her.

"Ladies, this is Kayden, my brother's friend. Move over and make some room for him." Mindy shooed them with her hands and the girls all shifted, moving away. I sat down and made sure my thigh touched hers. "You look great, Kayden." She licked her lips after saying my name. I knew I'd get what I wanted. I could see the lust in her eyes.

"Thanks, Mindy. You look beautiful, as usual," I said. I leaned over pretending to fix something on my shoe, and as I started to sit up, I brushed the skin on her ankle with my fingers. I could see her body react out of the corner of my eye. *Yeah, I had her.* "How's school? What are you studying, again?"

"It's good. I'm studying fashion design at the Art Institute. I have two more years before I can finally break into the field. I've been..." I tuned out at this point. She may have been beautiful, but she's boring as fuck and totally self-absorbed. "What are you going to do, Kayden?"

"I have an interview with a cell phone company to be a salesman," I replied. I was excited for the chance to work in sales. I knew it could be a lucrative career; cell phones were becoming popular, and I knew it was the next big thing – something everyone would have to have.

"They're too pricey for me, maybe when I make it big in the fashion industry... Maybe you can hook me up," she said.

"I'd love to hook up with you." I wink at her and redness filled her cheeks.

I sat with Mindy and her friends for a while and let them talk about college and the parties they attended. As Mindy spoke, she touched my arm, eventually holding on to my bicep. I flexed it a couple of times, and her grip would increase slightly. The rest of the girls slowly grew bored and left until it was just the two of us.

Kayden: The Past

"Want to go somewhere a little more private?" I asked, slyly grinning at her.

"I'd love to," she said.

I didn't waste a moment; I stood up and helped her to her feet. "Where ya wanna go, babe?" I asked.

"Let's go in the woods; it's dark and private," she said as she began to walk in that direction. She was a little eager by the speed in which she moved.

I grabbed her by the wrist. "Not so fast, walk slower so we don't draw so much attention." I placed my finger tips on the bare skin of her back. She wore a cute little belly shirt and jean shorts.

"You're right, I wasn't thinking." From what I knew of Mindy, she rarely ever had a thought that didn't involve material possessions or her vanity. We passed by a shed that was nestled only a couple of feet in the woods. Her parents kept all the power tools to keep the yard neat and tidy in the small wooden building.

"Let's go behind the shed... more privacy," I said, moving my eyebrows up and down. She didn't respond verbally, but she turned around with a smile and walked behind the shed. She faced me, waiting. I grabbed her by the back of the neck and stared into her eyes. "You want me?"

"Yes," she said all breathy filled with longing and placed her hand on my hip. "More than anything right now."

I crushed my lips to hers, smashing her body into the back of the shed. I grabbed her lip with my teeth and sucked it into my mouth, running my tongue along the smooth sweet skin. She moaned from the sensation becoming limp beneath my hands. I placed my leg between her knees, forcing them apart. I moved my knee up slowly making contact with her sweet spot.

I could hear her breathing change and her body twitched. I ravaged her mouth, searching it with my tongue as if looking for a lost treasure. I'd kissed plenty of girls over the last four years; I had this shit down pat. I pulled her body into mine, increasing the pressure she felt against my leg.

Her hands gripped my shoulders, her nails digging into my skin. I slowly moved my hand from her naked back to her smooth stomach. I could feel goose bumps break out across her skin. I placed my hand against her ribs and brushed my thumb against the underside of her breast—she didn't have on a bra. I increased the pressure and stroke of my thumb as my kiss grew deeper and more demanding. I waited to see if she'd tell me to stop, but she only gave in more, moving into my touch. She sucked my tongue into her mouth scraping her teeth against it as I drew it back into my mouth. My cock grew hard and my balls tingled at the sensation. I wanted to feel my cock in her mouth, buried balls deep down her throat. I cupped her breast running the tip of my thumb across her nipple as I moved my knee out, dragging it across her skin. The friction of her jeans and my knee caused a moan louder than I wanted to escape.

I broke the kiss, "Shhh, Mindy," I said as I placed my finger against her lips.

"Sorry, it felt so good and I want you so bad, Kayden."

"Suck my cock, and I'll give you more than you can handle," I said tilting my head waiting for an answer. I didn't need words. The full moon helped illuminate her face, and I could see her pupils were dilated, and she was ready to give me what I wanted.

She shifted and I removed my leg, letting her feet touch the ground. She dropped to her knees without a word of protest. "Unzip me," I said. She looked up at me, surprised by the tone in my voice; it was a demand and not a suggestion. Her fingers fumbled with my zipper before sliding it down slowly. "Pull down my pants slightly, Mindy." Her fingertips touched my side as she reached inside my jeans to slide them down my leg. As the jeans moved partially down my thigh, my cock sprang free. The look on her face was priceless. It didn't even come close to matching the look when she saw me tonight. In this moment, she looked scared at my size. "You can do it, Mindy. Look how hard I am for you, how much I want you."

She palmed it in her hands barely able to touch her finger tips together. She timidly licked the tip as if checking the flavor of a lollipop. My cock was like a Tootsie Roll pop; I had a surprise for her after we found out how many licks it took to get to the center or my end. She drew her tongue back into her mouth, looking up at me probably hoping I'd change my mind. I shifted my hips moving my cock closer to her, giving her the hint or encouragement she needed to continue.

She opened her mouth and moved towards my cock, placing it against her lips. I stared down at her. I could see her breasts through her top and her blond hair moving in the breeze. I waited years to feel her lips on my body, and I knew I wouldn't last long. The warmth of her mouth enveloped me, causing an uncontrollable shudder to run down my body. She slowly moved her lips up and down my cock, never deep enough to tap the back of her throat. I ran my fingers through her blond hair, playing with it, tangling it between my digits. She grabbed a little tighter with her hand making sure to use it as a barrier not to take me too deep. I stood there, feet planted shoulder width apart and became lost in the ecstasy. This obviously wasn't her first blow job; she knew the tricks. I let her work my cock for few minutes, enjoying the softness of her tongue on the sweet spot underneath. I wanted deeper; I wanted to possess her mouth... wanted to fuck her face.

"No hands, Mindy. Put them on your knees," I said. Her eyes shot up at me in a question without words with my cock still in her mouth. I was so close to coming from the innocent look in her eye, but I needed to control her. Her hand slipped off my cock, and she placed them both on her knees. I gripped her hair and began to move—slow at first, giving her a sense of security and false comfort. The tighter my body grew, the tighter my fingers gripped her hair, moving back towards her crown to give me better control. I pulled her by her hair, moving my hips forward causing my tip to tap the back of her throat. I withdrew quickly, hoping I didn't scare her off. I did it again, but this time, I jammed it as far down her throat as I could. She gagged, and I could feel her throat muscles close against my cock as she tried to breathe and swallow. I pulled it out again granting her a moment of reprieve.

"That feels so good, baby," I said in reassurance before repeating the movement. Drool ran out of her mouth and glistened on her chin. Every time my cock was buried in her mouth, her eyes would bulge out in shock, but she never said stop or made any motion for me to do so. My legs began to tremble as my balls tightened and my cock grew larger, more rigid in her wet sweet mouth. I let go of her hair letting her control the pace and depth. "I'm so close," I said giving her a warning, "I want to come in your mouth."

She sucked more feverishly... wanting my orgasm or praying for it to end. My body shook as warm liquid spilled from my body and into her mouth. She sucked it all, keeping the quick pace I had set earlier. She gagged slightly each time she pulled me into her mouth while my cock kept giving her my seed. I moaned; a blow job had never felt so good. I removed my cock, my legs shaky and unsteady, and watched her as she licked her lips and swallowed everything I gave her. I grabbed my jeans, tucking in my cock as I brought them up around my waist. "Thanks, babe, that was fucking fantastic," I said.

She stood up and looked as excited as a kid waiting for their favorite ride at Geauga Lake, an amusement park nearby. I made no move to touch her, and I started to walk away, "Hey, where ya going?" she asked. "What about me?"

"I'm sure someone here would be happy to give you what you want. I got what I was looking for, babe."

"You had me suck your cock and you're just going to fucking leave me here?" she asked glaring at me with hatred so pure I could almost feel the fist she wanted to hit me with.

"I got what I came for. You were a total bitch to me for years; you don't deserve what I'd give, how good I'd fuck you," I said with my arms crossed against my chest.

"You're a total cocksucker, Kayden," she said poking me in the chest with each word to drive the point home.

"No, that would be you, babe," I said with a smile, "Oh, and by the way, you have a little on your chin," I said pointing at her face chuckling softly at the situation. I watched as she wiped her chin and I turned and walked away, leaving her there like she deserved.

I left Mindy out of the story of my life when I sat down and started to tell Sophia about my high school years. It's not one of my shining moments, nor is it who I am today. It was a total dick move, but fuck, she's a bitch and deserved being used and thrown away.

We all know those girls in high school. The mean ones who think their shit don't stink and they have the right to treat everyone like they're disposable. Mindy is one of those girls. She never liked me or gave me the time of day until she came back home for our graduation. I knew when she saw me, the man I had grown up to become, that she'd be nice and friendly. She got every bit of what she deserved.

The rest of my youth was filled with dumbass decisions that caused problems at home. My dad was a dick who thought that using a belt was the best way to 'correct' my behavior. Major FAIL. It all ended when he learned that I was bigger, quicker, and stronger than he was. I wouldn't have hit him, but I wasn't going to sit by and take his bullshit any longer. My mom and I were better off without him. She found Joe, a loving man, and he became my father, the one that I looked to for advice as I grew up and learned how to become a man. My real father became more and more absent from my life; he left me behind. I may not have always agreed with him, but to be left behind and feel forgotten is not something anyone wants to feel during their life.

Chapter 2

My First Love ~ Bridget

I worked my ass off and became the best cell phone salesman in my office. The ladies were the customers I zoomed in on as soon as they walked through the door. I flirted with them and gave them my full attention. I gave sexy ones my card in case they had any questions and needed to call me, making sure to circle my personal cell phone number. I would always be available to help them with an issue, which was usually bullshit, but I let them come to me first. I installed phones in cars on my days off, making the extra bank to support my extra-curricular activities.

I met Bridget when she walked into my store looking to have a phone installed in her car. Bridget was petite with long blonde hair and almond shaped brown eyes. She looked sweet as apple pie and innocent, but the clothing she wore told me she was anything but. She batted her eye lashes at me, and I turned into a hard wreck. She had me by the balls before I even tasted her lips.

"May I help you, miss?" I asked trying to be a complete gentleman when my thoughts were anything but.

"I want to get a phone installed in my car. What kinda special will you give me?" she asked heaving her large chest on the counter. "Pretty please." Her teeth were brilliant white and perfectly placed.

I wouldn't waste the opportunity thrust on me. We were always allowed to play with the price, but in this moment, I was more interested in playing with Bridget. "I can knock thirty percent off and throw in the installation."

"Oooh, I like that. You've made me a very happy girl. When can we do it?" she asked.

Thoughts of doing her on the counter or bent over her car flooded my mind. Fuck, I wanted to take her in the bathroom and shove my cock in her. "Anytime you want."

Her lips twitched, and I could almost see her thinking. "I'd like to have it installed today."

Perfect. "Well I could put it in after work today. I could come over and do it for you. I get off around six." I smiled at her wondering if she would be put off by the idea.

"Yes, thanks," she said.

That night, I went to her house installed her phone into her late eighties model BMW. She had a pizza delivered while I was working and asked me to have some with her when the job was complete. Dessert was her against the living room wall and bent over her couch.

I made sure she had my number in case she needed any help or had any trouble with her phone. She called me a couple days later, and we became an item soon after. She worked at her dad's company as an assistant, but based on her luxury condo, I'd say she was paid more. Not many assistants barely in their twenties drove a Beemer and had such a high priced pad.

Bridget invaded my life, but in the best possible way. We spent every waking moment together when we weren't working. Our schedules often clashed as it does when one person in the relationship works in retail. I wasn't a traditional salesman with an office but worked in a store trying to sell people on the newest cellular technology available.

The months flew by quickly, and I fell in love with Bridget. She may have been slightly self-absorbed, but she adored me and was a generous lover. She didn't judge me based on my job or the car I drove; she loved me for the way I loved her. I gave everything I had in the relationship; swearing off my evening at the bar, unless Bridget was in tow. I was content and happy with our relationship and all the possibilities the future held.

I had to take the next step and meet the parents. Mothers usually loved me, and fathers weren't always my biggest fans. I never really had a steady girlfriend, and I was usually the flavor of the month, which was fine by me at that point in my life. Bridget was different than the other girls. I had fun with her and she couldn't get enough of me.

She couldn't wait to introduce me to her parents. They were having a family party at their home to celebrate her sister's birthday, and she came over to my place to beg me to be her date for the night. She had told her parents all about me and couldn't wait any longer. I avoided the topic of the party every time she brought it up, but it was D-Day, and I could no longer change the subject.

"Come on, Kayden. They'll love you. You have to meet them at some point," she pleaded. "My sister's birthday party is today and I want you to come. Don't make me go alone."

"Ok, Bridge. You're right. I'll go with you, babe." I leaned forward and kissed her on the lips.

She bounced up and down on the couch filled with excitement and hope. I wanted them to like me, and I needed their approval. I knew she was a daddy's girl, and without his acceptance we wouldn't have a future.

"What should I wear?" I asked unsure if it was a casual family barbeque, or if they were the type of family that dressed up for every occasion.

"I'll go pick out your outfit, okay?"

"Sure babe. Anything you want." I patted her ass as she stood. I grabbed her wrist before she was out of arm's length and pulled her back onto my lap as she shrieked.

"First, I want you naked in exchange for going to the party," I said as I kissed her again on the lips. I kissed her hard, pulling her to my body and sliding the tiny straps of her tank top down her shoulder and over her arms. I kissed her jaw, nipping slightly as I made my way down to her neck. I nibbled the flesh below her ear before sliding my tongue against the silky skin to her shoulder. I bit the muscle of her shoulder and instantly felt her body tense and shudder in response. I rolled her nipple in between my fingertips while holding her still with my free hand. She began to grind her pussy on my cock through the layers of material. Thank God the unit upstairs was currently vacant because Bridget was a moaner and screamer. I wanted to listen to her howl as I made her come.

Kayden: The Past

I captured her lips quieting her moans of pleasure. I slid our bodies off of the couch and onto the shag area rug never breaking the kiss. I hitched up her skirt and slid my fingers through her wetness. Her fingers dug into my shoulders, and I inserted two fingers pumping them in and out of her like a quick moving piston.

"You want my cock?"

"Mmmm," she said as she pushed my fingers deeper inside of her with her hand.

I flipped her over and pushed her stomach to the floor and pulled her up by the hips, positioning her with her ass in the air. I unbuttoned my jeans and pulled out my cock stroking it while looking at her pussy in full-view and waiting for the abuse I was about to give her.

I could hear her breathing shallow and filled with anticipation. I rubbed the tip, lubing it. I rammed it in to the hilt as her body jerked forward from the fullness. I held her hips, drawing her back and not allowing her to move away. "Is it too much for you, baby?" I removed my cock and jammed it in harder, deeper than I thought possible before she could respond. "Want me to stop?" I said as my body stilled. I reached down and placed my hand around my cock feeling her wetness and running my fingertips across her opening.

She didn't speak but moved against my cock, fucking me, moving on her elbows. I met her thrusts, and my body bounced off her ass allowing the speed to grow faster. I placed my hand on her bottom just above her ass. I rubbed my thumb against her asshole. It was so small, tight, and forbidden. The pressure of my thumb increased, and I could feel her body adjust and relax to the sensation. I wanted to hook her, gain control of the situation and fill her up a little more increasing the pressure against my cock.

I slid my finger inside. "Ouch," she moaned.

"Shhh, baby. It'll be good. Relax a little bit." I stilled my finger inside her allowing her body time to adjust as I continued to pound her pussy relentlessly. Her moans grew louder with each thrust, and I took it as the green light to move my thumb inside her. As my body slammed into her, it forced my thumb to go deeper.

"Oh God, yes." Her face was sideways in the carpet; her eyes half open and her eyeballs rolled back in her head. I held her hip, gripping tightly as my orgasm neared. I dug my fingertips into her ass, thumb firmly rooted, and laid my body across her back. My fingers trailed a path across her body to her clit. I rubbed it in a circular motion, feeling her pussy convulse around my cock. "Yes, fuck yes," she wailed. I kept the pressure firm, but not too hard as my balls tightened, and my cock grew harder on the peak of release. When her body became slack from complete relaxation and ecstasy, I reached up and grabbed her hair. She was my captive in this moment and my mercy. I fisted her hair and pulled her to me bending her neck back unable to see her face.

My release was so intense that my body shuddered and convulsed from the sensation. Drool dripped out of my mouth and onto her back, but I didn't give a fuck in that moment. I rested my forehead against her spine and waited for my cock to stop twitching inside her tight post-spasm core. Our bodies were both slick from sweat, and my skin glided across her as I caught my breath.

"Fuck, that was incredible," I said kissing her spine.

Kayden: The Past

"Mind blowing," she whispered into the carpet. I sat up and stared at her body as she laid there still with her ass in the air. I pulled my thumb out slowly. "Ouch," she said.

"Sorry, babe. Did I hurt you?" I asked.

"Just for a second, but damn, that shit rocked my world; No one has ever done that to me before," she said wiping her lips as she pulled herself up on her elbow.

"Good, cause I want to put more than my thumb in there." I rubbed my palm across her ass feeling the softness and a world of possibilities. "Now, go pick out my clothes," I said as I smacked her ass.

"What if I don't?" she asked.

"Then I'll shove my cock in that tight pretty ass hole of yours." I never saw a human move as quick, as she shot up from the carpet and was standing up within what seemed like a second.

"Fuck that. That shit is not fitting in there. Ever." She started to walk away and pulled down her skirt which had made its way up to her ribs during the floor pounding I just gave her.

"It will," I said smiling as she walked down the hallway towards my bedroom.

Bridget picked out a dress shirt, tie, and dress pants for me to wear to the party. The party wasn't going to be a casual affair. It was best though, since I was looking to impress her father and not look like I was heading out to fish for the day with the guys. Her parents' home was large and sat in a very exclusive subdivision in the area. It was nothing like the home I grew up in as a child.

The large grand staircase was the most noticeable structure when we entered the grand foyer –

outlined in black wrought iron with an intricate design featuring an O at the center. The O was the first letter to the family name, a sense of pride was evident. People were milling around drinking champagne while classical music filled the air. I instantly felt hot and uncomfortable. "Can I grab a drink?" I asked.

"Yeah sweetie, go on into the kitchen unless you want champagne."

"I'll go grab something else and come find you in a few minutes," I said kissing her on the cheek.

"I'll be out back; I'm sure that's where my parents are. Let me go warm them up a bit."

"Good idea. I'll find you in a couple minutes."

"Don't be long," she said as she walked away slowly pulling away from my hands until only our fingertips touched. She hooked her fingertips with mine and gave me a smile before breaking the connection.

She turned around and walked away. I stood there watching her walk through the room and stop to greet and kiss various people. *What the fuck am I doing here?* I was so out of my league. I was a poor kid from a split family who worked as a salesman. She was a rich girl who wouldn't get Daddy's approval when it came to me.

I walked into the kitchen and was greeted by the hired help. They were filling champagne glasses and small silver trays with appetizers to hand out to the guests. "Where can I get a beer?" I asked.

The room became quiet as a number of people stopped what they were doing to look at me, to see who wanted a beer in this home filled with caviar dreams. "Beer?" one man asked.

"Yes, sir. Just a plain old beer."

Kayden: The Past

"Let me look for you, sir," he responded and walked to the fridge searching through the contents for my drink of choice.

"Ah, I found a couple tucked away in the back," he said as his body became visible again from the other side of the door. He held out the beer for me, but I looked at it funny. It wasn't a beer that I had ever heard of before; I was used to Bud or Natty Light. It was an imported European beer with a name I couldn't read or pronounce. "Let me get you a glass, sir. The family would frown upon you walking around drinking out of a bottle."

"Lord forbid." I popped the top and took a large swig of the cool liquid. I'm sure if was pricey, but it tasted like any other beer I've ever had in my life. I just wanted something cool and wet, still thirsty from our earlier activities. I took the glass, emptying the contents of the bottle into the beautifully crafted silver vessel. At my mom's, I'd be lucky to find a clean plastic cup with Batman half worn off to pour my drink into. "Thank you."

I walked through the crowd and sipped my beer before finally finding my way to the backyard. I spotted Bridget with her parents standing near the pool. She must have been talking about me by the posture of her father. I approached slowly trying to overhear the conversation, but not draw too much attention to myself.

"Daddy, this is Kayden," she said smiling and pointing in my direction as I approached. Her father hated me from the moment he laid eyes on me; he didn't have to say the words, but I could tell by the way he looked at me. He studied my face before eyeing my outfit through critical eyes.

I held out my hand to shake his hand, "Hello, sir."

"It's nice to meet you, Kayden." He didn't shake my hand, but held his daughter a little closer and looked away from me. Bridget didn't seem to notice the unfriendly welcome that I received, or she was used to such a welcome by her father.

"I'm going to go greet the guests, baby girl. Find your sister; she's here somewhere." He kissed her on the top of her head before smiling at me and walking away.

"Well, that didn't go quite like I'd hoped."

She walked towards me and wrapped her arms around my waist. "I'm sorry, Kayden. He's just a little over protective of me. He'll warm up to you."

"Maybe someday, baby," I said as I grabbed her face lifting her lips towards mine. I kissed her lips gently, not wanting to get carried away in front of the entire family. They didn't look like the crowd that enjoyed public displays of affection.

I'd like to say that the relationship between her father and I progressed and a mutual respect formed over the years we dated, but it NEVER happened. I would never be good enough for his baby girl. He made it clear that I wasn't the type of person he saw her with in the future, and I didn't have the ability to give her the financial security she deserved. Money's great, but love's more important. Love is the foundation that all else teeters on, the great precipice that can bring you happiness or total torture.

Chapter 3

The Plunge and Fall ~ Bridget

Our lives became intertwined; we were a unit, and it was time to take the next step. All of my friends were planning weddings or having babies, and it felt right. Bridget had all the qualities I wanted in a woman. She has a heart of gold, beautiful, funny, ready to party, fucking mind-blowing in bed, sucked cock like a pro, and never judged me.

Her father was the only obstacle that stood in my way. I thought that someday I'd ask for a girl's hand in marriage, but I knew with Bridget, it would be pointless. Her father would never give me the green light; he'd never welcome me with open arms. I knew that Bridget loved me and told me time and time again that nothing her dad said could ever change that fact. I'd skip asking him permission and ask the one person that mattered in the actual decision, Bridget.

I couldn't make the proposal simple; most girls would be happy with simple, but Bridget would require a grand display of affection and commitment. Her family and friends would judge me based not only on the way I proposed but also by the ring I buy her. I spent weeks looking at diamonds, learning the ins and outs. I learned about the three C's, cut, clarity, and color. I knew as a salesman that the price on the item wasn't final, and I'd be able to get her a decent ring based on the amount of money I had to spend.

I found a ring that would suit her, please her, and not make her embarrassed to show her friends and family. I would spend over four months' worth of pay on the clear little stone, and I wanted it to be drop dead gorgeous, just like Bridget. The one point five carat princess cut diamond with only slight imperfections would be stunning on her long thin fingers. I didn't opt for the traditional yellow gold, but had it placed in a white gold band. I wanted the diamond to be the show stopper, nothing else to decorate or draw the eye away from the main attraction.

I spent more time thinking of how to propose than I did on picking out the ring she would wear during her lifetime. Every time I thought of the perfect setting, I always talked myself out of it, deciding it wasn't good enough. The only thing that kept popping in my head was our upcoming trip to New York City. We'd be there for New Year's Eve to watch the ball drop in Times Square. We were leaving tomorrow, New Year's Eve morning, and I couldn't wait any longer to ask her. I didn't want to waste another moment as just boyfriend and girlfriend; I wanted to call her my fiancé.

I barely slept; my mind tormented by the thought of flying and proposing to Bridget without fucking it up. You only get engaged once and can't ever take that moment back. I crawled out of bed as soon as the sun peeked over the horizon. Our flight was early, and I dragged our bags outside and threw them in the trunk of her car. I had the little black box in my coat pocket, not wanting to take the chance of my bag getting lost with the precious cargo inside. I waited on the sofa for Bridget to finish making herself perfect. She was naturally beautiful and didn't need to put on as much make-up as she did. I love her for everything she

Kayden: The Past

is and not her false beauty. Time ticked away slowly; my palms were sweaty, and I felt flush.

"Bridget, come on babe, we're going to miss our flight," I yelled from the living room.

"One more second," she yelled back.

I walked around making sure all the windows were locked, and everything was off in the house. Bridget finally made an appearance looking as beautiful as she always does. Her hair was fluffed just perfectly. She wore a long cream-colored clingy sweater and tight blue jeans with boots. "You look beautiful, Bridget."

She approached me with a lop-sided grin and stood on her tippy toes, reaching up to kiss my lips, "I love you, Kayden." My heart skipped a beat with her words.

New York City greeted us with its crowds, noise, and a party atmosphere. The taxi driver had a hard time navigating the streets with the sea of people and street closures for tonight's festivities. We checked in and threw our bags down, both falling on the bed in exhaustion. "Just five minutes," she said as I stroked her hair. I closed my eyes relishing the feel of her warm body pressed up against mine, not looking forward to the hours in the freezing New York winter air.

Fingers were running through my hair and woke me from my dream of a beach with rolling waves and Bridget at my side. "Wake up, sleepyhead. We have to get ready and head to Times Square. Come on, baby." Her words made my heart jump and start beating at a feverish pace remembering where I am and what the night held for us both. "I love your hair," she said as she played with my hair that had fallen across my forehead.

"Let's go, beautiful." I crawled off the bed, grabbed a beer from the mini-bar and waited for Bridget to winterize herself.

We stopped at a liquor store and grabbed a bottle of Champagne to crack open at midnight to celebrate the New Year and our engagement. I held Bridget's hand tight as we walked through the endless mass of people gathered in the streets, drinking and celebrating hours before the ball dropped. At times, I only had a grasp of her fingertips, but I made sure never to lose her. I'd never fucking find her in this mess.

"Stop here, Kayden." She yanked on my hand, "I want to be able to see the ball and the screens with the Dick Clark performances. I don't want to go any farther."

I held Bridget by the waist watching the countdown clock tick away. With every hour and minute, my pulse grew faster, and my palms more sweaty. The cold had no effect on me at this point; I was burning up inside my winter coat and hat. My mouth grew dry, and I felt like I was swallowing sand paper.

"Oh my God! I can't believe we're here on New Year's Eve." She almost jumped up and down in my arms filled with excitement.

"There's no place I'd rather be than here with you, love."

"One minute, get ready. Hurry, open the champagne." I quickly worked the contraption that held in the cork and pointed the bottle away from Bridget, aiming it high in the air. Other people around us were readying their drinks and watching the clock with urgency. "Thirty seconds."

I reached into my pocket and grabbed the ring. Bridget didn't see anything as I moved because she was focused on the ball. She started to yell the countdown with the crowd. I sank down on one knee and waited for her to look at me. Fucking hell, thank God I only had to wait a few seconds – Any more than that I might have had a panic attack. She looked in my direction and a panic looked flashed across her face before she looked down. Her eyes became as big as saucers and her mouth opened in shock.

"Kayden." I could see her mouth moving, but I couldn't hear a damn thing.

Fuck. I didn't anticipate the noise and her not being able to hear my words. People began to cheer and kiss all around us. I held the ring up, not wanting to waste another moment. "Will you marry me?"

She shook her head yes and crumpled to the ground in front of me. I gently grabbed her hand and slid the ring on her finger. Tears began to form in her eyes, and she wrapped her arms around my neck. We looked into each other's eyes as the world around us disappeared. Bridget and I were engaged, and we'd become man and wife. I kissed her hard, demanding entrance, marking my territory. She would be mine forever.

Bridget was the first great love of my life. The details about our relationship or the engagement aren't important; our downfall is what changed my view on love and fidelity. When I'm in a relationship, I'm in it one hundred percent; I only have eyes for my partner. I never will be a cheater.

Our wedding was a month away. Bridget's father still grumbled under his breath every time I walked in the room; that someday we'd hoped for when I first met him still hadn't arrived. Her parents had booked the Cleveland Botanical Garden as the venue for our vows and reception. It was beautiful and way out of my price range. Everything was purchased, and we were just counting the days until we'd become husband and wife.

I went for my final tuxedo fitting and decided to go home early to surprise Bridget. She's been so stressed with all the planning. She and her mother didn't see eye to eye on the dresses, flowers, and just about everything. She needed some downtime – a night filled with fun and I knew just how to help her to relax.

I walked through the front door and followed a trail of clothing. They led me to her, but she wasn't alone. I heard the noises coming from the bedroom. The sounds weren't those of sadness but of lust and passion.

"Fuck me. Harder!" My heart broke in that moment. Shattered. I pushed the door open and a naked male body filled my vision. He was standing up thrusting into her as she kneeled on the bed like a bitch in heat.

"You're my slut," he said as he smacked her ass.

There are only two options in this moment. Option one involved screaming, making a scene, and beating the fuck out of him. Option two would be to wait for them and let them squirm when they realize they've been caught red handed. Option two was the winner. I was too devastated in this moment to do anything else but drown my sorrow in a bottle of Jack. Fuck it! The damage was done; Bridget and I were over.

I should have picked up on the queues that I missed or overlooked because of the stressful nature of planning a wedding. She seemed distant at times, not as into sex, and was often out 'shopping' for the big day. I didn't pay attention, too wrapped up in the dream of what we were going to become instead of clutching what we are.

Kayden: The Past

I left the door ajar and walked into the kitchen. I quietly opened the liquor cabinet pulling out the bottle of Jack. I didn't wait to get a glass; I popped the top and took a large gulp. I walked to the couch facing the hallway and waited. I sat there watching for the adulterer and her boy toy to make their grand entrance. I downed half the bottle before they emerged from the bedroom.

Bridget turned paler than I thought she ever could and came to a dead stop as he slammed into her back, causing her to lurch forward. I sat there with my leg over my knee, hand across the back of the couch, gripping the bottle of Jack and void of expression.

"Kay-den," she stuttered, adjusting her bra and panties, the rest of her clothes were still all over the house.

"Save it. Who the fuck is he?" I placed both feet on the floor and leaned forward on both my elbows.

She looked at him, but I didn't need an answer. Now that I was able to see his face, I knew exactly who he was. Jim or Tim, something bland and boring, worked for her father. He was an executive in his office and made large bank. "Lemme explain," she said.

"Explain what? That you're his slut?" I could almost feel my blood boil in my veins. I watched as he gathered his pants, dress shirt, and tie off the floor as he headed to the door almost entirely naked. "I should have known you were a whore. I fucked you the first day I met you." He stopped dead in his tracks.

"Shut your mouth, asshole. That's not how you talk to a lady," he said as he turned around.

"A lady? I thought she was your slut, just a fuck toy. She used to be just that to me, too."

"Tom, just go. Kayden and I need to work this out." She pointed towards the door. Tom, I knew it was some short boring ass name that fit him to a tee.

"Are you sure you're going to be okay with him? Don't let him talk to you that way. No one should talk to you that way, ever."

"Go fuck yourself, Tom. Get the fuck out." I stood up moving towards him. If he wouldn't leave willingly, I'd gladly show him another way out.

Bridget jumped in front of me placing her hand on my chest. I moved my body out of reach; I couldn't stand the thought of her fingers that were just touching his naked body now touching me. "No, Kayden don't." She looked hurt, but I didn't buy the look on her face. "Just go, please Tom."

He walked out the door without saying another word. I looked down at her; she didn't look like the girl I'd fallen in love with. She looked like a dirty whore, used up, not worthy of my love or my attention.

I backed away from her; my mind clouded from the liquor. "Why?" I asked. I didn't know what else to say, and it didn't matter what her answer was.

"I don't know, Kayden. I've felt us slipping away." tears began to stream down her face, making my stomach turn. "I think I just got scared with the wedding coming up."

"You're going to blame it on the stress of the wedding? The wedding made you stick your ass in the air for any random cock? Don't insult me."

She walked toward me and I backed away, I didn't want her hands on me. "I'm sorry, I..." she placed her face in her hands and began to weep.

"Save the explanation. I can't believe you threw us away, me away. I hope he's worth it," I set the bottle of Jack down, feeling deflated. Nothing I said or she begged mattered at this point. "At least your daddy will be happy if he doesn't already know."

"Don't go, Kayden. We can work this out," her mascara smeared on her face caused her to look aged, "Don't walk out on me," she pleaded.

"I'm not the one that left this relationship first, Bridget." I grabbed my keys as she crumpled to the floor. She latched on to my leg as I touched the door handle. "Get off me." I looked down at her feeling nothing but disgust. She slowly removed her fingers, drawing out the ending of our relationship in her eyes. I turned the door handle and walked out into a new life – a blank slate, a fresh start that didn't feel so full of possibilities but felt like a death – she was no longer the center of my universe, but the master of my destruction.

My break-up with Bridget left me raw and reeling. Life felt a little less sweet, and little things no longer brought me joy. I drowned my loss in the bottom of a bottle. How could you claim to love someone and want to spend the rest of your life with them, but suck another man's cock? I never looked back. Bridget called me, but I never answered the phone. I had nothing more to say to her. I needed to move forward with my life. I could never believe another word that came out of her mouth, and that's no way to be in a relationship.

After a week of closing myself off from the world and tormenting myself with the pornographic replay of Bridget and the suit, my friends dragged me to a bar in Kent. I agreed to go only because it was a bar. I wanted to wash away all the images and events of the past year with booze.

I walked into the dank smoky college bar with my buddies in tow around midnight, and my heart stopped in my chest… Literally. I couldn't feel a beat, just a void. My eyes caught sight of Bridget across the room sitting in the lap of some mother fucker laughing like she didn't have a care in the world. Her world didn't shatter, only mine.

"Mother fucker," I said, unable to take my eyes off her.

"What?" Ron said.

"The cheating whore is here." I pointed across the room as Ron looked over.

"Fuck! I'm sorry man. Want to go?"

"Hell no! I want to watch the show." What can I say? I must love torture. I live in my sadness and wallow in my self-pity. "I want a fucking drink."

We headed to the bar, and I ordered a pitcher of beer for myself. Yes, for myself – I wasn't sharing. I washed down the beer with shots of Tequila trying to drown out the hurt I felt with her in my sights. She worked the room, draping herself over various men like she knew them in a more intimate way. I would have never believed that she would even step foot in a bar like this, let alone look like a regular. I didn't know Bridget as well as I thought I had; I felt duped.

Half way through my pitcher and four shots of Tequila later, Bridget spotted me. Instead of walking away or leaving like a cheating bitch should, she walked in my direction with a look of hurt. What the fuck did she have to be hurt about?

She stood in front of me; yet, I couldn't say a word. There were so many things running through my brain. I had so much to say to this whore in front of me, but none of it would come.

"Kayden." She sounded like she just saw me the other day and was saying hello like we were friends. "How are you?" I saw red, pissed doesn't even explain what I felt in this moment.

Kayden: The Past

"You've got to be fucking kidding me. How am I? HOW AM I? That's all you have to say, you vile bitch." Eyes started to look in our direction, but I ignored everyone, keeping my eyes pinned on her, not worthy of even saying her name.

"I'm sorry. I fucked up," she said staring at the ground.

"You fucked something, and it sure as hell wasn't me. Get the fuck out of my space."

She grabbed my arm, and my flesh instantly felt the coldness of her hands, just like her heart. "Get your fucking hand off me." I stared at her hand not wanting to look her in the eye. I could barely think straight; my insides were raging.

"You can be such a prick."

I looked at her; my eyes glaring unable to believe the words coming out of her mouth. I could see someone standing next to her out of the corner of my eye, and I turned my attention towards him. He was staring at Bridget with a look of concern.

"Bridge, are you okay? Want me to get rid of this asshole?" the cock sucker asked her. Somehow I became the piece of shit in this situation, how in the fuck did that happen. I wasn't the one spreading my legs to every Tom, Dick, and Harry like the lovely Bridge standing before me.

"Yes, poor little Bridge, are you okay?" I stared at her wanting to hit something or someone.

"What's going on over here, Bridge?" Another male voice asked.

What in the fuck? Was she on a first name basis with every asshole in this shit hole, "Yeah, I'm fine. Just give me a moment guys." They stared at me for a moment before walking away.

"Doing more than one at a time, now?"

"Fuck you, Kayden. You're the one who destroyed us."

Dumbfounded. "I don't remember shoving my cock into any hole that would grant me access."

"You're drunk. You fucker! Your drinking was more important than me. Look at you now, shit-faced drunk."

"Nothing was more important than you. You're delusional to put the blame on anyone but yourself. You're a whore, and I never knew it." I clenched my fists becoming more and more pissed off with each moment.

Her hand connected with my face as my neck snapped to the side. I licked my lips tasting iron from the blood that was trickling out of a small cut the slap had caused. I would never, no matter what, ever hit a woman. If anyone in the world ever deserved it, she did. I grabbed the remaining pitcher of beer at my side and dumped it over her head. She began to scream, "I can't believe you. You're a mother fucking dick." The beer was dripping off the tips of her hair and her tank top was drenched.

"What the fuck?" Echoed from across the bar, and I knew the two guys that were all up in my shit were about to be in my face. A hand wrapped around Bridget's waist and moved her out of my sight.

"Come on, fucker," I said ready for a fight. I needed to beat the shit out of someone and who better than a guy she's probably already fucked in my absence. His fist connected with my face; I allowed it to. I wanted to feel the pain. He moved to hit me again, but I ducked and slid off the bar stool.

My fists flew in rapid succession, smashing the guy in the face and ribs. He landed a few more punches before I knocked his ass out. He lay on the floor at my feet before I was able to look around. The entire bar had erupted into a fight. People were punching each other all over the room, and the girls were ducking under tables and heading for the doors.

I knew my body would be sore, and I'd feel every simple movement tomorrow. Every stab of pain would be worth pouring that pitcher of beer over her head. How dare that whore blame me for literally fucking up our happy ending; she was the one with her legs spread – not me.

My life was like an inescapable black hole. I worked hard and played harder, needing to lose myself in booze, women, and drugs. I wanted to dull the pain, escape reality, and just forget everything. The problem with my method is that it's only a momentary Band-Aid for the scar that stays with you a lifetime or eventually bites you in the ass.

Chapter 4

Don't Shit Where You Eat or Fuck Where You Work ~ Jessica

Seeing Bridget only made things worse, drove me farther down the tunnel of despair and deeper into my addictions. I went from booze to smoking weed almost regularly. The mixture was the only thing that allowed me any rest; without it, I laid in bed almost in a catatonic state. I used cocaine to help me get through the day, giving me the buzz and energy I needed.

All I wanted to do was to take a couple of weeks off work and drown myself in liquor and drugs, but I couldn't. We were opening a new store, and everything had to be set up for the grand opening. I'd climbed the proverbial ladder of the retail world and made it to assistant store manager. Jessica, the manager, and I had the sole responsibility to make sure everything was perfect and ran smoothly for the big reveal. It was a prime spot on a busy street, and everyone was chomping at the bit for it to open. They all saw dollar signs with the potential for increased sales and a larger customer base.

We had less than twelve hours until the doors opened to the general public. Jessica and I were the only ones left in the store; we had a bigger stake in the

Kayden: The Past

success or failure of this store. Everyone else worked their eight hour shift before walking out the door and leaving us behind.

"I'll be right back, Jess." I needed another bump of coke, something to get me through the countless hours of prep ahead of us. I snorted a small amount, not wanting the effects to be too noticeable to Jessica. I looked at myself in the mirror and the person staring back was almost unrecognizable. I rested my hands on the sink and gave the soft white powder time to work its way through my system and fill every ounce of my being.

"What do you want to work on next?" I asked as I walked back into the main showroom.

Jessica was bent over with her ass in the air stocking a shelf with cellular accessories. I never really paid much attention to her sexually, but in this moment, it was the only thing I could think about. She was my boss, and I never crossed that line, but for once, I didn't give a fuck. Maybe it was the coke in my system or my 'who gives a fuck' attitude, but I wanted her. She didn't move to stand up when I asked her the question but continued stocking. I stood there and stared at her ass without shame or remorse.

"What are you doing?" Jessica must have noticed I wasn't moving.

"Just looking at something."

"Grab that box and move your ass, Kayden."

"Bossy much?" I liked her sassy mouth.

"I just want to get out of here, Kayden. We've been here all day, and tomorrow isn't going to be any easier." She stood up and turned around catching me staring at her. "Do I have something on me? What are you looking at?"

"There's nothing on you, Jess." I grabbed the box off the counter and moved it to an empty shelf for her to unpack. "I'll move all the boxes where they need to go, and we can cruise through the rest."

"Doing anything is better than staring at my ass," she laughed.

Jessica's a smart girl; you don't make it to the top without brains. She knew exactly what she was doing – she wanted me to look. She was stooped down like she normally would be, but her ass was pointing upwards instead of down towards the floor. She had put it on display for me wanting me to notice her sexually.

"I have a couple things that are better than just staring." The statement crossed the line of employee/boss relationship, but I think Jessica liked the flirtation. She didn't say a word back to me.

I moved all the boxes around the store; there were only a couple left. We finished quicker than we both expected. I turned off all the lights in the store as Jessica waited for me in the backroom to walk out. I didn't want her to leave alone; the back was dark and not entirely safe. The lighting was dim, only a security light illuminating the room as I walked in. Jessica made the first move and kissed me. I put her on the counter and held her legs in a V, wide open for me to take her. We had sex that night and only that night.

Our working relationship felt strained after that night. I never asked her out or had sex with her again. I felt shitty afterwards, not because we had sex, but because I had to see her every day, and I think she wanted more. I tried to act as normal as possible around Jessica. I went on with my life as normal. I flirted with the customers, got some numbers, and went on some 'dates'. I did my job and tried to nicely decline any

Kayden: The Past

offers that Jessica threw my way, but none of it mattered in the end.

My cock mixed with the cocaine would be my ultimate downfall. Jealousy reared its ugly head, and its name was Jessica.

I still remember it clear to this day. It was a Friday, two months after opening day, and I was about to beat my monthly sales goal for the third straight month. "Kayden, you have a phone call. Please take it in my office."

"I'm with a customer, can it wait?" I asked.

"No, I'll help them while you take the call." She had a smile on her face. I've never been called away from a customer for a simple phone call.

"Excuse me Ma'am; Jessica will help you for a few minutes. I'll be right back with you." I walked away, leaving Jess to make my sale. The feel of the entire situation put me in a shitty mood.

"Hello, Kayden Michaels." I kicked back in her comfy oversized office chair.

"Mr. Michaels, a grievance has been filed against you relating to sexual harassment, and we've decided to terminate you." My stomach dropped and I instantly felt ill. There was only one person who would file said grievance.

"Excuse me?" I needed a moment to gather my thoughts. Angry isn't even a great descriptor for what I felt in this moment. I wanted to break shit.

"We cannot have employees sexually harassing customers and other employees. It may turn into a legal matter. You'll be paid for your time worked, but as of this moment, you are no longer an employee."

"I've been the top salesman in this office more times this year than anyone else, and you're just going to fire me without my side of the story? Who filed the complaint?" I slammed my fist on the desk.

"Top salesman or not, we cannot open the company up for a lawsuit, Mr. Michaels."

I argued for a few more minutes before hanging up the phone. I sat there a moment and tried to gather my thoughts. There is only one person who would file the grievance against me with the district office, Jessica. I rubbed my temples trying to calm my anger. She fucked with my livelihood and my career. I wanted to be a manager someday and sticking my dick in her fucked it all up. She wasn't going to get off without a word or two from me.

I walked into the showroom and ignored everyone else. Jessica had finished with my customer and didn't close the deal. She stood at the desk pretending to be busy, but I could see her watching me out of the corner of her eye.

"You fucking reported me?" I wanted her to confess, I needed it.

She looked at me with a shitty ass smirk on her face. "I did."

"They fired me. What the fuck is wrong with you? What did I ever do to you?" I asked trying to keep my voice down to not cause a scene, although I almost didn't care. They couldn't fire me again.

"You used me, Kayden. You had sex with me and then ignored me."

"Jessica, YOU came on to me not the other way around. I never sexually harassed you." I moved closer and put my lips against her ear, "Maybe I fucked you too good. Did you enjoy my cock a little too much?"

Kayden: The Past

Her head moved away quickly; the words hit a little too close to home. "Fuck you, Kayden. You're a dick. You used me."

"You never asked to be my girlfriend. I thought it was a plain and simple moment of passion; guess you're just a conniving bitch." There wasn't more to say.

I didn't have any other skills. My job filled my days and kept me from drinking too much, but now I had nothing, no reason to hold back.

I went to the bar with my friends that night. The city would be a flurry of activity, and I needed to lose myself in the excitement. I was picked up by one of the guys since I was already shitfaced from my afternoon binge. I can't recall which bars we wandered in and out of through the haze of people.

A giant party bus filled with women caught my attention as we walked down the sidewalk looking for our next destination.

"Gentleman, I think we've hit the mother load," I said. "It's a bachelorette party." I knocked at the door and waited. All the giggling and chattering stopped; the doors opened, and I was greeted by a beautiful brunette with a short dress and fuck me pumps. "Ladies, are we celebrating?"

"Hell yes we are. Natasha is getting married tomorrow," said the girl in the little red number. Her words were slurred, and she swayed on those mile high heels.

"Feel like a little male company?" I asked with an eyebrow raised and a grin on my face.

"It's up to the girls. Ladies, what do you say? Look out the windows... do we want to invite the gentlemen in?"

Female faces filled the windows and eyed us, checking us out like a potential meal or victim. "Come on in, boys."

We had a couple drinks on the bus and talked with the girls. Everyone paid attention to a different girl and shared the love. I paid strict attention to the bride. I wasn't looking for love but a night of fun. "Are you sure you want to get married, beautiful?"

"I do; he's a nice guy." Those words are the kiss of death. It was code for boring ass mother fucker, but he's kind and makes good money.

"We're here," yelled a girl from the front trying be heard over the chatter and music.

"Want to dance with someone the polar opposite of your husband-to-be?" I held out my hand, and she stared at it for a long moment.

"Let's go, hot stuff." Maybe she wasn't as committed as she let on.

We entered the crowded dance club filled with smoke and music so loud it made your chest throb with the beat. I took the bride on the dance floor and grinded against her. I fucked her through her pretty little dress with her veil on. She blushed but pushed her body against mine. We stared into each other eyes, and I saw the spark. My cock grew hard from the friction of her body against mine and the look in her eyes. It was sensual, and no nudity was involved. I would've never fucked her. I was on the shit end of that stick before and wouldn't wish it on another soul.

The moment was ruined by an asshole who bumped into me causing her to fall to the floor. "What the fuck is wrong with you, dickhead?" I yelled at the bastard as I helped her off the floor.

"Fuck off, dude." He started to walk away. Fuck me? No apologies to the lady he knocked over. I needed someone to take my anger from the day out on, and this guy fit the bill. I grabbed his shoulder before he was able to take another step.

"Fuck off? Apologize to the lady. NOW."

He looked at my hand with a look of disgust. He grabbed my hand, and I used that moment to punch him in the face. It was a sucker shot, but I didn't give a shit. I landed a couple shots, having the advantage of surprise. The fists flew between the two of us, and the rest of the world drifted away. Tables moved, and chairs fell as we made our way out of the club and continued to fight on the sidewalk.

The sound of sirens didn't mean anything good, but I kept my attention focused on the cock sucker I'd been pounding my fist into for the last few minutes. Hands grabbed my arms and pulled us apart. My face smashed against a metal fence as a man tried to restrain me, but I fought back. My anger had blinded me, and all I could think about was taking my feelings about being fired out on this guy who just bumped into me.

"Stop struggling," the guy said as he held my hands behind my back and slammed my face into the chain link again. My mind didn't communicate with the rest of my body as I continued to struggle. My face met the concrete in the most unfriendly way as a knee pushed into my back, and my arms were being pulled away from my body. My face throbbed, my arms burned, and my mind was a jumbled mess.

"You're under arrest, anything you say or do..." He read me my rights. I had steered clear of the police since I was a teenager but not tonight. The officer pulled me up using my hands as a motivator.

I sat in the back of the car as they ran my name through their database on the ride to the police station. I tried to think of a way to get out of this. I didn't need to add jail to my list of troubles. "Guys, come on. We can work something out. Maybe we can stop by the ATM on the way."

"Are you trying to bribe us, son?" The man didn't even bother to turn around and face me.

I leaned forward trying to plead my case. "Sir, please, I just lost my job. I can't sit in jail. I'll give you anything you want."

I received no response. My ass would be spending the night in jail, and I couldn't do anything to change it. I was booked, fingerprinted, photographed, and given a new set of clothes to wear. It would be a long night as I lay on the hard wooden bench that lined the holding cell. I closed my eyes and shut the world out.

"Mr. Michaels," a voice woke me from my nightmare.

My body ached as I sat up. Every muscle and bone screamed when I tried to move. "Here."

"Let's go."

"Where?" I asked as I stood propelling myself up with my hands holding the hard bench.

"You're getting out, kid," he said.

I walked without knowing my feet were moving. I was getting out. I hadn't placed my one phone call, but maybe one of the guys had bailed me out. I walked through the wing door and jumped as it slammed behind me. It scared the shit out of me and even the softest sound sounded like a semi horn with my hangover.

"The guy is from out of town and didn't want to come back for court. He's decided not to press charges." The cop walked in front of me and didn't bother to turn around. Jail is part of his everyday life, but to me, this was a nightmare I wanted to escape.

Kayden: The Past

"That's it?" I shook my head, still not believing I was free. "I don't have to come back?"

"That's it, kid. You're lucky, try to stay out of trouble or next time you won't have such a happy ending."

I'd like to say that I followed his advice, but I didn't. The next month of my life was a downward spiral. I stayed in my house and drank myself to sleep each night. I snorted coke and washed it away with Vodka. I didn't give a fuck about anything or anyone. I chased the next high and used the liquor to help calm my mind and sleep at night. I lost over a month of my life in my addiction; time I'll never get back or remember.

I was self-destructive.

Chapter 5

Roaring Twenties ~ Candy

I found a job after I stopped drinking myself into oblivion – a friend from my previous job had switched companies and told his boss about me. I received a phone call without even applying and was asked to start the following week. I needed to celebrate and felt like a night out with the boys.

We spent our weekends in the Flats, a section of Cleveland that was filled with bars and nightlife, usually ending our evenings in a strip club. I needed the cash for drinks, dates, and the G-strings of some smoking hot piece of ass dancing on the stage. Tonight, we were spending our hard earned money at Tiffany's, a multi-level strip club in the heart of the Flats sitting on the bank of the Cuyahoga River.

Candy would be our waitress tonight. She had waited on us before and we always flirted with each other, little touches and innuendo passed back and forth. It'd been days since I had sex, and my body craved the release. "What can I get you, gentlemen?" she asked, placing little napkins on our table and brushing her fingers against mine when she set it down in front of me. The guys rattled off drinks while she wrote them down on her notepad. "And you, sugar?" she asked tapping me on the shoulder.

"I'll take a Jack and Coke, doll," I said grabbing her fingers stopping their barrage against my flesh. The game between us for months had become too much and grew old. I needed it to end tonight.

"Coming right up, gentlemen. Be back in a jiffy." I watched her walk away, her ass swaying from side to side, and she turned around twenty feet away to see if I was watching her. I wasn't trying to be coy or hide what I wanted from her.

"She wants you, man," Tony said.

I looked at him, but not out of surprise. "I know and I'm going to give her what she wants tonight," I said. "I'll be right back." I stood up and moved towards the bar area where Candy stood waiting for our drink orders to be filled.

I stood in the open spot next to her and lightly touched her arm as I rested my free arm against the counter. I leaned towards her, putting my lips close enough to her ear that they almost touched. "I'm done with games, Candy. Wanna fuck or what?"

With my words, her shoulders began to move up and down as if her breathing became heavier. She turned her face; her lips almost touching mine. "Yes," she whispered her eyes wide and pupils dilated. "I get off in a couple hours. Hang out til then," she said looking me in the eyes.

Her eyes were a beautiful shade of blue, like an aquamarine gemstone, framed by wisps of her blond hair. "I'll wait for you," I said as I touched her cheek. I grabbed my drink off her tray before walking away.

The guys looked eager to hear what happened as I sat back down. "What did you say?"

"Wanna fuck?"

"You said that to her?" Bobby asked looking shocked. He obviously had no balls.

"Fuck yes. I said I'm done with games, wanna fuck? It's that easy, Bobby." I picked up my drink and polished it off.

"She said yes?" I always thought Bobby had a pair, but obviously I was wrong.

"Why wouldn't she?"

"I didn't think there were girls out there that would actually say yes to that statement." He shook his head in disbelief.

"It may not work for you, but for me, it works like a charm," I said. "You need to be confident when saying the words. I knew Candy would say yes. You need to know your target before you stick your neck out. Be calculated in all that you do – think of it as closing a sale."

"Hmm, just not my bag. I want to be in love or at least dating the girl before I stick my dick in her," Bobby said as Candy approached the table with the drinks. She placed the drinks down on the table.

"I brought you another one, Kayden," she said as she set the drink down over my shoulder, crouching down slightly and brushing her arm against mine.

"Thanks, Candy."

"Anything you want," she whispered in my ear.

"I'm counting on it," I said, turning my face slightly so my lips were almost touching her flesh. She stared into my eyes for a moment before winking and walking away.

We sat around drinking and watching the girls dance on the stage in the center of the room. I like the girls with the petite frames and small tits that filled my hand. Most of the girls dancing for money had extremely large chests, usually enhanced through surgery. Candy didn't go the extra mile and stuck to serving the drinks instead of shaking her tits on stage to make a buck. She still dressed the part with skimpy shorts and a bra, but never topless or nude – I planned to change that soon.

Ever since Bridget ripped my fucking soul, leaving me with blackness, I tried everything to fill the void. My body became acclimated to the liquor, requiring more and more to make me forget the loneliness. The endless stream of women filling my bed helped while my cock was buried deep but caused the emptiness to become more prevalent the moment they walked out the door.

I walked towards the bar slowly watching the beautiful view in front of me; Candy stood there leaning against the bar with her right foot up on the piping that ran underneath. The high heels she wore showed off the strength of her calf muscles and created an amazing outline of her legs. I watched as she laughed with the bartender and played with her hair while waiting for her order to be placed on her tray. I wanted to press my body firmly against her and whisper in her ear but touching of any kind is a no-no in a strip club.

"You wanna come over to my place, Candy, or want me to wait here?" I leaned against the bar watching her expression intently waiting for a response.

"I'm about to go on break, gimme ten, okay?" she asked me looking hopeful that the answer was good enough for me.

"Sure, babe, just come and get me."

"Ten," she said with a look of seriousness and want.

"Can I get another Jack and Coke?" I asked the female bartender. I didn't see the sense in wasting a trip to the bar. Candy walked away, and I turned around staring at the scene before my eyes. The dimly lit room was filled with smoke. The stage was illuminated in a blue hue to draw your attention. Two girls were each working separate sides of the stage, and girls were moving around the room giving lap dances to the fools willing to pay the extra price to get a hard-on with no payoff.

I stayed at the bar and polished off my drink while I waited for Candy. I didn't want the guys to make Candy feel awkward or slutty by having to come and get me. My cock grew hard thinking about being inside her. We'd never have a relationship, but the flirting and innuendo for months has been driving me crazy.

I was tired this evening after working all day hustling for a sale, more mentally exhausted than physically. I wanted to crawl into the bottle of Jack and let it soak through my skin taking all thoughts and memories with it.

"Ready?" her voice startled me dragging me from of my thoughts. "Sorry, you okay?" she asked.

"Never better. I'm always ready for some Candy." I smiled, "Where do you want to go?"

"Backstage to the employee area, come on." She motioned for me to follow her, and she approached the security guard standing at the door to the employee

Kayden: The Past

area. He smiled at her and looked me up and down before stepping out of the way. The hallway was dimly lit with half naked women walking around and bitching about the amount of tips they were given for the night. A knockout red-head caught my eye in passing. She was dressed in a white lace with stiletto white high heels. She looked up as I walked by, and our eyes locked. She looked familiar, but I couldn't place her. Candy looked back and noticed my attention averted away from her. "Kayden, are you coming?" No truer words have ever been spoken in the moment.

"Right behind you," I said as I picked up the pace not wanting to be left in the dust.

"Let me grab something out of my locker. Give me one second, wait here."

The red-head approached me with a look of curiosity. "Hey," she said. "Don't I know you?"

"I was just thinking the same thing."

"I heard Candy call you Kayden. I think you know my boyfriend, Ron. I've heard him talking about a Kayden." she asked.

Ron, he is one of my best friends. We spoke often, but he had disappeared recently and now I know why; he was keeping himself busy with the hot piece of ass in front of me. "Yeah, Ron and I are friends. I haven't spoken to him in a couple of weeks. Tell him to give me a call when he has a chance. What's your name?"

"My name is Danielle. I'll tell him when I see him tonight. Nice meeting you, Kayden." She said as Candy emerged from the locker room, and Danielle walked away quickly.

"What was that all about?" Candy asked looking a bit jealous.

"We have a mutual friend, nothing else." Candy grabbed my hand and opened a black door that could almost be missed if strolling through the hallway for the first time. I followed her into a bathroom, not exactly the location I thought we'd be going to this evening, but I was game for anything.

Candy pulled out a tiny vile from her pocket and twisted off the cap. I didn't have to ask what it was as she placed a small amount on a metal stick and sniffed it. Her eyes rolled back slightly and a look of calm and euphoria became visible across her face. "Want some?" she asked.

Nothing was more alluring at the moment than a bump of coke and Candy's pussy. "Sure, thanks," I said as she passed me the container and stick. I didn't think twice or bat an eyelash; I scooped some out and inhaled it quickly.

I felt like my head was spinning as I let the cocaine fully penetrate my brain. I closed my eyes and let the coke and Jack mixture course through my system. The mixture was exhilarating and made my heart pound feverishly in my chest. I felt hands against my neck and moving through the collar of my shirt, grabbing my shoulders.

All sensation in my body was amplified. It felt like more than one set of hands caressed my skin. I licked my lips and began to open my eyes as she placed her lips against mine. "I want you here and now, Kayden."

"In the bathroom?" I asked. I mean I'd fuck her anywhere, but I wanted to be sure she felt the same. I didn't receive a verbal response, but that of her lips against mine, feverishly moving and trying to gain access to my tongue.

I responded, the cocaine taking full effect on my thoughts and feelings. I had energy that I hadn't felt in a long time; I wanted to rock her world and fuck her right through the dry wall. I wanted this to be at my pace and not hers. I grabbed her hair making a fist and pulled her face away from mine. She stared at me for a moment confused. "I'm in charge, baby, just enjoy the ride," I said and kissed her. Her break couldn't last very long, but I'd use every minute of it.

I tilted her head giving me better access as I dipped my tongue inside her mouth. She tasted as sweet as her name, like cherry soda. I kissed her jaw moving down her neck as I pulled down the straps of her lace fitted bra-like top exposing her breasts. They were perky and petite and fit her frame perfectly. I bent down and placed my lips on her nipple as I used my hand to pull her body closer to mine. I drew her entire breast into my mouth moving my tongue across the surface and flicking the hard pebble at the tip. I felt warmth on the outside of my pants as she rubbed my cock. She squeezed my cock causing it to grow harder. I ached as my cock throbbed to be buried deep inside her, and I didn't want to waste any more time kissing her.

Reaching down, I unbuttoned her cutoff jean shorts and pulled them down past her knees, making sure that her panties went along for the journey south, too. Her movement was restricted by her shorts as I ran my hand up her leg to the inside of her thigh. I straightened my body returning my lips to hers and slid my fingers through her folds. She was wet and ready and I couldn't hold out any longer.

"Turn around," I said, using my hands to help her turn her body. She complied and didn't speak a word in protest. I could see her face in the mirror above the sink as she positioned her body resting her weight on the sink. Her eyes looked slightly glassy from the coke she did early, and the look of anticipation on her face was clearly visible.

I unbuttoned my pants and the sound of my zipper, Candy's breathing, and the bass from the club music were the only audible noises in the room. I stroked my cock, pumping it, making sure it would be rock solid when I thrust inside her. I pulled the condom out of my pocket that I had waiting ever since Candy said yes to me. I opened it quickly, throwing the wrapper on the floor before rolling it over my cock. With my free hand, I trailed my fingertips down Candy's back causing her skin to break out in goose bumps.

With my cock still in my hand, I placed it against her opening rubbing the tip against her wetness. It slid in easily as I moved my hand away from my shaft allowing my cock to glide all the way inside. She moaned from the fullness, and I exhaled from the relief I felt being deep inside her. I gripped her hips with my hands and pumped in and out of her quickly. I dug my fingers into her skin, and her head went limp, falling forward. Her body bounced away from me every time my cock was fully seated inside her. I reached up with my right hand and gripped her hair, pulling her head back and stopping her body from moving away from my thrusts. In the mirror, I could see her tits bouncing from the motion, and her nipples were tight pink buds against her beautiful pale skin.

Her voluptuous ass stopped me from being buried as deep as I possibly could. I slowed my pace and stopped with my cock inside her. I used my shoe to pull her shorts down to the floor. "Step out of them, Candy," I said to her as I held my foot against the cloth. She moved her legs one at a time and kept her body against the sink to help her balance on her stiletto heels. "Place your knee up on the sink. I want to be buried balls deep, baby," I said in her ear.

She placed her knee on the white porcelain ledge, spreading her legs wider. I gripped her foot and

Kayden: The Past

began to move faster, chasing the release I wanted and needed at this point. The high from the cocaine was fading, and I didn't have time to waste. I heard cracking but didn't pay any attention as I thrust inside her. I watched her facial expressions, the ecstasy noticeable – her open mouth and eyes rolled back into her head.

Our bodies fell to the floor with a thud and the sound of shattering pottery. The sink had detached from the wall and laid in pieces around us, but my cock never left her body. Her hands and knees were firmly planted on the wet floor as I continued my pursuit. She moaned louder, neither one of us wanted to stop – no matter how messy our surroundings now were. I thrust harder and deeper than I had before moving with determination. My balls grew tight, and the muscles in my body grew rigid as a tingling sensation ran down my spine landing straight in my cock. The orgasm was amplified from the drugs and liquor in my body, helping to dull the usual bland orgasm caused by a condom. My movement slowed, and I opened my eyes trying to catch my breath. The room was a disaster. Candy's shorts were in a puddle, white shards filled the floor in varying sizes, and water was everywhere, and in some places, it was tinted pink from the blood that had escaped from our skin during impact. In front of me was Candy still on all fours and not moving.

"Sorry about that, Candy," I said as I pulled out of her. "Are you okay?" I grabbed the condom and ripped it off my skin, it was suffocating at times to wear.

"Fuck yes! That was the craziest damn thing ever, but you didn't miss a beat," she said as she started to move.

I stood up, zipping up my pants as I watched her struggle. She didn't know where to put her hands, and her grip was slippery from the mess. "Let me help you up." I grabbed her hand, pulling her to her feet.

"Fuck, we can't leave the room like this," I said. I needed to turn the water off and looked around for the shutoffs. I turned the knobs, stopping more water from filling the space.

Candy looked down surveying the damage her body sustained during the last fifteen minutes. "Can you go out and ask one of the girls for a robe?" she asked.

"Yeah, I'll be right back." I looked down making sure everything was back in place, although my pants were soaking wet. I walked out the door to an empty hallway. I saw light streaming into the hall and approached the doorway and found a group of women inside doing their makeup and chatting about men. I stood there for a minute, not wanting to interrupt their conversation.

The redheaded beauty from earlier looked over and spotted me in the doorway. "Shit, what in the fuck happened to you?" she asked.

"Um, just a minor problem in the bathroom. No worries. Would one of you ladies have a robe Candy could borrow, please?" I asked with a slick smile. I knew these girls would know what happened, well not exactly what happened... I mean who fucking would believe the sink came free from the wall.

Danielle smiled at me sweetly as she stood up from her chair putting down her makeup brush. "I got one she can use." She opened up a small door behind her and grabbed a red satin robe. "Give her this," she said as she held it out for me to take.

"Thanks, Danielle," I said as I grabbed the cover-up and hustled back to Candy before someone found her inside the bathroom naked, bleeding, and wet.

Kayden: The Past

I knocked on the door, not wanting to scare her. "It's me," I said before turning the handle and entering the room. "Danielle gave me a robe for you."

"Thanks," she said wrapping it around her body securing it with a bow. "You better get out of here before my boss sees this mess and you in here with me. He's going to be pissed, but I'll tell him I leaned against it, and it just fell off the wall," she said before kissing me on the cheek.

"I'll pay for it if he's a dick and says anything."

"Nah, he'll be pissed, but he'll get over it. Don't worry, now go," she said opening the door and waiting for me to leave. I did as she instructed making my way out of the employee area and walking back towards the guys still drinking at the table.

"What in the fuck happened to you?" Tony asked.

I shook my head and laughed as I sat down in my chair, "Candy."

"What'd she do? Kick your ass in a swimming pool?"

"The sink broke off the wall while we were fucking." I took a drink from the leftover liquid still in my glass, "She looks worse than me, though. I think I'm gonna jet. I need to get home and out of these dirty ass clothes."

"I don't blame you, dude. I'm going to head home, too," Bobby said.

I threw a fifty on the table to cover my tab and a tip for Candy before gathering my keys and wallet off the table. I said goodbye to the rest of the guys before heading to the door. Exhaustion overwhelmed me. The buzz of the Jack and coke had worn off, and I was spent from Candy.

The drive home was a blur as I adjusted my wet clothing as it clung to my skin. I walked through the door and immediately undressed throwing them on the tile floor in the entry. The blood from the cuts on my knees had dried on my skin, and the hair on my legs was matted down. I walked into the kitchen and grabbed a beer from the fridge before heading to the bathroom to shower. I placed the beer on the sink counter as I waited for the water to warm up. I climbed into the shower, grabbing a wash cloth to clean out the wounds on my knees and scrub the filth from my flesh. I let the water trickle down my skin, washing away the dirt of the day.

Candy and I never fucked each other after that night. Neither of us wanted a relationship. She had a boyfriend; I found out after the fact, and I didn't want the complication in my life. It was an experience, and I wanted to leave it at that. Fucking on a bathroom floor isn't what most dream of, but as a guy, I'm quite proud of the way we destroyed the room.

I did share some of this story with Sophia. She asked about one of the craziest sex experiences in my life. I told her about breaking the sink off the wall but didn't give her the other details. I still don't feel right sharing stories that involve other women, but she's so damn persistent at times. I chased the high – the ability to forget the fucked up mess my life had before. Cocaine had become a necessary part of my life.

Chapter 6

Clusterfuck ~ Ron & Danielle

Ron and I had been friends since middle school; we grew up in the same neighborhood. He was there when my mom caught us drinking; well, I should say he was there to drink the liquor but ran like a little girl when my mom ran started to yell.

He didn't go off to college like the other guys but hustles his ass off to make a buck. We didn't hang out every evening like I did with the guys at work, but we saw each other a couple times a month. He told me he'd started seeing someone new and that she was taking up most of his time, but we could go weeks without speaking and pick right back up where we left off.

Danielle must have told Ron she saw me at Tiffany's, because my phone rang the next day while I was in bed still nursing my wounds and my slight hangover.

"What the fuck happened with Candy, dude?" Ron asked. "Danielle told me that you were both bloody, covered in water, and that the sink was in pieces."

I laughed thinking about how the room looked as I left last night. "Shitty construction, the fucker wasn't attached too well to the wall. Guess it wasn't built to lean on."

"I guess not. Shit, and the blood?" he asked.

"We both hit the floor when the sink collapsed."

"Danielle said there was a lot of blood on the floor, more than just a simple fall," he said.

"We didn't stop when we fell on the floor." I laughed. Ron knew that I was an animal and didn't let simple things stop me in my pursuit of carnal pleasure.

"That's funny as fuck; I know you're one crazy ass mother fucker." I thought about all the crazy shit Ron and I had done through the years. He was there when Fred dared me to walk into the police station, the liquor, and the endless stream of women in my life. "Candy didn't seem to mind. She actually bragged to the rest of the girls. Guess you made quite the impression on her. You were the talk of the club last night."

"It's hard to believe that chicks are worse than guys when talking about sex. I always thought they didn't talk much, man was I totally fucking wrong," I said.

"I listen to those girls every night when I pick Danielle up from work. Their mouths are so damn filthy. They put us to shame, dude. I can tell you more shit than I ever wanted to know," he said making a puking sound. "Candy told all the ladies about your size, bend, and stamina."

Kayden: The Past

Ron had seen me naked more times than I could count. The wrestling team showered after each meet in a giant room and in gym class. Guys see each other's cocks, and eventually it just becomes normal. I always felt horrible for the guys with little nubs, the size of a small pickle. They tried to hide it, but the guys just couldn't help but notice. "Well as long as she did my cock justice," I said smiling at the knowledge that my shit was well represented and advertised amongst the other ladies at the club.

"Danielle's off tonight. We're going out for drinks. I wanted to know if you want to join us tonight. I want her to meet you under other circumstances."

"Yeah, Ron, I'd love a nice evening out with you two. Anyone else coming?" I asked.

"No, just the three of us; Danielle seemed curious about you after hearing all that Candy had to say. Let's meet down in Ohio City around eight?" he asked.

"Yeah, where you want to meet?"

"Great Lakes Brewing Company;" he replied.

"I'll be there, man," I said before hanging up the phone.

I laid there and thought about Danielle. Something about her caught my eye. She was strikingly beautiful. I was never really attracted to red-heads; I'd always been in love with blonds, but Danielle's look was fiery. I needed to remind myself that she's Ron's girl, and I needed to keep my hands to myself and remind my cock to behave while in her presence.

My cock already grew hard with the thought of seeing her. I reached under the blankets and wrapped my hand around my stiff cock. I squeezed it hoping that I could get it to go down or behave, but it had a mind of its own. I moved my hand slowly up and down and thought about her glossy red lips wrapped around my shaft. The thought of her mouth touching my skin caused my balls to tingle.

I gripped harder and moved my hand faster, paying extra attention to the head. I stroked it with my eyes closed and thought only of Danielle. I twisted my hand the closer I got to the top; the unusual curve to my cock made a straight up and down motion almost impossible. I moved my hips, making the visual in my head match the movements of my body. I had Danielle bent over the sink last night, not Candy. I could almost feel her pussy grip my cock as I increased the speed in which I thrust into my palm. I squeezed the head a little harder with each stroke, chasing the orgasm my body craved. My movement became more fluid, and I touched every inch of my cock with my fingers, twisting and squeezing. My body shook as the orgasm ripped through my body causing my eyes to roll back.

I prayed the release was enough to satisfy my hunger for Danielle when I saw her tonight. A girl was not worth ruining the life-long friendship that Ron and I had. I closed my eyes not ready to face the day and wanting the night to come just a little bit quicker.

The streets of Cleveland were busy, and people lined the streets sitting at small café tables outside restaurants and coffee shops. I walked in only a few minutes late after searching for a parking spot on the street. Ron and Danielle were at the bar sitting close together, laughing as I approached. I sat down in the empty high-top chair next to Ron.

"Hey Ron. Nice to see you again. Hello Danielle," I said as I moved my chair.

Kayden: The Past

"We were just talking about you," Ron said.

"Laughing at me is more like it." I gave them both a hurt look, but I knew better than to think Ron would be making fun of me.

"Nah, man, Danielle was talking about Candy. You literally fucked her silly. She was a total mess after you left," Ron said as Danielle touched his arm.

"When she walked in the dressing room, everyone stopped to look at her. You know how she looked when you left her in the bathroom. A total fucking train wreck. She seemed to be talking to herself mumbling about Kayden. She told the entire story, every second – almost a play by play. She cleaned the cuts on her legs with tears streaming down her face but never stopped talking about you. I can't explain it, but she was fucked up," Danielle laughed and her whole face lit up and her lips seemed to almost kiss the corner of her eyes. "You must have scrambled her brains with that cock of yours."

I sat there in shock but not about Candy. The casual way that Danielle tossed the word cock around was surprising. Women were usually a little more tactful when talking about sexual parts, but I guess in her line of work, it was par for the course. "It was a crazy scene with Candy," I said as I shrugged my shoulders and started to laugh. "Candy was a trooper through it all. I'm going to be a gentleman and not say anything else."

"Oh, come on! Candy told us everything. You have no secrets when it comes to sex. Just know next time you come into the club, every girl knows what's in your pants," Danielle said.

I felt uncomfortable talking about my cock with my friends' girlfriend, especially with him sitting right next to me. It must have been clearly visible on my face.

"It's okay, Kayden. It's some funny shit. You're like a rock star at the club," Ron said.

I swallowed hard; my mouth dry from the conversation as the bartender approached us. "What'll you guys have?" she asked.

"Shot of Jack and beer for me, what do you guys want?" I asked.

We ordered our drinks and talked about work. I was astounded to find out the amount of money the strippers were pulling down each night. I was definitely in the wrong line of work and lacked the parts necessary to make the crazy cash they were making each year. Most of the women were making six figures a year, literally shaking their money makers. Many of them were paying their way through school or like Danielle, trying to bank as much as possible before they aged out of the business.

Ron's newest hustle involved a rapid weight-loss system in powder form that could be added to any drink to inhibit appetite. I knew his ability to sell, and I'm sure a majority of his clients didn't need to lose an ounce of weight but freely gave their money to Ron with a smile. He could sell anything, but usually would burn out on a product before jumping to the next business. Pyramid schemes were usually the type of hustle he was involved in, his current venture included. Not only did he sell the shit out of the product, but he recruited others to sell and kick back a portion of the profit.

"Hey, there's Kyle De Luca over there." Ron pointed across the bar to a guy who looked vaguely familiar, but I couldn't place where I knew him from. "I see him downtown all the time; I think he lives around here, now. He used to play against us when we wrestled."

Kayden: The Past

Kyle was a wrestler from our rival high school. I never wrestled against him; he was in a different weight class, but Freddie often went against him and usually lost. "I remember him now. What's he doing?" I asked as Ron caught Kyle's eye and motioned him to come over and join us.

"Something you'd never expect, but he's a salesman like us," Ron said as Kyle approached our seats.

"Ron, I haven't seen you in fucking weeks." Kyle wrapped his arms around Ron giving him a manly smack on the back. "What the fuck are you up to?"

"Having a drink with my girl and best friend, Kayden. Kayden wrestled with me in high school," Ron said.

"Hey, Kayden, I remember you. We were at some parties together, but it's all hazy to me," Kyle said as he held out his hand for me to shake it.

I thought back to the countless parties I've attended, but I couldn't place his face. I was probably shit-faced and had my mind on pussy more than talking with an old rival from high school. "It's nice to see you again, Kyle."

"You guys need anything for tonight?" Kyle asked Ron. The question confused me. Did he own the bar?

"Yeah man, that would be great. Hook us up," Ron said reaching in his pocket for some money.

Kyle put his hand on Ron's arm, "Not here. Meet me in the bathroom after I walk away," Kyle said looking around the room.

"What are you doin' for work, Kayden?" Kyle asked.

"I sell cell phones and install them in cars on the side and you?" I asked.

"I'm in sales, too. I could use a cell phone. Do you have a card?"

I reached into my back pocket and pulled out my wallet. I always carried a handful of cards, any good salesman always does. "Here, call me anytime. I'll hook you up."

Kyle placed the card in his suit jacket. His hair was jet black, and he had blue eyes with a round face. He had a tattoo on his neck, which I found odd. It wasn't the typical salesman look, but maybe he worked for a company that had lax rules or he was like Ron and hustled for a living. "See you in a minute, Ron. Nice to see you again, Kayden." He leaned over and kissed Danielle on the cheek, "It's always a pleasure to see you, Danielle."

"I'm sure I'll see you soon, Kyle." She winked at him as he walked away. She looked at me with a sinful smile, and her eyes were alight with mischief.

Ron fidgeted with his drink and watched as Kyle disappeared through the bathroom door. "I'll be right back," Ron said before standing and following the same path.

I moved over to Ron's seat, "What are they doing in there?" I asked. "What exactly does Kyle sell?"

"Ron went to get us a little something to party with tonight, you'll see." She placed her hand on my forearm and said nothing more about Kyle. Her hand was warm, almost scorching my skin. I could smell her perfume, sweet but with a hint of something I couldn't place. She smelled like cotton candy, edible. My mouth watered, and I could feel my cock growing hard.

"You have a girlfriend, Kayden?" Danielle asked.

"Danielle, if I did, I wouldn't have fucked Candy last night. I'm a one woman guy."

"She has a boyfriend, but that didn't stop you."

"I didn't know anything about that. She's flirted with me for months. I offered and she accepted, simple as that." I sipped my drink. "What other people do is their business, but when I'm taken, I'm fucking taken. I've never been, nor will I ever be a cheater."

"Hmmm." She stared into my eyes and licked her lips. *Fuck, she's killing me.* I swallowed hard watching her tongue glide across her lips, wishing they were licking my cock. *This is Ron's girl, stop the dirty fucking thoughts.* I needed to remember who she is and that my cock would never be entering that pretty sweet pussy I knew she would have.

I looked away unable to take the torture any longer. Ron walked back toward the bar with a stupid ass grin on his face. I scooted back to my seat and my rightful place. I needed the barrier, the reminder of who Danielle was and that she most certainly wasn't mine.

"Did Kyle have anything good?" Danielle asked.

"Beautiful shit... clean," Kyle leaned over and kissed Danielle on the lips. I felt a pang of jealousy, a small punch to the gut, watching him kiss her. I thought about all that had transpired and read between the lines. Ron liked to party; he used drugs recreationally and during sex. Ecstasy was becoming the go to drug along with cocaine.

I had polished off my drink and needed another. The bartender made her way down to our side of the bar and started to place the clean glasses on the shelf above the liquors. I watched her trying to take my mind off Danielle. She had a tight ass, and the tramp stamp on her back was black and tribal. I waited patiently for her to turn around, not wanting to be a dick. "Can I get another drink, please?"

"The same?" she asked with a beautiful smile, but it was ruined by the large piercing in her nose. I preferred my women to have piercings that only I could enjoy and that weren't the most noticeable thing on their face.

I shook my head and watched as she grabbed the bottles and started to pour. "Finish those off and let's get out of here," Ron said nudging me in the arm. "We'll have another round here, too, Miss."

"Where are we going?" I asked lifting my eyebrows.

"My place, some place more quiet, and we can sample the perfect shit Kyle gave me," he patted his jacket and grinned.

"I didn't know you and Kyle were friends. Do you guys hang out often?" I asked.

"I see him at the clubs all the time. He does a lot of business down here." Ron grabbed his beer and took a sip, "He's dating a girl that works with Danielle, and her stage name is Sunshine."

Sunshine is a stripper who had the same body shape as a Barbie doll. She has big tits, long legs, tiny waist, and long blond hair. She had plastic surgery to get the look of societal perfection; no one is that perfect naturally. "I don't think I've seen him there."

"Oh, he's always in the VIP room or in the back. He doesn't sit out in the audience. He does a lot of business from there, supplies the girls and owner, so he gets special treatment," Ron said.

Drugs are a part of the stripper life that is often over looked and happens in the shadows. Not all the girls are hooked, but many of them are a train wreck. "I'm sure he makes a bundle there."

Danielle rubbed Ron's thigh but kept her eyes on me while Ron and I spoke about Kyle and his business venture. We all took different paths in life, but we were all looking to make a buck, who am I to judge someone on how they make a living. Ron started to talk about his current business and never stopped. He loved to talk about his latest scheme. I pretended to be listening but couldn't help but watch Danielle as she stroked his thigh and squeezed his knee; I was mesmerized.

"Hey baby, can we get out of here?" Danielle interrupted.

He snapped out of his business mode turning towards her, "Sorry about that. I get so caught up when I start talking about work. You need to stop me when I get on a roll. Ready to hit it, Kayden?"

If he only knew how fuckin' true his words were. "Yeah, I could use a little something extra," I replied. "I got the bill since you took care of the after party."

Ron and Danielle stood up as I threw a fifty down on the bar. I needed to get the fuck out of here; I needed air and separation from Danielle. I started to feel like the biggest asshole in the world, she's Ron's. I followed them out the door breathing in the cool evening air. I inhaled deeply holding it in for a moment before blowing it out slowly. "You want to drive with us or meet us at my place?" Ron asked as we approached his car.

"Nah, man, I'll meet you there. It'll be easier later." I headed down the street to find my car and cursed myself during the walk. *Why the fuck are you going to his place? I'm such a fucking moron, a stupid ass mother fucker.* I had to go to Ron's or else he'd know something was wrong. He knew I liked to party and would never turn down an invitation.

Chapter 7

Three's Company ~ Ron & Danielle

"The shit Kyle sells is the best on the streets," Ron said as he cut the coke. I sat on the couch and watched as he made plump lines on the glass coffee table. Danielle kneeled at his side with a look of hunger in her eyes. I sipped my beer and watched them closely. They seemed happy in the most beautifully fucked up way.

"Baby," Ron said as he handed the straw to Danielle. She smiled and looked like a little girl at Christmas. I watched her inhale, and the change in her facial expression was a sight to behold. Danielle is a stunningly beautiful woman. The change in her face and the euphoric look made me wonder what she looked like while coming.

Ron quickly grabbed the straw and snorted two lines holding his nose after each one and pausing. The entire situation was surreal. "Kayden?" Ron asked holding the straw out for me. I climbed off the couch and knelt on the opposite side of the table and looked at them both while they touched their noses and made sure not to miss a drop. I leaned forward pausing for a moment. I didn't pause because I didn't want the cocaine splayed out before me, but more because I didn't know where this would lead.

Ron and I had a past – one that I rarely mention. Sophia knows about it, and it's something I can't escape or leave out. When we started talking online, I told her about it briefly. Naturally, she had more questions over time, but I never went into details about us and the girls we've been with. We'd shared woman in our past, mainly in high school. One girl, her name escapes me now, was a regular for us.

Looking back now, it just wasn't right, but when you're a horny teenager, you don't think about it. She wanted it, and we gave it to her, plain as that. She wasn't the only girl who we shared. There were more after high school, and I don't know why or how they even happened. Ron wasn't well endowed and that may have factored into the equation, but I know if I wasn't hung, I sure as fuck wouldn't want a guy with a bigger cock fucking the girl I'm trying to nail.

Ron walked down the hallway, leaving Danielle and I alone. I looked at her, and as she did another line, and watched as her tongue darted out licking her lips. We were both sitting on the floor with a table full of coke between us. She looked at me and smiled before scooting a little closer.

"We want to know if you want to have a threesome, Kayden," Danielle asked with a hopeful look in her eyes.

The words shocked me coming from her mouth, and I almost choked on my drink. "He's having you ask me?"

"Yes, he said I should ask you. We talked about it, and he felt it was the right thing to do. He said you've done it in the past."

Kayden: The Past

"In the past, yes, and all with girls who meant nothing to either of us... We've never shared a woman we've been dating." I shook my head not believing the words that came out of her mouth.

I would NEVER share Sophia with anyone, ever. She's mine and only mine. When I told her the story of Ron and Danielle and the other girls we'd shared, I told her it would never happen with her. I love her too deeply, and the jealousy would kill me.

"You piqued my curiosity with Candy. Ron knows you aren't looking for a relationship, so he feels you're safe with you, with us." She moved closer, almost crawling to me around the coffee table. "Don't you find me attractive?"

I swallowed hard and licked my lips, my mouth salivating at the thought of tasting her. "I find you extremely attractive, maybe too attractive. It's dangerous."

She laughed at my words. "I thought you liked a little danger in your life," she said moving close enough I could smell the scent of her perfume – a sweet flowery scent. "Ron won't trust me with anyone else, please."

My cock answered the question for me, growing harder in my pants and straining against the material. I sat there and didn't move. I didn't want to make the first move or give an answer. I didn't know what the right thing to do in this moment would be. Ron's one of my best friends, but he did give his blessing. It's not like he wouldn't be there or this would occur behind his back – it was purely consensual.

Danielle leaned forward and stopped a breath away from me and stared into my eyes. I could feel her waiting for a protest, but I didn't give one. She placed her hands on my knees; I could feel the warmth of her skin as she kissed me. Her lips were warm and soft, and she tasted like strawberry lip gloss. I didn't touch her back. I needed to know Ron was okay with this, that he sanctioned it.

I heard Ron in the room and opened my eyes to see what he was doing. He touched Danielle's shoulders and started to kneel down next to her. He looked at me and nodded his head, giving me the sign of approval before kissing her on the sweet spot where her neck meets her shoulder. Her body shook, almost convulsing, from the sensation. Her hands slid across my pants and stopped at my thighs. She squeezed my legs, gripping tightly as her kiss grew more intense. I no longer wanted to be a passive participant; I wanted to be the aggressor. I wanted her since the moment I saw her.

I ran my hands across the skin of her arms towards her shoulders and placed my hand against the back of her neck. Kissing her was too intimate and personal, and all I wanted was to be buried inside of her. She wasn't mine to kiss or linger but to use enjoy and leave. I lightly pulled her hair downward breaking the kiss and exposing her neck to me. I kissed her perfume infused skin and could feel her pulse vibrating beneath my lips - it felt like the vibration of music coursing through her veins.

Her hand touched my cock and palmed me through the cloth. I moaned wanting to feel her skin against mine. Her shirt hit my chin as I licked her throat. Ron pulled her shirt, and I moved, allowing him to remove it. He unhooked her bra, and I slid the tiny straps down her arms exposing her breasts. She didn't have large ones but small beautiful tits. I ignored Ron and whatever he was doing from behind. I wanted to see her face and look into her eyes. She was too pretty not to look at.

I returned to my pursuit of her flesh needing to work my way down to her breasts. I placed my hands against her ribs and moved them slowly up her skin,

Kayden: The Past

stopping just below her breast, and grazed her nipple with my thumbs. She shuddered and moaned, squeezing my cock in her hand. I leaned forward licking a trail with my tongue down to her nipple and sucked it into my mouth. I flicked it with my tongue before dragging my teeth across it.

Her body shifted as she rose slightly, and my mouth instantly felt the loss. Ron pulled off her skirt while she adjusted to make the transition easier. She didn't have panties on underneath, and her mound was completely bare. Ron pulled her backwards and leaned over her face, kissing her deeply and filled with passion. She stretched out her legs granting me full access to her body.

I ran my fingertips over her skin from her shoulders down to her knees. I could see tiny goose bumps form as she reached up and grabbed Ron's face, holding him to her like a lifeline. I leaned forward and laid my tongue against her flesh moving it slowly. I could taste her, and the sweet tang of her pussy danced across my tongue. I laved her flesh with my flat tongue, soaking up every drop. I grabbed her ass and tipped her hips wanting to get deeper. I could feel her wetness dripping down her ass and onto my fingers.

I sucked her into my mouth running my tongue across her swollen clit. She pushed herself on my lips, grinding against my face. I squeezed her ass and dug my fingers into her skin. I sucked and licked until I felt her body shake from pleasure.

I couldn't wait any longer – my cock ached, and I needed to be inside her. I let go of her skin as she bucked not wanting me to stop. She sat up slowly and moved to face Ron as I unzipped my pants and pulled off my shirt. Ron laid her down on the floor and unzipped his pants releasing his cock. He held her legs in the air, and he pushed himself into her already lubed pussy. She reached up in search of me. I pushed my cock forward giving her something to hold on to. She eyed my cock, surprised by the size. She was used to Ron's size, but I knew she had to see plenty of cocks in her twenty something years.

I leaned forward wanting to feel her soft tongue and warm mouth on my cock. Her lips parted, and she sucked me in, taking all of me. My cock hit the back of her throat, and she didn't even gag. She cradled my balls, and she worked my shaft in and out of her mouth. I pumped my hips forward and back, controlling the speed and the depth. I didn't want to come, not yet at least. I watched as Ron's cock disappeared inside of her wet core. Her mouth did amazing things, but I wanted to feel her insides.

I waited patiently, watching the scene before me, trying to hold out for my turn. It felt like an eternity waiting for Ron to switch and give me my just reward. We never did sloppy seconds. He liked blow jobs more than pussy, and I knew that's how he'd finish. He didn't want her to swallow my come and claim her mouth in that way.

She turned and lay on the floor splayed out before me. The position was the same, but the cock in her mouth had changed. I was thankful that I'd get to see her, although her face would be partially blocked by Ron.

I pushed my cock slowly inside her, relishing in her tightness. Her body gripped my cock like a vice, clamping down on it with each pump. My cock has a slight bend to it; it's the secret to the pleasure I'm able to give. It hits just the right spot inside a woman causing the experience to be great and the pleasure more intense.

Her eyes grew wide as I began to move quicker and relentlessly pursued my release. I held up her legs gripping them in my hands and placed her toes in my

Kayden: The Past

mouth. I sucked them causing her to writhe against me. I licked the bottom of her foot as I pulled her legs a little higher and moved faster. This was about me, my release.

My body tightened and began to stiffen from the building pressure, and my speed became erratic. I was at the tipping point, the precipice of pleasure. Three more hard thrusts, and I spilled my seed inside her.

No one discussed condoms or birth control. In the heat of the moment and the drugs in our system, it never entered my mind. I prayed Danielle was on birth control. I didn't need a child being born from this one night of pleasure.

I pulled out as I watched Ron fuck her face. He withdrew and began to pump his cock in his hand, spilling himself onto her face and chest. She licked her lips and collected every drop off her skin, putting it into her mouth and swallowing it like it was the most delectable morsel. I stood up and gathered my clothing before walking to the bathroom. I needed a moment to gather my thoughts before heading home.

I stared at myself in the mirror, and I prayed to God that I wouldn't regret this night, that it wouldn't ruin the friendship Ron and I had shared. Sex can cause problems, emotional problems and complications. She was off limits unless Ron was part of the picture. I didn't feel as free sexually with the other person being a significant other. Jealousy can make things ugly.

I dressed and found Danielle and Ron curled up on the couch. "I'm exhausted. I'll catch you guys later."

"You need a ride home, K?" Ron asked.

"Nah, man, I'm good. I worked that shit right out of my system. I'm fine," I said.

"Danielle left you a party favor by your wallet, bro."

Danielle stared at me, looking almost mesmerized. She seemed to be paying more attention to me than the man at her side. I grabbed my keys, wallet, and coke off the counter before heading to the door. I wanted to make a stop for some beer on the way home and checked my wallet for cash. Inside was a tiny piece of paper that read "D" with a phone number and a heart. *Fuck it.*

Chapter 8

Breaking the Rules ~ Danielle

I should've thrown her number in the trash and never gave her another thought. I wish I had, but I didn't – something pulled me to Danielle. Maybe it was her beauty or her wildness – I have no clue. I thought with my dick back then, and I didn't use my head. My mind was too clouded, and my heart too broken to make an intelligent and thought out decision.

I put her number on my fridge and stared at it for days. I didn't call her. I would never betray Ron in that way intentionally. I couldn't avoid her forever, and her place of work was a regular hangout for me and my friends. I convinced my friends to go to the dance club in the flats instead of the strip club where Danielle worked.

Aqua was a late night club that stayed open until six in the morning and was the trendy spot to hangout. It sat on the edge of the Cuyahoga River and had a beautiful outside area and deck overhanging the water. The building faced the water and was covered in glass, showing the spectacular view of the city at night. Girls danced on the speakers; people made out on the couches, and sex happened in the bathrooms. It was crowded and loud and the perfect spot to get lost and dance my ass off.

We ordered drinks and stood at the bar watching the girls on the dance floor. I didn't want to be the guy asking a girl for dance; I'd wait until someone came to me. The music blared through the speakers playing the song 'I'm Horny' by Mouse T. Most of the girls were dancing with their friends, showing off their bodies, almost offering themselves up to just the right taker. I watched as men approached them and started to dance only to be turned away. I didn't want to be the creep being rejected tonight.

The guys and I weren't talking; the music was too loud to be heard. Bobby nudged me and pointed to the patio doors and held his fingers up to his mouth. I shook my head wanting to get some fresh air and talk - not much was happening inside the club for me to stick around. I followed him outside and watched as he lit a cigarette. "It's packed tonight, bro," Bobby said as he took a long drag off his cigarette. "Want one?"

"Thanks." I took the cigarette and lighter, cupping my hand when I flicked the lighter, trying to block the wind. "It's packed, which gives us all more options." I looked around the exterior. White lights were strung between the trees overhead, illuminating the grassy area and lights dotted the deck on the riverbank. A couple hammocks filled the open space, and couple lounged on them kissing and getting to know each other a little better.

"How's work at the new place, Kayden?" Bobby asked. He worked at my previous employer and knew what a lying rat Jessica was - how she lied to get me fired.

Kayden: The Past

"It's going really well. There are no females working there, so I know I won't have that bullshit happen again. How about you? I'm sure you were all happy to see me go – more sales for everybody else."

Bobby chuckled, "We weren't happy to see you go, but yeah, we're all making more money now that your smooth selling ass is gone." He inhaled almost sucking down the remaining portion of his smoke. "I got some good news that will make you happy."

I raised my eyebrows, not much made me happy lately, but Bobby thought he had a morsel that would bring me joy. "Shoot."

"Jessica," he said sucking down the cigarette to the filter before throwing it on the ground. "She was fired yesterday. I almost called you to tell you the good news, but I thought I'd wait until I saw you; I wanted to see your expression."

A smile crept across my face, and my insides grew warm with the knowledge that her ass was out on the street. "What happened?"

"I don't have the entire story, but from what I hear, someone called corporate and complained about your firing, and Jessica's role in it. Somehow they convinced them to pull up the security camera footage, and they saw her come on to you and not the other way around. She was fired for filing a false complaint."

I smiled and laughed thinking about the video someone had to watch. Neither of us knew that the store had been outfitted with cameras. I'm sure we wouldn't have fucked if we knew they could see us, and she sure as hell wouldn't have filed the false complaint. "Bitch deserved it. You've made my night, Bobby. She got her just reward."

"Trust me; everyone is happy as hell to see her go. I might make assistant store manager now. Will you come back if they call you?"

I know Bobby wanted me to come back, in a way, but no one really wanted the competition I brought to the table. I couldn't go back. She ruined my reputation, and I'd feel like I had to look over my shoulder constantly. "Nah, I like where I am now. I'll leave the hustle to you in that store."

He pretended to be sad, but I knew otherwise. "Sorry to hear that, man. We miss you," Bobby said. "Let's get back inside with the other guys and find some grade A pussy."

"Did you find your manhood all of a sudden? I thought it wasn't your style to be so forward?" I asked surprised by his complete one-eighty.

"My way just wasn't working. I'm sick of watching you guys have all the fun while I sit on the sidelines being a fucking altar boy."

I slapped him on the back, "Welcome to the dark side. Let's go find what you seek my friend."

I ordered another drink, watching the clock carefully. All liquor sales stopped at two am and were replaced by bottled water. Cleveland didn't allow liquor to be sold after two am and most bars shut down at that time, but Aqua found a way around it. I turned my back on the dance floor; I didn't want to watch anymore bumping and grinding. The club was more crowded than when we walked outside. People poured into the place after one looking for somewhere else to dance the night away after everything else closed.

I felt a tap on my shoulder and slowly turned my head to see who I caught. My stomach sank as my heart began to pound in my chest. Danielle – *Fuck*. I didn't turn around, taking a moment to gather my

Kayden: The Past

thoughts. Maybe she got the picture when I didn't call her; I hoped she just wanted to say hi.

"Hey Kayden," she said in my ear, leaning forward pressing her breasts against my back. My cock grew hard as I remembered her mouth on my skin and the feel of her tongue on my shaft. "You never called me."

I turned around slowly, and my arm brushed against her body. I stared at her for a moment and could see hurt in her eyes. I leaned in and smelled her hair as my lips touched her ear, "I didn't think it would be right to call you, Danielle."

"Ron and I were never serious, or I wouldn't have given you my number." I felt like shit. I wanted her. The rub of it all is that I knew Ron had girls on the side. Danielle isn't the only girl he was seeing or fucking. He had never been a one-woman man. Would he care if he lost one of his girls or if he shared her with me again? "I knew I wasn't the only one Ron was seeing; we made no commitment. We broke up a couple days ago."

I didn't know how to respond. Ron's still my friend, and I wouldn't throw his business out there for others, including Danielle, to know. "I just don't know, Danielle." Even if they did break up, you never date your friend's ex. It's just an unsaid rule.

"Come on, at least dance with me." Her lips brushed my ear causing a shiver to run down my body. I didn't see anything wrong with dancing with her. I've been balls deep inside her, what's a dance? She held out her hand and waited for me to respond. I enveloped her fingers in my grasp and ushered her quickly on the dance floor before my conscious got the better of me.

Danielle danced like music's part of her soul. I'd watched her on the stage, but the songs were always slow and sexy and chosen to help show off the female body and bring in the most cash. The speakers lining the dance floor pumped music into the air, the techno beat causing my insides to move with the vibrations. Danielle smashed her body against mine. We danced with our bodies intertwined as she wrapped her arms around my neck, and my body reminded me how much I wanted her.

She rubbed herself on my leg, grinding on me, as her leg rubbed my cock. All willpower I had of avoiding being with Danielle, wanting her, had evaporated. She smelled too good and felt amazing in my arms – I couldn't resist her any long. She turned in my arms and rubbed her ass against me moving with the music. She threw her head back and placed it on my shoulder as I held her waist, and we moved together to the music. Dancing with Danielle was the most erotic moment I've had on the dance floor and with clothes still on my body. She turned her face and ran her tongue along my jaw. I turned mine and captured her tongue in my mouth. I ran my hands up the side of her shirt brushing the underside of her breasts with my thumbs. I nuzzled my face into her hair and let our bodies move together as one.

We lost track of time as the songs changed, and we touched, danced, and kissed on the dance floor. She cupped her hand and motioned she wanted a drink.

We ordered a drink right before the two o'clock stop time. It would be water the rest of the night if we stuck around. "Now what, Danielle?"

"I drink my drink."

"Smartass, I meant us. Where do we go from here?"

"I'd say we need to get to know each other, Kayden. I know you're an amazing dancer, a great kisser, and fucked me better than anyone else in my life. I want to know you, Kayden. Who are you?"

Kayden: The Past

"If you figure out the answer to that question, please let me know." I laughed, what was there to say? I'm not a normal guy, but I didn't think any of her past boyfriends fit the average scale. "Can I take you out for dinner tomorrow night?"

"I work tomorrow night, but I'm off on Monday."

Fuck. Her job would be an issue with me if we became a couple. I didn't like the idea of another man looking, let alone possibly touching what's mine. I swallowed hard and put the thought out of my mind. "Monday then, I'll pick you up at seven."

"It's a date."

We stayed the rest of the night at the club dancing and talking. We found an empty hammock close to closing and laid together to watch the sunrise over the city. It was amazing. The glass windows all illuminated in shades of red, orange, and yellow. I'd never watched the sunrise with someone, spent a night awake dancing and talking, and a night with a woman without sex.

"Sleep well, Danielle," I said. I kissed her goodnight, and I longed to be with her, but we needed to wait, at least until our first date. She wrapped her arms around my body and held herself to me.

"Kayden, can I ask a favor?" She looked up searching my eyes praying for something.

"Anything."

"Will you come home with me and hold me until I fall asleep?" She blinked slowly, and her face looked heavy with worry.

An internal warmth emanated throughout my body and the corners of my mouth rose almost touching my eyes. "I'd love to. Are you sure?"

"Yes, I'm sure. It's been ages since I've just been held by a man." She planted her face in my shirt and wrapped her arms tighter around my torso. "I'm not looking for sex. I just want to be wrapped in your arms. I want to sleep peacefully."

I kissed the top of her head. "Let's go. I'll follow you home. No sex. I'd love to just hold you." Some of that statement wasn't true, but I could keep my cock inside my pants for one night. I wouldn't allow myself to come on to her and fuck her if that wasn't what she wanted.

She lived in an apartment above a store in an up and coming neighborhood of Cleveland. It wasn't safe like the suburbs or the area that I lived in, but it wasn't crime ridden. We parked on the street, and she walked to my car and waited for me to get out. When I looked at her face, she looked relieved. I followed her up to her tiny one bedroom flat. The front door looked like it had been painted dozens of time and the paint was chipping off. I knew she could afford more than the rent in this place had to cost.

The apartment smelled of flowers, and the scent was so strong it hit me as soon as I entered the space. It was a girl's place, and there was no mistaking that fact. Everything was a shade of pink with sprinkles of black throughout. She grabbed my hands as I looked around the room immersing myself in all things Danielle.

"This way." I would've found it without her taking my hand; the place only had two doors, but I could've easily spent an hour just trying to figure her out by things she surrounded herself with and gotten lost.

She went in the bathroom and came out in a long night shirt with a bunny on it. Not the sleep time attire I'd think a stripper would wear. It looked too childlike and didn't fit the sexy image I had in my head.

Kayden: The Past

She crawled under the covers and held them out for me. I took my clothes off and thankfully, maybe for the first time in my life, I had a pair of boxers on, because a naked me with Danielle in the bed would've been a bad combination, not that a tiny scrap of cloth would stop me. I lay down on my back and let her situate her body against mine before wrapping my arms around her. For the first time in months, I'd fall asleep with the scent and warmth of a woman. I'd missed it more than I realized and having her in my arms made my heart ache for the love of a woman.

We found that we had a lot in common, but the worst were alcohol and drugs. She was a user, but I wouldn't classify her as an addict. I knew it was a bad idea; my addictions could spin out of control and I could fall deeper into the world I had already stepped foot inside. I ignored my conscious and listened to the little devil on my shoulder telling me all the reasons I should be with Danielle. I was blinded by her beauty, mesmerized by her body, and infatuated with the woman.

Chapter 9

Lost & Found ~ Danielle

Ron and I talked before Danielle and I officially became an item – I needed his blessing, the okay from an old friend. She meant nothing to him. He had his choice of any girl out there; he was successful, good looking, and a catch. Danielle was just a fuck toy for him. She was his arm candy for events, but he had no real use for her and didn't see a future for them. I took his blessing and grabbed the reigns making Danielle mine.

Danielle rescued me from my loneliness. We didn't get to see each other much, but the time we did spend together meant everything to me, but I never did get passed the issue of her being a stripper. We talked about moving in together, and I felt it was right, but my only hang-up was her line of work.

I learned everything I could about Danielle. She came from a broken home, and her mom was on her second marriage, much like my mother although I had my father for most of my life. She started to dance to save money for college but never found the time or motivation to go after she started making the big money

Kayden: The Past

and becoming immersed in the adult industry. She'd never been engaged and had a couple boyfriends through the years. She was like me – a troubled home drove her to addiction at an early age. We were a matched set of fucked up reality.

"D, I want to live with you, too, but I need you to do something for me first." We sat on the couch facing each other talking about the pros and cons of getting rid of one of our places. We spent all of our time off together, and it seemed a waste of money.

"What, sweetheart?" She fidgeted with her hands and looked at her fingers.

I touched her chin and moved her face upwards; I needed to look into her eyes. "I need you to stop stripping. I can't stand other men looking at you and seeing you naked."

"I make such good money, though."

"Baby, we'll be living together. I make great money. Isn't there something else you can do? I'm too jealous of a person to have you continue. It's been killing me."

"I know how to make drinks. I guess I could bartend or something." She shrugged her shoulders. "I'm just used to the cash I get dancing."

"You aren't a dancer. Guys don't come there to see your moves; they come there to see your tits and ass. It's my tits and ass now, and I won't have you naked in front of strangers. I can't, or we'll never make it."

"Okay, Kayden. I'll put my notice in and look for a bartending job. Anything to be with you. I didn't think I'd be 'dancing' this long. The money made it too hard to quit, but for you… I will." I smiled at her last two words.

I felt an overwhelming sense of relief. Every night that she worked, I'd do anything to keep myself busy and not think of her naked on the stage. I usually turned to the bottle, although her working at a bar wasn't the best solution either, but at least her clothes would stay on. I grabbed her face and kissed her passionately. She'd made me happy with the knowledge – soon a major stress in our relationship would be over.

"It means the world to me, sweetheart. Your place or mine?" I didn't want to live at her place. It was cute but cramped and all chick.

"Yours is bigger, and I can break my lease anytime. I don't have much stuff to pack up, and it would just be easier. I hate this neighborhood, too."

"I won't argue with you on all those points. I'll help you pack when you're ready." I stroked her cheek and felt at peace, but I was still anxious to take this step. Bridget had ruined me to totally trusting a woman. She stabbed me in the heart at the last moment, but I should have known better, I wasn't on her economic rung of the ladder.

"I can start packing this week and maybe move in on the weekend?" She raised her eyebrows waiting for my seal of approval.

"I'll come help, too. You can't do it all on your own, babe."

The next weekend Danielle incorporated all of her pink knick knacks and pillows with my mostly brown interior. My sports memorabilia was quickly overtaken by her love of stuffed animals, something called Beanie Babies. They looked useless to me but who am I to judge. My apartment was a shrine to Cleveland sports, and they hadn't won a damn thing since before I was born.

Kayden: The Past

Danielle gave her boss a notice the day after we decided to move in together. She found a job at a hip new bar down the street and would be able to walk to work, and it allowed me to be close enough to keep an eye on her – more for her safety than my sanity.

I received a promotion at work too; I was now the assistant store manager. The company that I worked for knew of my sales skills at my old job, and I hadn't disappointed since my hiring. I was being groomed for the manager position and would replace someone in another location when an opening became available. I had skills when it came to selling people on an item and I could always up-sell them and spend more than they had planned. Everything seemed to be going my way. A beautiful woman in my bed each night, a salaried job with bonuses, and life seemed to be looking up for the first time in what seemed like an eternity.

We never talked about marriage in the months following her moving in. I wanted to take the relationship as slow possible, but the universe had other plans; grander ones that were out of our control.

"Kayden, I'm late," she said walking out of the bathroom in her sexy teddy and rubbing lotion into her skin.

"For what?" I looked at her confused by the statement.

"Dumbass, my period." My stomach instantly flipped over as I sat against the headboard staring at her in disbelief.

"You're pregnant?" I was dumbfounded, and the dumbass label totally fit me in the moment. My mind started to race with the thought of a baby and how it would change our lives and eventually our relationship.

"I don't know. I just know I was supposed to get my period days ago, and it never happened. I've always been regular and never missed a period before." She crawled under the covers and faced me with her head lying on her pillow.

I probably looked like an idiot with a million emotions crossing my face at once – happiness, shock, amazement, and fear. Fear was the winning emotion at that moment. I know she was looking at me waiting for my excitement, but I didn't think we were ready to be parents. We both drank regularly and used drugs. I quit using coke on a regular basis, and we both smoked weed almost nightly to help us sleep. Sleep was something that was never easy for me to do, but the relaxation marijuana brought me helped me enter a peaceful slumber. It wasn't the way I thought I'd bring a child into this world.

"Wow. I don't know what else to say. What now?" I asked.

"I'll make a doctor's appointment and see if there is something else wrong. Let's not get too worried until I hear what they have to say." She rubbed my stomach trying to offer me reassurance, but I knew Danielle; I knew she had to be a nervous wreck at the idea of a baby. She didn't have a job that offered maternity leave, and she worked on her feet all day. It wasn't the best job to have with a belly and body aches.

"Okay. Either way, I'm here for you. I love you, Danielle." I kissed her lips and pulled her into my arms.

"I love you, too, Kayden."

I held her in my arms that night and barely slept a wink. I stared at the ceiling for the entire night. I can tell you every spot and shape on that colorless surface. Were we ready to be parents? Could we be good parents? I didn't want to bring a child into a relationship without being husband and wife. It's one thing I'm old-fashioned about. I believed a child should be born in wedlock. I can understand why it happens, but we didn't have anything from stopping us.

The doctor confirmed her suspicions the next day. We were going to be parents in a little over seven months. I thought about nothing else all day and came to terms with any fear that I had. We'd make the best out of the situation and show the baby all the love in the world. I always wanted children, but I thought they would be planned. "I know this isn't romantic, but will you marry me? I love you, Danielle, and I want our child to be born into a family. Will you be mine?"

Tears formed in her eyes and the corners of her lips crept up her face, causing her eyes to form little slits allowing the drops to cascade down her face. "Oh, Kayden. I'd love to marry you, and I'll be yours always."

I kissed her lips filled with all the love that I felt and joy to make her mine with a bundle of joy on the way. "Do you want a big wedding?" I prayed she said no. We had money saved up, but I felt that we'd need that for when the baby arrived. We couldn't live in this tiny apartment forever.

"No, I rather just elope or something. Just us. I don't have a big family, and I stopped talking to my mom about the time I started dancing. I don't give a fuck about anyone, and we need to save our money, Kayden."

"I'll do anything you want." I meant those words. "The sooner the better." I wasn't going to drag out the engagement and allow this relationship to fall apart. I learned my lessons usually the first time and try to never repeat the mistake again.

"I don't see a reason to wait. I can't believe I'm going to be Mrs. Kayden Michaels." She seemed proud when saying our names mingled together.

"You'll be mine. How about a honeymoon?" I asked. We could both use a little time off and get away from the real world for a while.

"I've always wanted to go to the Poconos, is that okay?"

"Anything you want. I'll make the reservations."

Within two weeks, we were standing in front of the justice of the peace saying our vows. Getting married at the courthouse isn't the large drawn out production that I'd been accustomed to attending. It took under five minutes for him to go through the lines and for us to repeat them, sealing the deal and officially making us husband and wife. We were legally bound together. It was a shotgun wedding, but the impending birth of our child made me take the leap that I'd avoided with Bridget and for that I'm grateful.

"What are you doing?" Danielle screeched as I scooped her up into my arms.

"Carrying you over the threshold." I didn't think of myself as a romantic, but I know it's a custom. She wrapped her arms around my neck as I opened the front door, and she kissed my cheeks as I carried her into the apartment.

"We have a couple of hours before we leave for Pennsylvania. What do you want to do?" I only had one thing on my mind. I wanted to make love to my wife. I wanted to consummate the relationship.

"I'm going to consume you, ravish you, and make you sore." Her head fell back, and her body went limp.

"You know just the right thing to say to me to make my entire body quiver at the thought." I made slow passionate love to her. I did it face to face at an

Kayden: The Past

excruciating slow pace. I savored every inch of her body and stayed nestled inside her for over an hour.

We were spending the following three days shacked up in a beautiful room in the Poconos. When I was a kid, it was the hip and trendy place to go for a romantic weekend. I remember hearing the adults talking about their weekend escapes. The room had a large champagne glass that doubled as a hot tub and a heart shaped bed with mirrors on the ceiling. It wouldn't have been my first choice, but it's what Danielle wanted.

Getting away from our real life, even if for a short time, was such a stress reliever. The pressure at work had increased and getting the days off had been difficult, but I didn't really give them an option. A weekend in bed with Danielle is exactly what I needed.

I had this intense need to claim every inch of her body. How to broach the topic with her? She was on top of me kissing my lips and grinding her pussy against my cock. I pushed her away a bit wanting to see her face when I brought up the topic. "I want to claim all of you. I want to know I've laid my seed in every available part of your body." All the blood drained from her face.

"Oh, I don't know, Kayden." She started to move off of me, but I held her on top of me, keeping her close.

"I promise I won't hurt you, babe." I would do everything in power for it to be pleasurable for her. "I'll go slow and be gentle." She gnawed on her lips and stared at me with puppy dog eyes. "Have I ever hurt you?"

She shook her head, "No."

"When it becomes too much, just say the word and I'll stop. I promise." I pulled her face down to mine and sucked her lip into my mouth. I ran my hands down her hair and trailed my fingertips across her back. I touched her everywhere with my hands. I could never get enough of her skin, the smell, the feel, everything about it. I licked the skin of her neck down to her breast. I spent time sucking and licking her tits. I needed her really turned on for this to be pleasurable for her. I grabbed her ass and touched her puckered hole, and I knew it wouldn't be an easy process. She moaned at the sensation of my fingers touching her. She was tight and nervous. I had to find a way to relax her and get her used to something smaller before putting my cock inside her.

I moved Danielle off of me and onto the bed, placing her on her stomach. I could see her body instantly tense and become stiff. "Not yet, baby. Relax." I stood on the bed above her and reached down and pulled her hips into the air. She was like play dough in my hands and moved with ease. I rubbed my cock through her wetness before sliding it inside her pussy. I didn't move at first dragging my fingers across her lips collecting lubrication for my fingers. I moved slowly at first while rubbing the moisture from my fingers on her tight hole. I could feel it convulse under my tips. I increased the speed of my cock thrusting inside of her, filling her mind with nothing but lust and my cock. I pushed lightly waiting for it to yield to the pressure. I pushed deeper as I felt the muscles relax, and her body shook from the sensation. She yelped, but it was quickly followed by a moan.

I worked my finger and my cock in unison, confusing her mind by the sensation and erasing any pain she may have been feeling. I moved my finger twisting it as I pulled out, expanding the size and stretching her. I needed more lube to work in a second finger, but nothing was close at hand, and I couldn't stop. I dropped saliva from my lips letting it fall and plop on her ass, running down her crack and onto my fingers. I withdrew my finger and heard a slight whimper. I rubbed both fingers through the saliva before inserting a single digit again. I slowly worked in the second. Her body pulled away, but I held her in place with my free hand. Her movement stopped, and she moaned. Her face was turned sideways on the bed, and I could see the expression on her face change. She was on the edge, close to orgasm, but I wanted to make her come with my cock in her ass.

I slowed my rhythm, not letting her fall over the cliff of ecstasy, before withdrawing my cock from her quivering core. "Stay there," I said smacking her on the ass. She stayed still, not moving a muscle, she didn't even turn her head to see what I was doing. She had to be a jumbled mess and filled with worry. I grabbed a bottle of lube off the floor. I filled my palm with the silky fluid and palmed my cock rubbing it over every inch and ridge. I held the bottle against her ass and squeezed a generous amount letting it dribble down her crack over her hole and drip off her pussy onto the sheets. I threw the bottle on the bed and stroked my cock paying attention to covering the tip.

I placed my hand on her ass and spread her, giving me easier access. I rubbed the liquid on her hole and used my fingers to spread it inside her. I pulled my fingers out and grabbed my cock and rubbed it against her hole, pushing gently. "Relax, sweetheart. Didn't my fingers feel good?"

"Yes," she said all breathy but with shakiness in her voice.

"Relax and it will slide right in." I knew I was lying; it wouldn't slide right in without force on my part, but it would go in. I started with just the head, and I could feel her ass squeeze my cock with so much force I almost came on the spot. I stopped moving to let her body adjust to my size. "Are you okay?" I rubbed my hands down the skin on her back.

"Yes, I think so. Just give me a minute." She held her breath and blew it out slowly. When she exhaled, her ass released and I started to inch in slowly.

"It'll get easier. I promise it will feel good." I seated my cock inside her fully and the force from the muscles inside her were like a vice squeezing the life out of me. I arched my back laying my body against hers. I wrapped my arm around her waist and stroked her clit, rubbing it just the right way to make her world explode, with each swirl of her clit, she became more relaxed.

"Fuck, yes," she moaned. "Don't stop. Oh God."

"So damn tight. I fucking love your ass." I applied more pressure shrinking the size of the tiny circles I made on her skin. I moved slowly inside her, quick on the out and slow on the in. I relished in the feel and concentrated on the movement of my hands trying to draw out my release.

Her body tightened; every muscle became rigid and the sounds coming out of her mouth were the sexiest I'd ever heard. I started to squeeze her clit lightly with a rhythmic pulsating motion. Her eyes rolled back into her head, and her mouth grew slack. I didn't think her ass could get any tighter, but it put me over the edge.

"Fuck." My movement stopped as a tremor overcame every muscle in my body. The experience so intense I became powerless in the moment. My rhythm became jerky as her body writhed beneath mine.

"Oh my God. Uhhh," she moaned into the sheets.

I collapsed on top of her. Our bodies were slick with sweat, and I'd now claimed every inch of her. I left no stone unturned and no surface untouched in my conquest of her body. I waited for the swelling of my cock to subside before removing it.

"Ouch," she said as I pulled her with me onto our backs. She rested her head on my chest, and I laid there unable to speak. My breath was ragged, and my heart hammered at a rapid pace beating against my chest. My legs felt like rubber, and my entire body was a puddle of goo.

"I'm sorry, love. Did it hurt too much?" I ran my fingers through her hair, rubbing her scalp.

"Not too much. I don't think I've ever come so hard in all my life. Damn. Kind of threw me for a loop."

"So we can do it again?" I asked with a grin on my face.

"Not now."

"I know, babe. Someday?" I wanted to make sure I didn't shut that door forever. It's too good to wall it up and never be granted access again.

"Someday." She still hadn't moved and I watched her chest move up and down as her breathing slowed.

"I don't want to go home tomorrow," she said stroking my legs.

"Me either, but we'll go away and do something before the baby is born." I knew life would never be the same once the bundle of joy arrived. No more days or nights of marathon sex; they would be filled with feedings and diaper changes.

She rubbed her stomach resting her hands across her abdomen. "I can't believe I'm pregnant. The doctor always made me think it would almost be impossible."

My life seemed to be filled with the impossible becoming reality. I was happy about the upcoming birth of our child; it brought us together and sealed our future that I was too chicken shit to face.

"We have so much to do." My mind would become so overwhelmed when I thought about all the things we needed to do to get ready for it. We didn't know the sex, and we didn't want to know. I, we, wanted to be surprised – it should end like it started.

"One step at a time; we'll be ready."

I placed my hand on her belly and could feel her heartbeat. There was a tiny piece of us alive inside her, and I was in awe. I don't think my mind would truly be able to comprehend the reality until I held the baby in my arms. "You got to stay clean, Danielle." I know I didn't have to say the words to her, but I couldn't help myself.

"I know, but I can't do it without you. We both have to stay clean." She looked up at me with pleading eyes.

"I will." I meant those words. It had been years since I lead a clean lifestyle, but for the future of my child and my family, I would try my hardest. Danielle drifted off to sleep in my arms against my skin. I moved her off me and put a pillow under her head. She looked so peaceful, and the hard living disappeared off her face during sleep. I rubbed my fingers across her belly and put my face up to her stomach. I had so much to say, so much I wanted this baby to know.

"Daddy loves you. I'll be the daddy you deserve," I needed to get my shit together and get my addictions in check. "I can't wait to meet you, but take your time." I laughed quietly with those words. I lay down next to her body and pulled her into my arms. I laid her back against my front and held her stomach until I drifted off to sleep. Life was looking up for the first time in longer than I could remember.

Danielle and I cleaned up our acts after we found out we were going to be parents; we helped each other through withdrawal and the cravings. When I thought my life had finally turned around – God had other plans. Who knows why things happen in life? Is there an ultimate plan, is it written in the stars and are we predestined? I don't know about any of that bullshit, but I know we have no control over our lives at times. Even the best laid plans can fall apart and lay in tatters at our feet.

Chapter 10

First Comes Love, Then Comes Marriage, Then Comes...
~ Danielle

Danielle looked so small and breakable lying in the hospital bed. She was asleep or passed out from the medication that was still coursing through her system. My heart was broken. I thought I'd experienced loss in my life, but it was a piece of me, a piece of us that died tonight. I didn't have any memories to look back on, no joyful moments filled with kisses, nothing – just emptiness.

She called me at work hysterical that something was wrong and that she was bleeding heavily. She was at the end of her trimester. Long enough for us to both fall head over heels in love with idea of being parents. We started to buy clothes, blankets, and all the little things you need when a baby's on the way. We already planned and dreamed of what life would be like in six short months.

Kayden: The Past

I'd lost friends and family in my life, but nothing cut a hole in my heart like the loss of a child, my child. The loss of a vision, a dream felt something entirely more, something soul destroying. I know at first I was scared shitless about this baby, but in this moment, I felt nothing but complete loss and utter sadness.

"Mr. Michaels." A voice behind me pulled me out of my emptiness. I turned to face the doctor with a deep exhale. There really was nothing more to be said. "I'm sorry for your loss."

"Thank you for your kindness, doctor. How's my wife?" I asked.

"She'll recover, but the trauma of losing a child will take her some time to deal with." I was traumatized, and the baby wasn't even inside of me; I couldn't imagine what she'd feel when she finally came to. "She'll be able to get pregnant again. There's no permanent damage." It's a funny phrase – no permanent damage. Maybe not in the physical sense, but my heart had a chunk removed that I'd never get back. "Wait a couple of months before trying again."

We didn't try this time, and eventually, I looked at it as a blessing; now, it was an event I couldn't wipe from my memory. "Okay, thank you. When can I take her home?"

"Give her today to rest and make sure there are no other issues; you should be able to take her home tomorrow."

I shook my head at a loss for words; something I've rarely experienced. I couldn't keep thanking him. It wasn't a joyful event, and I had nothing to be thankful for, except for Danielle. I walked away from him and towards my wife, my life. I sat in the chair next to her bed and held her hand. I rested my head on the bed and ran my hand across her now hollow abdomen. I needed to be strong for her. I needed to be her shoulder to cry on; she was more important than me.

I stared at her, waiting for her to wake up. Would the right words come to me in that moment? I hoped they did. Most would pray in this moment, but the words I had for God, if there's one, weren't pretty. I had no baby to whisper to while mommy slept; it was only her and I.

Her hand squeezed my finger, and I looked at her. Tears were streaming down her face, but no sound escaped her lips. I wiped the tears from her cheeks. "Kayden, the baby?" Danielle asked.

"Shhh, sweetheart." I crawled in bed and held her in my arms. "They couldn't save the baby; it was too little, D." I held her face against my chest and let her weep. She wailed, and the tears soaked my shirt, but I never let go of her.

"It's my fault. I did something wrong," she cried. I held her tighter not wanting to let go.

"You did nothing wrong. Don't say such crazy things. It just happened, love." I rocked her as she wept.

Tears led to exhaustion as she fell asleep against my chest. I feared the sadness would ruin us, drive us back down into addiction. I knew I was on the edge and craving something, anything to forget and dull the sadness I couldn't escape.

I stayed with Danielle in the hospital that night. I couldn't go home to an empty space and look at the baby stuff lying around the house. I knew the sadness would lead to drinking, and I couldn't go there now because Danielle needed me. I called my mom and asked her to go to our place and put any baby items in the nursery. I didn't want Danielle to see it when she walked through the door. We'd have to face it eventually. I just didn't want it to be the first thing she saw when she walked through the door. I didn't want it to be the first thing I saw; the thought of it made my stomach hurt.

Danielle was almost catatonic, answering in one syllable words and short phrases and not holding a conversation on the drive home. I helped her inside and thought about the vision I had of one day walking through the same door as a family, but it had vanished.

She looked around the apartment, "Where's the baby stuff?" She looked to be panicked.

"It's still here. It's all in the bedroom." I couldn't use the word nursery. It wasn't one anymore; it was a bedroom just like it was before Danielle ever came into my life. She pulled away from me, "No, D, don't go in there now."

She didn't answer me and walked straight into the bedroom and crumpled in the center of the room. I wrapped my arms around her. She grabbed a teddy bear off the chair and held it and rocked back and forth. I didn't know how to deal with the situation or what to do for her. I just let her cry and feel the sadness she needed to.

When her crying slowed, and she became limp in my arms, I picked her up and carried her to the bedroom. She stared at me as I started to remove her clothes while she sat on the edge of the bed. "Come on, baby doll. You need some rest. Let's get you out of these clothes."

"Don't leave me," she said with a broken voice.

I held her face in my hand, "I'm not going anywhere, Danielle. You're mine, my wife, everything I have in this world. I'll always be here for you." She wrapped her arms around me and held on to be so tightly she almost choked me.

"In the bed, come on." I pulled her arms away from my neck and helped her lay down. I removed my clothes, letting them fall to the floor in a heap with hers. I climbed in next to her and wrapped my body around her, enveloping her in my warmth and love.

My mom stayed with Danielle the first couple of days when I went back to work. She never really liked Danielle and didn't agree with her line of work; my mom wanted a June Cleaver type for a daughter-in-law, but those weren't the ones who I lusted after. My mom put her feelings aside and wanted to be there for us; she'd lost a grandchild and mourned with us.

Danielle had changed. The funny spitfire I'd known before she had dreams of booties and bottles. The connection we had before, the electricity that filled our relationship was only a flicker. Everything between us seemed strained as we tried to put our life back together. I didn't know how to fix the fracture that formed in our bond. Weeks passed slowly, and everything was stagnant. Something needed to change... I held on to every shred of hope I had that we'd survive. A month passed, and she was a shell of her former self.

"I want to move, Kayden... I hate it here." I was thrown for a loop. She never expressed those feelings before, and I didn't know how to respond.

"You do?" I didn't know if she meant another apartment or a different city.

"I want to get the fuck out of Cleveland. I need a change. There are too many memories and temptations."

Kayden: The Past

I sat there and stared at her. "Where do you want to go?"

"I don't care, out of state. A fresh start for us." She sat down next to me on the couch. "I need this. I can't walk into this apartment anymore. I think of the baby and all the happy memories we would've had and never will."

"Okay, sweetheart. I don't know where we'll go or what I'll do. We have to be able to survive."

"My friend, Trish, called yesterday while you were at work. Her husband is the manager for a cable company, and they're looking for installers. You'd be a contractor and basically be your own boss. She said there's a lot of money in it. We should go there."

"St. Louis? What the hell is in St. Louis?" I asked. I had dreams of Florida and warmth, not another Midwestern state covered in snow.

"All I know is it's not here, and you'd have a job waiting for you."

How could I say no? There really was nothing to hold us here. My mom had Joe and his family, and Danielle hadn't talked to her mother in ages. The rotten woman never even bothered to come around when we lost the baby. She didn't give a fuck about her daughter.

"I guess we can go there, if that's what you want."

"I want it, and I'm not going to change my mind either." She looked at me with a face of stone. I didn't have a reason to change her mind. If it didn't work out, we could go back to Cleveland; it would always be our home.

"I'll call her husband and find out about the job. See if it's really worth going to St. Louis, okay?"

"Yes. You've made me happy today, Kayden." I wanted to make her happy every day, but it was exhausting lately.

Danielle and I made love that day for the first time since the loss of our baby. It was slow, gentle, and face-to-face. I needed that physical connection with her, the hole in my heart closed a little. I loved my wife and would go to the moon and back for her, but I was just as heart broken and damaged as her.

Everyone seems to forget about the father of the lost child. I didn't carry the baby, but I had just as much love and emotion tied up into the loss of it. The Danielle who captured my attention long ago was no longer there; the façade was the same, but her insides had changed forever. She didn't look at me with the same sparkle, and her face didn't light up when I walked into the room. I hoped the change of scenery would help put the spark back in our relationship and help us feel like a couple again.

Chapter 11

Meet Me in St. Louis ~ Danielle

This had been a mistake. I came to St. Louis without Danielle. I had training and needed to find a place to live while she packed up our belongings. The problem with St. Louis was where I lived and whom I lived with. The house was stuffed with eight guys who all worked for the same company. They left their wives behind for quick money and flew home periodically. It was a frat house filled with temptation.

I bought a work truck and the tools I needed to get the job done. The days were long and grueling out in the elements. I did like the work. I didn't think I'd like it as much as working sales, but I liked working with my hands and being outdoors. I wasn't tied to a single space; the city was my workplace.

I missed Danielle, missed our life we had together. I didn't know where anything was in this fucking city. I had my roadmap and had to study it at every turn. It slowed me down. I kept her and our time together in my thoughts to help me make it through the day.

I was so lost in my daydream driving to my next job I almost missed my exit. I quickly cut across three lanes of traffic to just make it and avoid an extra half hour of driving. Sirens immediately filled the air. I shook my head. *Naturally there would be a cop to see me.* I pulled off to the side of the exit and rolled down my window.

He approached my truck with his hand on his gun. "Sir, license and registration, please." I reached over and grabbed my wallet off the seat.

"I'm sorry, officer. I'm new to the city. I didn't mean to do that."

"License, please." He held out his hand and didn't want to engage in small talk, I guess. I handed him my license and watched him walk away and climb back in his car.

I had a bad feeling about him. He didn't seem to be the type to give me just a warning. I hoped he would; my license was still registered in Ohio. I hadn't lied to him. The wait felt like an eternity as he returned with his pad of paper.

"I'm giving you a ticket for reckless driving." I closed my eyes trying to not let my temper flair. "You can pay it at the police station or go to court." He tore the yellow piece of paper off the pad and stuck it through the window with my license.

"No warning?"

"No, sir. It was reckless of you to cut across the highway in that manner. You could've caused an accident. There is no leniency for that."

I took the paper and threw it on the front seat. Pissed doesn't even begin to describe what I felt. I

Kayden: The Past

waited for him to return to his car before continuing on my way. I had a full day ahead of me and couldn't let this get to me.

I got more pissed the more I thought about the fucking ticket. Why can't some cops ever give a guy a break? I'm just trying to make a living and find my way through this maze of a city. I had four jobs ahead of me and wouldn't be done until well after dark.

I walked through the door after nine exhausted and dirty from crawling through attics and climbing on roofs. The guys were gathered in the living room and dining room, drinking and eating dinner. Everyone finished late and came home starving and thankful the day was over.

"Drink, Kayden?" one of the guys asked. I thought about it for a moment. I had a couple of drinks here and there, but tonight, it was the only thing I wanted to do; I needed it.

"Yeah, I'll take one." I watched as he filled the cup with more Jack than Coke. I drank it quicker than I planned. My thirst and hunger for the buzz overcame my will power. I'm weak and have no other excuse.

The night slipped away, and my cup was never empty. These guys could drink in volume. Most of them walked through the door at night with their gas station cups already infused with liquor. Work all day, drink all night, and repeat. That is the life of a cable guy, and I felt myself slipping into the pattern.

I opened my eyes to a blaring light above my bed. I don't remember coming into my bedroom or falling asleep; I just remember laughing and drinking. The alarm was blasting in the room, and everyone was starting to move around the apartment. I looked at my phone; I'd missed five calls from Danielle.

The phone rang four times before I heard her sleepy voice, "Hello."

"Baby, sorry I missed your calls last night," I closed my eyes and waited for her response.

I could hear her exhale into the receiver, but it wasn't a happy sound. "What the fuck happened to you last night, Kayden? You always call me."

"I'm sorry. I got home so late from work, and the guys were sitting around talking. I fell asleep."

"Were you drinking?"

I swallowed hard and thought about lying, but I just couldn't do it. "I had one."

"Which means you had five, Kayden. You've never fallen asleep and forgot to call me. I thought you were with someone else and not passed out in bed."

"I fucked up, babe. I wasn't with anyone. I'm only yours. I need to be with you. It's been too long since I've touched you. When will you be here?" I wanted to change the subject.

"I'll be there next week. Is the apartment going to be ready?"

"Yes, I have it all set up with the landlord. It's furnished, so we just need our personal stuff. It's not fancy, but I don't care as long as you're with me."

"I'm leaving on Sunday, so I should be there Monday or Tuesday. Depends on how far I can drive."

"Do you want me to fly home and drive you here?"

"No, I'm good. I'm a big girl, Kayden." She said it with such a sassy tone I was taken aback, and it wasn't sexy at all.

"I know you are, babe. I just want to see you."

Kayden: The Past

"I'll be there soon. Don't forget to call me tonight, got it?"

"I'll call right when I get home from work, I promise."

The phone clicked, and all that was left was quiet air. She hung up on me, and I knew I was in trouble; I had a lot of groveling to do to make things right.

I never fully grieved the loss of our baby when I was with Danielle – I had to be strong for my wife. My time in St. Louis without Danielle was a disaster. I fell back into easy habits, back into Jack. I couldn't stop myself without her there to remind me of what I had instead of what I'd lost. I hoped when she came to me that we'd be healed, and our new home would make us whole again.

I didn't forget to call Danielle after that night. I called her every evening as soon as I walked in the door. Did I continue to drink? Yes, the temptation was too great, and my loneliness almost strangled me. The days were too long not to fill my nights with liquor. I counted the days, hours, and minutes until I'd hold her in my arms again.

She called me along the way to tell me how far she'd driven. I stopped in the morning and grabbed the key to our apartment and did a quick walk through. She'd be here around noon, and it couldn't get here fast enough. I constantly checked my watch; time ticked away slowly, and I wasn't a patient man. I sat on the steps to the building waiting for her.

My heart skipped a beat when I saw her pull into the parking lot. My girl was finally here. I tried to walk casually up to her truck, but I couldn't walk slowly, the excitement overcame me. She opened the door and started to climb out when I grabbed her and held her in my arms. I inhaled the scent of her hair, a smell I had missed at night when lying in my bed.

"God, I've missed you." I kissed her lips not waiting for her response. I smothered her with my kiss, not wanting to pull away. She wrapped her arms around me and held on to me like a lifeline. I lingered on her lips before backing away slowly.

"I missed you, too, Kayden," she said with a smile on her face. She looked like the Danielle I met in the club, the one full of life and happy. "Should we unpack now?"

I held her hand and kissed the top, running my lips across the soft skin, "No, sweetheart. I want to show you our place. I need some time alone with you before we start working."

"Show me the way, handsome."

The apartment walls were covered in white, and the furniture was comfy, but it lacked personality. "It's nice," she said as she looked around the space. The kitchen was a decent size for an apartment with plenty of counter space and light wood cabinets. It was a complete blank slate, just like our relationship in St. Louis.

I grabbed Danielle and threw her on the couch. I couldn't wait another moment to make love to my wife. "Kayden," she squealed as her body bounced. I stripped off my shirt and threw it across the room.

She started to laugh, "Wow, excited, tiger?"

"You'll see how much." My cock strained against the fabric of my jeans, wanting to break free. I unzipped my pants slowly humming a tune and gyrating my hips performing a mini striptease. I swirled my hips before pulling my pants down at a slow rate until my cock sprang free. I ached to be inside her. I kicked off my pants and pounced on her, ripping the clothes from her body.

Kayden: The Past

"Kayden, stop," she said in a weak voice with words I know she didn't mean. I didn't listen. I started to kiss her neck and feverishly undid her pants. I used my feet to move them down her legs and out of the way. I pulled her body down and laid her flat on her back. I wanted to look into her eyes while I made love to her. I wasted no time, rubbing my cock against her wetness before slamming it into her.

"Fuck, you feel amazing," I moaned. I grabbed her legs and folded her up, pushing her knees against her chest. I needed to be deeper inside her.

"I fucking love your cock."

"Take all of me," I said as I slammed back into her, nudging her cervix. Danielle liked it rough and fast.

I didn't last long. The weeks apart were too great for me to bare and tugging it myself while apart didn't help prolong my release and she came when I did. I collapsed on top of her, and we lay there together catching our breath.

I kissed her forehead and lingered over her face a moment. "You're so beautiful, Danielle. I don't ever want to be apart like that again."

"It seemed like forever, never again, I promise."

We drifted off to sleep for a bit, just a cat nap. I couldn't help it with her in my arms. My bed had been so lonely and cold. We spent the rest of the day unpacking and eating Chinese food and talking about St. Louis.

"I'll start looking for a job tomorrow after I'm finished unpacking."

"Okay, babe. I have to work tomorrow, but I can cut my day short. I'm done with training and on my own now. I can work however many hours I want and need." I chewed the noodles that were laced with curry.

"There seems to be a lot around here. I'm sure I can find something pretty quick. I don't want to sit here alone all day."

"Want to go walk around a bit and see what's close by? Let's take a break from unpacking. It doesn't need to all get done right away, love."

"Great idea." She said with noodles hanging out of her mouth.

We walked the neighborhood and grabbed a cup of coffee down the street to keep us warm. I held her hand and never let go during our walk. I felt complete with her by my side.

Danielle found a job at a small bar down the street. The tips weren't as great as the place in Cleveland, but it filled her days and made her happy. I made great money, more than I did as an assistant manager at the cellphone store. I would drink when I was home alone at night. It was the worst part of her job, working evenings. Our time together began to be minimal over the following weeks. I'd feel her crawl into bed and wrap her arms around me. Sometimes I'd hear her sniff me, trying to smell the alcohol that was undoubtedly on my breath.

Danielle didn't drink anymore, but she still smoked pot; we'd smoked it together since coming to St. Louis. I only smoked it with her, preferring to turn to my drink of choice instead. I was happy that Danielle was with me, but the invisible distance between us didn't disappear. She wasn't entirely whole; she had lost more than a child that day.

I walked into the cable warehouse to grab my supplies and tried to think of ways to get it back, our

Kayden: The Past

love, the groove, the thing that drove me to her to begin with.

"Kayden," my boss yelled across the warehouse.

"Yo." I turned and headed in the direction of the voice.

"Get your ass over here, now." He usually wasn't so demanding and rarely yelled.

"What's up, boss?" I walked up to his office door and saw a police officer inside waiting in a chair. "What happened?" I'd never seen a cop here before.

"You, kid. Do you remember getting a ticket a while back?" he stared at me.

My mouth instantly went dry, "I do now, but shit, I forgot all about it."

"Well the cops haven't. You missed your court date and a warrant was issued for your arrest, Kayden." He shook his head in total disbelief.

"Fuck, I totally forgot about it. Can't I just pay the fine or some shit?"

"I don't know; you'd have to ask him," he motioned to the man waiting in his office.

"Damn it! This is the last fucking thing I need right now."

My boss knocked on the window and the cop stood up and walked out of the tiny room. "Mr. Michaels?"

"Yes," I answered.

"There's a warrant for your arrest. I need to take you in, son." I wanted to ask if this was the best use of law enforcement time, but I kept that tidbit to myself.

"Can't I pay the fine or something? I have a big day of work ahead of me. This will put me behind." The thought of having to spend countless hours at the police station made my stomach twist.

"Sorry, you'll have to come with me. I can read you your rights outside to avoid any further embarrassment."

Well thank God for small miracles, who needs embarrassment? Everyone already overheard our conversation and knew what was happening. He didn't spare me anything with his generous offer.

He followed me outside, read me my rights and placed me in the back of the police cruiser. Danielle would be livid with me, and I dreaded having to make that phone call. This wasn't an easy in and out, arrest means I'd have to go in front of the judge. I knew the routine all too well.

It took hours to have my fingerprints completed, go through booking, and get a fresh set of itchy jail clothing to wear. I'd see the judge at nine am tomorrow morning, and I'd find out if I could pay a fine and be released. This was ridiculous for a simple traffic ticket. Missing court wasn't intentional on my part; I simply forgot about the entire incident. I had to call Danielle and break the news to her.

"Danielle, baby?"

"What's up, Kayden? I was just leaving for work." She sounded like she was rushing around as I heard glasses clinking together.

"I have a tiny problem." I wanted to puke having to tell her this; how can I say it without her getting mad at me? I couldn't think of anything, totally blank.

"What now?" The now was drawn out and snarky.

Kayden: The Past

"Um, well, I forgot to pay a ticket that I got when I first moved here. The cops were at my work this morning, and I'm in jail waiting to see the judge."

"What the fuck? Are you serious?"

"Baby, I wouldn't kid about something like this. I swear to God."

"God, you can be such a fucking train wreck at times. How do you forget to pay a fucking ticket?" I could almost hear the venom in her voice. Danielle was the type who typically got quiet when she was pissed off but not today.

"I don't know. I just did. I swear it wasn't intentional, babe." I rested my head against the pay phone.

"Jesus Christ! I mean really, Kayden? How can you be so damn forgetful?" she yelled into the phone almost blasting out my eardrums. I held the phone away from my ear to let her finish. "Oh yeah, probably because you were too busy drinking Jack than running down after work to pay your fucking fine."

"I'm sorry! What else can I say?" I felt like a child – tiny and stupid. "I fucked up, babe. Now I have to sit in jail until tomorrow. I didn't want this to happen."

"When do you see the judge?"

"Nine am tomorrow morning and then I'll be home."

"I'll be there to get you." With that, the phone clicked, and she was gone.

There was anger and a hatred that I never heard in her voice before. Danielle wasn't the most put together and organized person. I thought she'd understand and maybe even laugh at me, but I never expected the amount of anger that I felt slap me in the face.

I was thankful when morning came, and I walked into the court room. The night seemed to drag on, and I was cold and lonely without Danielle. I saw her sitting in the court room, and I smiled when she looked at me, but I didn't get a smile in return. The smile quickly left my face and worry filled my insides. A knot formed in my stomach as I waited for my name to be called.

"Mr. Michaels?" The bailiff called out to the crowd.

I rose to my feet and approached the small podium in handcuffs. "Here, judge."

"Mr. Michaels, you stand before me now because you failed to appear before me for a traffic violation."

"Yes, sir." I swallowed hard, and my mouth grew dry just by the look of him. He didn't look friendly or forgiving.

"You were cited with reckless driving, and there is a heavy fine associated with the offense." He riffled through his paperwork before speaking again, "You'll serve three days in jail, Mr. Michaels, for failure to appear and pay a five hundred dollar fine for the reckless driving charge."

I stood there trying to process the words. Three days in jail. I wouldn't be getting out today. "Judge, I forgot about the ticket, please. I have a job and a wife, please."

"Maybe next time you'll remember, son. 'I forgot' is not a reasonable defense." He slammed down the gavel, and the officer walked toward me to bring me to the court room. I turned around needing to catch a glimpse of Danielle, but she was gone.

Kayden: The Past

The only thing I could think about while I watched the minutes tick away on the piece of shit clock on the wall was Danielle. How in the fuck did she just leave me there without a goodbye or even a last look? She just vanished without a trace. I felt like I was going to climb the walls. I was trapped inside, and Danielle hadn't answered any of my phone calls. She shut me out and turned me off.

Chapter 12

It Doesn't Only Happen in the Movies ~ Danielle

I walked out of the county jail around noon. Three days felt like an eternity stuck in a small cell eating bologna sandwiches and staring at a plain yellow wall. The one thing that jail is great for is thinking and self-evaluation. Danielle leaving the courtroom, without so much as a last look, was an eye opener. I needed to change my ways; I needed to get my shit together for the sake of my future, our future.

I looked around the parking lot, but I didn't see her or our car. My stomach twisted at the realization that she wasn't there to get me. A car slowly pulled up in front of me, and it was one of the guys from work. He rolled down the window, and I know I looked totally confused.

"Dude, I'm here to get you," Derek said. Derek and I lived together when I first moved to St. Louis and went through training together. He was in his work vehicle and didn't look entirely happy to be picking me up. We became friends during the couple of months I've been in St. Louis. When you're new to a city, you gravitate to those you know and become friends quickly.

Kayden: The Past

"Where's Danielle?" I asked still looking around the parking lot.

"She said she had to work and couldn't get out of it. She gave me twenty bucks to come get your sorry ass and bring you home." I didn't like the feeling of the entire situation. Noon wasn't a peak hour in the bar; she could've easily taken an hour off to pick me up and bring me home. My heart hurt; she was still punishing me. I know I fucked up, but my indiscretion wasn't worth all this suffering she'd been inflicting on me.

"It's fine man. Thanks for getting me. I can't wait to get home."

"Get in, let's roll. I have a couple jobs to get to this afternoon."

I climbed in his truck, and we chatted on the way home. "Does Don still want me back at work?" I asked.

"Fuck yeah, man. We're slammed and shorthanded. You're on the schedule tomorrow."

Thank God for little miracles. "Good. I was worried that I wouldn't have a job to come back to. I'll give him a call when I get home."

Derek dropped me at the curb, and I climbed the stairs to our apartment. I unlocked the door and walked into an empty space. I hoped that Danielle would be there waiting for me, that Derek was just a diversion. I had dreams of her waiting for me in a little teddy at the door, but my daydream was just that, a fantasy.

An envelope caught my eye on the kitchen table. Kayden was written in cursive, and it wasn't sealed. I opened it and withdrew the single white sheet of paper.

Kayden,

I can't do this anymore... I can't do us. We're two different people, and it doesn't work for me anymore. I think it's time for us to move on with our lives and go our separate ways. I didn't know how else to tell you.

We only married because of the baby, and I don't see a reason to move forward in this relationship. I don't feel I'm your number on – the thing you can't live without. I've always come second to alcohol. Losing the baby destroyed me and made me look at our life together. We weren't right for each other then, and we aren't now. I've felt detached from you after losing our baby.

I met someone, and he's helped me realize that we aren't meant to be. I can't devote my life and my heart to someone who I don't love anymore. I thought my heart shattered and died months ago, but I realize it was only temporarily frozen. When I'm with you, all I can think of is what should've been but will never be.

I've taken my stuff home and will be moving in with my mother; we started speaking after you left for St. Louis. She flew here and helped me gather my things, and we left yesterday.

Thank you for the memories and the chance to have a family; we just weren't meant to be.

-D

The letter slipped from my fingers and drifted to the floor. I stood there with my heart beating out of my chest. My body frozen in place. *She left me?* I knew that things weren't great, but I never expected this. *She met someone?* It was her idea that I go ahead and get settled, and she'd meet me when the time was right. I left her alone just long enough in her grief to find someone else to love.

Someone without all the painful memories.

Kayden: The Past

I sat down at the kitchen table and stared out the window. My mind still hadn't processed the finality of the situation. Could she really leave me with a Dear John type letter? I thought that shit only happened in the movies not in real life.

I didn't cry. I sat there in shock for what felt like hours. The loss of our child had been gut wrenching, but the loss of Danielle had felt earth shattering. I held my shit together with the loss of our baby because I had to be strong for her. Who did I have now? I was alone.

Using alcohol as an excuse was bullshit. Danielle was every bit an addict as me; it was a cop out. I picked up my phone and called her, but it went right to voicemail. She took the easy way out with the letter, the coward's way.

I went on a bender. I don't know exactly how much time passed after coming home to an empty house and waking up on the couch. Days probably, it's all a haze to me today. I consumed all the alcohol I could find in the apartment – which is more than I'd like to admit. I woke up smelling like shit, sweaty, and in the same outfit I walked out of jail in. I lost time... days which I'll never get back. How could she walk away from me? I never made her feel like my number two, but in her eyes, the booze always came first. Drinking ruined my life or at least it was the reason that was used, but what else did I have in my life?

I crawled off the couch and needed a shower. I needed to rid myself of the funk and clean my act up. I needed to get the fuck out of this place.

My phone rang, and my heart leapt. Danielle wanted me back. The time away made her realize she was wrong. I looked down at the screen, but it was my mom.

"Hey mom."

"Where have you been? I've been calling you for days, and Danielle hasn't been picking up her phone. I've been worried to death, Kayden."

"She left me, mom."

"What?"

"I fucked up, mom. I came home a couple of days ago to a letter that said she left."

"You're too good for that girl, anyways, babe. Come home."

Home was no longer Ohio. My mom and Joe moved to Florida to live the dream of every retiree. They wanted sunshine and beaches to fill their days instead of shoveling snow and freezing for six months out of the year.

"I don't know what I'm going to do, mom." Tears filled my eyes. How could my world collapse in such a short time? I'd swear I had a black fucking cloud that followed me around and fucked with my life. "I'm a little old to live with you, and maybe Danielle will come back."

"You've always got a place here. It's warm all year, and winter's coming. The door is always open."

"Thanks, mom. I need to figure this out for myself, but I'll get back to you."

"Where have you been the past couple of days?"

"I forgot to pay a ticket and had to spend three days in jail." I cringed holding the phone away from my ear.

"What? Kayden, I thought I taught you better than that. How could you be so damn forgetful?"

"It happened when I first moved here. I fucked up. I know, mom."

Kayden: The Past

"Well, I won't harp on you. It seems like you have enough shit on your plate right now. Just think about it, a fresh start. Love you, baby."

"Love you, too, Mom. I'll call soon."

St. Louis was supposed to be a fresh start, but it ended up being the finish line.

I called Don and quit. I couldn't go back to work. I needed to get the fuck away from this apartment and anything that reminded me of us. I spent the rest of the day packing up my shit and loaded it in my truck. I needed to find Danielle. I needed her to tell me face to face that we were over, fuck the letter bullshit. I wanted to remind her of what she threw away – me.

I left early in the morning after sleeping one last time in our bed. I slept with my head on her pillow, smelling the perfumed shampoo she used. The more miles that passed; the more pissed off I became. When she came to St. Louis had she already found the other man in her life? She was sneaky and never let on. I didn't know we had a problem until I was arrested, and she left me in court. I never would've imagined that I was disposable.

I pulled into her mother's around four in the afternoon. Danielle's car was the only one in the driveway. I parked down the street and casually walked up and knocked on the door.

"One second." Her voice was muffled by the door.

The door opened, and her smile slowly faded to a look of shock. "Kayden, what are you doing here?"

"You think you just leave me a letter and I'd let us die that easy? I'd just accept it and walk away?"

"No, but I hoped you would. I don't know why you're here. I'm not changing my mind."

"Can't we at least talk about this? Don't I get a say in any of this?"

"No, there's nothing to talk about. I want out."

"You don't love me anymore?"

"I don't know if I ever loved you, Kayden." My heart shattered in a million little pieces with those words.

"Why did you marry me then?"

"I don't know. I guess I thought it was the right thing to do with a baby on the way. I lusted you."

"You lusted me?" I tried to keep my voice down trying not to draw the attention of the people in their front yards weeding their gardens.

"Lust. Maybe I was infatuated with you."

"Can I come in so we can talk? I feel like an asshole standing out here having this conversation on your mom's front porch. I promise to behave. I just need to understand, Danielle."

She opened the door enough for me to enter and backed away trying not to get too close. I knew the attraction and pull was still there, that she still lusted after me. I walked into the kitchen and sat at the table, and she sat next to me.

"You found someone else?" I wanted to puke asking that question. I hoped it was just a lie that she used to get me to go away.

"Do you really want to know all this?"

I swallowed hard and thought only a moment before answering. "Yes."

Kayden: The Past

"I did, but I would've left with or without that person in my life. I didn't mean for it to turn into anything it just happened."

Again that mother fucking statement. It just happened. "Cheating doesn't just happen, Danielle. No man just falls into your pussy by accident."

"I was in a shitty place after losing the baby," she said as tears began to prick the corner of her eyes, "then when you left, I found comfort talking to someone else. It was nice not to have the reminder of what I lost."

"What we lost."

"When I'm with you, all I can think about is what could've been."

"We could've tried again."

"I'm not ready to try again. I can't take the heart break." I reached out and touched her hand trying to comfort her. The electricity still flowed between us.

"I know, Danielle. I felt every bit of that loss with you. It was my baby, too." I leaned over and wrapped her in my arms.

She pushed me away, "I'm not yours anymore, Kayden."

"You're mine until the judge says otherwise. You're still MY wife."

"I'll file the paperwork. I've already talked to a lawyer. I'm sorry, Kayden. We're just going different ways in life. You need to grow up."

I didn't have anything really to say to her. I could tell that I wasn't going to win her back. "Okay, Danielle. I'll sign whatever you want. I hope he makes you very happy, but I know he won't love you like I do." I stood to leave, but a thought came to me. I wanted to ruin her, and I knew just the way to do it. "Where's mom?"

"Working."

"She won't be showing up and waiting outside for me, will she?"

"Oh no, she's working until midnight tonight." Brains weren't always her strong suit.

She stood and walked me to the door but didn't open it. I wrapped my arms around her and enveloped her in my scent and warmth. I loved this woman, but she's wrecked me. As she started to pull away, I grabbed her face and looked into her eyes. I searched them for the love that I once saw, and I swear I still could still see it. She didn't pull away, and her lips parted slightly. One thing Danielle and I always had was a sexual chemistry that couldn't be matched.

I placed my lips on hers, waiting for her to say no. I pressed my lips harder and ran my tongue along them, looking for the access I wanted so badly. She opened to me and ran her fingers through my hair. I knew if I could only get my lips on her that she couldn't resist me or the lust that made her say 'I do'.

I fisted her hair controlling her movement; it was a weak spot for her. I commanded her like a puppet on a string; she was mine in this moment. I possessed her mouth and controlled her body with my kiss alone. I backed her up until her legs hit the cushions. Her body lowered onto the couch with mine, helping her fall gracefully. I grabbed the bottom of her shirt and began to lift it. I broke the kiss needing the space between us to remove her top.

"This doesn't mean we're getting back together, Kayden." She stared at me as she raised her arms allowing me to remove her shirt.

Kayden: The Past

"I know. I just want to bury my cock in you one more time. Think of it as a going away present." She didn't respond to my words verbally but began to unbutton my jeans. I removed my shirt and threw it to the ground. "Let me grab the door." I stood up and watched as she kept her eyes on me and kicked her pants off as I locked the door.

She looked like a wild animal staring at her prey as I walked back to her. She may not love me, but I knew she fucking loved my cock. I stroked it giving her a little show before I crawled back between her legs, placing my knees on the floor. Her torso was slouched down, and I had perfect access to her beautiful pussy. I grabbed her legs and yanked her body, pulling her closer to my face. I licked my lips before placing them on her. I devoured her. I licked and sucked until her body shook and was covered in perspiration. She laid there like a heap of skin, pliable and sedate.

I crawled up between her legs and ran my cock through her wetness; my saliva and her juices mingled. I crushed my mouth to her as I rammed my cock into her heat. I was merciless. I wasn't making love to my wife. I wanted her to feel my cock for days. I pumped into her hard and fierce. I held her legs in the air and spread them as far as they would without breaking them off her body. I pumped rapidly and didn't let up. I wanted to get deeper, needed her to feel me at her core. I wanted to bust her cervix.

I turned her over on her stomach, moving her like a rag doll. She was always putty in my hands. I grabbed her hips and hoisted them in the air. She clung to the couch, knowing what was coming next. I pushed her head down into the couch; I wanted maximum depth.

She was face down ass up, and I loved the view from above her – her slender waist an hourglass and her skin white as snow against her reddish hair. I wrapped her hair around my hand and fisted it as I stuck my cock inside her. I held her against me like a captive, but a willing one. Her moans grew louder and more intense as her muscles tried to push me out. I held her steady with her hair and slammed into her over and over again.

"Oh my fucking God," she yelled.

"You feel my cock inside you?" I asked slamming into her so hard the top of her head hit the arm rest.

"Yes," she moaned drawing out the s.

"I want you to feel me for days." I pulled her hair back, causing her eyes to look right into mine. "I want you to remember my cock inside you forever. You'll never get cock as good or anyone who will fuck you as hard and long like I do."

I pumped faster, faster than I thought I had in me. I was propelled by anger and vengeance at this point. It would be the last time I'd have my wife. "I want your pussy swollen, and you to only think of me."

"Fucker," she screamed as I slammed into her pussy one last time before pulling out and spilling onto her back. She didn't deserve to have my come inside her, and I didn't need the possibility of a surprise pregnancy either. I watched as it slid down her skin while I climbed off the couch.

Her body swayed back and forth as she tried to climb off the couch. "Thanks for the pussy, babe." I pulled on my pants as she stood glaring at me.

"You hurt me, bastard." She touched herself and winced.

"I didn't hear you tell me to stop." I buttoned my jeans and grabbed my shirt off the floor, pulling it over my head.

Kayden: The Past

"I hate you." She stood there naked looking like a lost puppy. She was torn; I could see it in her eyes. There was hatred there, certainly no love, but I fucked her so good that the lust still burned in her eyes.

"Feeling's mutual." I opened the front door, and I could hear her screaming as I shut it behind me. I walked out of Danielle's life that day. I didn't even show up for court when the day arrived. It would go through either way, and I didn't need the reminder of what I lost.

Chapter 13

Free Bird ~ Jennifer

I stayed with my grandmother and helped her around the house before skipping town. I decided to listen to my mother for once and join her and Joe in Florida for the winter. My grandmother was getting old, and I wanted to make sure the house would be ready when the cold, long winter began. After a week, I was ready to leave. I needed a change of scenery.

My mom greeted me at the door with hugs and kisses. She had dinner on the table waiting for me after the two-day drive south. "It's so good to see you, baby."

"Mom, stop calling me that." I shoved a forkful of meatloaf in my mouth and swallowed.

"Well, you'll always be my baby, but okay, fine. How are you?"

"Shitty, but I'm glad to be here. I've missed you."

Kayden: The Past

"Me, too. I got the names of some companies for you to call down here for work."

"Thanks. I'll start making those calls tomorrow. I need to work. I can't sit around this house all day."

"I know. They're dying for good workers down here. So many lazy bastards out there."

"Hopefully. So, tell me how things are with you and Joe? Does he treat you right, mom?"

"You know Joe, Kayden. He treats me like a princess. He got a part-time job and so did I; we don't see each other as much as we used to, but it's been good for us, trust me."

"Where are you working?"

"I started helping out at a club in town, serving drinks and helping in the kitchen."

"A club?" I stopped eating and looked at her.

"Not a club like you're used to. It's just a social club with people my age. People get lonely down here sometimes, Kayden. You should come one day this week and meet everyone."

"Yeah, maybe, mom. I'll see what happens tomorrow. I'm exhausted after that long drive." The drive wasn't the only reason I felt exhausted. I felt mentally worn out from the change my life had taken in such a short time.

"You look tired. Finish up and go to bed. I have plenty to do to keep myself busy, and we have plenty of time to catch up now that you're here." She kissed me on the head and walked to the sink.

I shoveled the last forkfuls of food into my mouth and carried the plate to her. "Thanks, mom. I'm happy to be here with you."

"I know you are, now scoot." She shooed me away as she grabbed my plate and started to wash it. I grabbed my bag from near the door filled with everything I needed for that night. I brushed my teeth and crawled into bed, hoping the future looked brighter than my past.

The process to be hired took more time than I would have liked. Background checks and drug tests took time to process. You'd think I'd applied for a job other than cable installer, but I guess everyone wanted to be safe. I spent my evenings at the club as my mom liked to call it. It was a bar that required membership to enter and be able to enjoy the food and drinks. I fell into old habits and spent my evenings drinking with my mom's friends and listening to their stories. It helped fill my nights with something other than loneliness.

The small town didn't have much to do, and it was packed every night. The bartender was decent looking and kept flirting with me. I tried to ignore it; last thing I needed in my life was another woman to fuck it up. I needed to not put my dick in her; my mom worked here, and I wanted to be able to show my face in this place for the near future. I walked up to the bar and she had a drink waiting for me. I leaned forward and whispered in her ear, "I can't."

She looked at me funny, "Can't what?"

"I can't sleep with you. I just want to put it out there. It's not that you're not hot, but I just can't. My mom works here, and it wouldn't be right."

"It's okay, darling. I just like flirting with you." She began to wipe the counter as I picked up my drink.

Kayden: The Past

"You're at least twenty years younger than any other man in this place."

I laughed and looked around. We were the youngest people in here; I guess I read into it a little more than I needed to. "I'm sorry. I just didn't want you to think I was leading you on, Cara." I read her name tag before speaking.

"It's okay. I love your mom, and she's told me a lot about you. Sounds like you've had a rough time lately."

"Yeah, you can say that." Fuck, was my mom airing my dirty laundry all over the place?

"Go enjoy your drink. I'm here if you ever need to talk. I can keep a secret, too," she said as she winked at me.

"Thanks, Cara. I'll remember that." I walked away and sat back down with the small group of my mother's friends. I felt like they were my new family. They welcomed me and talked to me like they've known me my entire life. I never felt like an outsider but one of them.

"So, Kayden, when do you start working?" Sal asked as he grabbed a handful of peanuts from the bowl.

"Tomorrow, actually." Not a moment too soon. I swear I was about to lose my shit in this town with nothing to fill my days.

"That's excellent, son. Good luck."

"Thanks, Sal. I can't wait to get back to work."

The chatter from the table filled the room. Everyone started talking about their past jobs and how happy they were to be retired. I couldn't imagine sitting around all day with nothing to do. The last couple of weeks had been torture; I couldn't imagine an endless barrage of days that held nothingness with no end in sight.

I finished my beer and said goodbye. I needed to get some rest and be ready to work my ass off in the Florida sunshine tomorrow. I was excited, like a kid for the first day of school. The shiny newness would wear off eventually, but for now, I'd ride the high.

I didn't need to go through training, just a quick rundown on how they handle paperwork. I had enough experience under my belt in St. Louis that the boss felt comfortable sending me out on my own the first day. Thankfully, he scheduled me only half a load to get day one under my belt. It was uneventful and went smoothly. I was good at my job and learned the little tricks to make life easier. Some people did everything the hard way, the longest way possible to cut down on their work, but I wanted more. I wanted to have the most jobs possible booked in a day. I called the office after each install to check in and give my work order. A sexy voice answered the phone each time. "Jennifer, what's your number?" I'd rattle off the digits and all the details, but into our third phone call of the day, it turned into chit chat. "You can text me the information too if it's easier for you."

I hate having to wait on hold; it was a colossal waste of time my time. "That would be great, Jennifer. Same number?"

"No, take down this number and put it in your phone. It's my private line, a couple of the techs send me the info that way. It's easier on everyone and quicker, too."

"Thanks. I got it. I'll send my last one through text."

"No problem. Bye." She said the bye in a sultry voice that caused my cock to twitch. I wondered what she looked like. The girls who worked the tech line didn't work in our warehouse but in another location offsite. I'd never have a chance to run into her without a reason. I finished my last job and texted in the activation code to Jennifer to close out my day without waiting on hold.

Over the next couple of weeks, Jennifer and I began texting beyond activation codes and confirmations. The texting started innocently but over time led to flirtation.

> Jennifer: One week and I finally get to meet you.

The company Christmas party was coming up, and I'd finally lay eyes on Jennifer. Flirting on the phone with a faceless person is easier when you have your own mental picture of their face and body.

> Me: Why haven't you sent me a picture?

> Jennifer: I can't do it on my phone. Hey, are you on Facebook?

What the hell is Facebook? I've never heard of it before; I've been so immersed in my own little world I often missed some of the newer things out there.

> Me: What's that?

> Jennifer: It's a website. I have a profile on there. You can see pictures of me on there.

I'd been told by some of the guys in the office that she's good looking, but I wouldn't believe it until I saw her with my own eyes. I rarely trusted the judgment of others when it came to women; my standards were usually higher. Although, it had been longer than I could remember since I've had my cock in someone. Danielle was the last girl I fucked, and I needed to move past her and open up a new world of possibilities. I needed to get on my game and live life like I did pre-Danielle.

Me: I'll check you out when I get home tonight. ;)

Jennifer: I've got to get back to work, hit me up on there later.

Me: Will do, J.

I hoped that her picture matched the vision in my head. I almost forgot that night to look her up, but she texted me when she didn't hear from me.

Me: I'm signing up now. Be patient with me. I've haven't really used the internet much. Give me ten minutes.

I entered my personal information and skipped some questions not knowing exactly what the website did. After hitting submit, I started finding people who I hadn't thought about in years. It asked me if I knew these people, and some I did. I sat there and stared at the screen surprised by the faces that filled it. Most of the people I hadn't seen since high school. I hit the Friend Request button next to a couple of them and ended up at a blank screen.

Me: How do I find you now?

Jennifer: I'll find you, one sec.

I sat there, and within a moment, I saw a tiny red notification at the top of the web browser. Jennifer's name with a little picture appeared and I clicked confirm. I clicked on her name to find out more about her and to finally get a glimpse of her. She was pretty, not drop dead gorgeous, but doable. She had dark brown hair that stopped around her shoulder with blue eyes. She had on too much makeup, and her body was average.

Jennifer: Hey. I found you.

Me: I see that. What do I do on here?

Kayden: The Past

I clicked on the search bar and started to look for people. I started with the guys from the wrestling team: Scotty, Freddie, and the others. They were all on here. I realized how behind I was.

Jennifer: You find people and can talk with them. Put your picture up. I want to see you. The girls in the office have a bet.

I chuckled. Had the girls been gossiping about me?

Me: A bet?

Jennifer: Yes, kinda like a hot or not bet.

Me: What did you say?

Jennifer: Hot. Your voice is so damn sexy, have to be hot.

I've known plenty of people in my life with the sexiest voices but train wreck of a face. I found a picture and uploaded it to my profile.

Me: Done. Hope you win the bet.

I kept searching for people I knew, people from my past. It recommended people to me, and I knew them. I started clicking on everything. Was this a hook up site?

Me: What is this? Is it a dating site?

Jennifer: Sigh, I win. I definitely win. No, it's not a dating site. Just a place to talk and share your thoughts with others.

The flirting had been great, but I didn't want a girlfriend. I didn't need the hassle or the heartache. I needed sex more than anything.

Me: Jen, I need to tell you something. I'm not looking for a relationship.

Jennifer: Who said relationship? I'm just looking for a little fun. Look, I was in a relationship for years, and I'm not looking to jump back in.

Women always said shit like that but never really meant it. Feelings always got involved when it came to sex. For some people, it was hard to separate the feelings after being with someone in such an intimate way. It was like a switch was flipped when the cock goes in. I needed to be clear with her and not lead her on in any way.

Me: As long as we're clear about this.

Jennifer: Perfectly.

I checked her profile out in more detail after she reassured me that she's only looking for sex and nothing more. She had pictures of herself in her bikini posted, but what caught my eye were the groups and other things that showed up on her profile. Groups with sexual names and graphic pictures. I followed the links and scrolled through the photos and postings. Some of this shit was hot, and my cock grew hard just thinking about them.

Me: Interesting groups you belong to, Jen.

Jennifer: A girl can look too. I'm not ashamed.

I wasn't in a position to judge anyone. What she did was her business. All I cared about is what she wanted to do with me. Facebook felt like an endless world of possibilities.

Jennifer: Sex is something I've never been ashamed to talk about or express. What's good for guys is acceptable for girls, fuck the double standards.

Kayden: The Past

She had me there. I smiled as I re-read her words.

Me: So, you want to hook up?

Jennifer: Yes, after the Christmas party. You game, big boy?

Me: You have no idea on both parts of that question.

I wouldn't say I had the biggest dick out there, but I'd seen plenty of cocks in my time. Changing in a locker room allowed one to see more cock than they ever wanted to.

Jennifer: I hope you're man enough to handle me.

Did she just challenge me? I could break her. Little girls shouldn't play with new toys unless they read the disclaimer first.

Me: We'll find out. I think I can 'handle' you just find. You'll never be the same again after me, just warning you now.

I may have picked the right girl for some fun. She didn't talk about feelings but wanted to talk about sex. We spent the night talking dirty; the conversation quickly going to the kinkier side of the fence. We shared our wildest experiences and hers kind of outweighed mine. I sat there stunned. I didn't think a woman ever threw her dirty laundry out there like she had. She liked sex rough, and she made that perfectly clear to me. She didn't want me to make love to her.

By the time I walked into the company Christmas party, I was ready for her and what the night held. She talked about things I've only seen in porn, *fucking hell*, I was game to try it all.

The party was being held in a local Italian restaurant. The company rented it out for the entire evening, and all drinks and food were on their dime. The company wasn't extremely large, but there were a group of about fifty employees who did various steps in the installation process to make it run like a well-oiled machine. I joined the guys I'd become friends with at the bar and ordered a drink. I looked around the room looking for Jennifer, but I didn't see her. Would she chicken out? Was she all talk and no action?

We swapped stories about some of our nightmare customers. Some women would answer the door in their robe and panties; I knew what they had on underneath because their robe was draped across their body, but they didn't tie it closed. Some were so overt with their sexuality and flirtation. I never crossed the line and didn't even think about fucking a customer. It's instant ground for dismissal. The money was too good, and they were the only game in town. If I lost this job, there was no other company to turn to.

A tapping on my shoulder drew my attention away from the conversation. I turned my head, and Jennifer was standing there with a big smile on her face. "I didn't think you'd show." I turned around and soaked her in. Her picture did her justice. She was decent looking, and her kinky side drew me in where her looks might not have gotten her a second glance.

"Hell yes! I wouldn't miss tonight for anything in the world." She smiled at me with a devilish grin.

"Drink?" I asked.

She shook her head yes. "Margarita, please." I studied her for a moment. A tequila girl, I like that. She had on a cute little polka dot sun dress and sexy red stilettos. She looked like a normal girl, but based on her sexual fantasies and experiences she shared with me, she was anything but normal.

"Margarita it is." The guys seemed to know her, maybe she did it with all the guys, and I'm just not in the loop, I didn't give a shit either way. Everyone stood around and talked about work. It was the one thing we all had in common. Our jobs didn't give us time to chit chat about our everyday lives. We saw each other for only a few minutes while stocking our trucks in the morning and doing our inventory in the evening. Our vehicles were our office, and the road our worksite. It was the best type of job. No one gossiped or knew much about each other; everyone kept to themselves.

After dinner, we moved on to shots. Everyone was getting their last couple of drinks in before the end of the party. Jennifer did shot for shot and kept up with the boys. We'd be a massive disaster if we were to become anything other than fuck buddies. I didn't need a wild child with drinking issues like myself.

"My place," she slurred.

"Are you sure?"

"Never been so sure about anything. Take me home. Show me what ya got." She grabbed her purse off the bar and handed me her keys.

I wasn't in the best shape, but I knew I could drive.

"You live far?" I asked.

"Just a couple miles away." She hiccupped. Please don't have this girl puke on me.

"Are you drunk?"

"Fuck no, takes more than that. I'm buzzed and feeling fucking fantastic. Are you stalling?"

"I never stall when it comes to pussy. Let's hit it." I grinned at her. I wanted to tear her shit up.

She held my arm as we walked to the car; she closed her eyes and sang as I drove. I didn't know the song, but she knew every word. She rolled down the window and sang into the air as her hair whirled around the car. She danced in her seat and kept moving the bottom of her sundress higher up her thigh, giving me a glimpse of her naked pussy.

I squeezed the steering wheel as I pulled in her driveway. "Ooo, we're here." She said as I turned the car off, and the music stopped.

"Last chance to back out, princess."

"Fuck you, you're being a pussy. Sure you can handle all this?"

"Out. Let's go. I'm going to give you more than you can handle."

I followed her into the house. The lights were off as she grabbed my hand and led me through the space to her bedroom. She flipped on the lights, and I was momentarily blinded by the brightness. She immediately started to take her dress off. She wasn't shy about her body. I removed my shirt and tossed it on an empty chair in the corner. She sat on the bed and ran her fingers across her naked skin as she watched me intently, waiting to see what I had in my pants. I slowly unzipped my pants, and my cock was already rock hard. I moved the material just the right way to let my cock spring from the top, giving an amazing visual.

"My word." She touched her lips as a smile crept across her face. "You sure don't disappoint." She leaned forward and touched the tip of it with her finger.

"Sure you want what you said, now that you've seen what I have to offer?"

She shook her head and looked at me from head to toe. "I want all of it."

She climbed off the bed and crawled like a tiger, stopping in front of my cock. She grabbed it with both hands and began to stroke it while swirling her tongue around the tip. I fisted her hair as she placed my cock in her mouth. She palmed my balls and licked my shaft and sucked me into the back of her throat. I could feel her swallow against my cock, and I almost exploded. The force against the tip was so intense I felt like she would swallow it right off my body. She was an expert at sucking cock, a true master.

"Stop unless you want me to come," I said as I pulled her head away from my body.

"I want you to come... You'll last longer for what I want." Fucking hell. This girl was all sex.

I released her hair and let her work her magic, sucking, licking, and pumping my shaft until my balls tingled and my body tightened. She sucked all of me, pulling out every last drop as I watched her take it all. She swallowed and licked her lips. "Mm, you taste so fuckin' good. Now, I want mine."

She didn't mince words. I'd give her what she asked for, every bit of it. She placed her body on the bed, leaving her legs dangling off the side. I lay down next to her and started to kiss her skin and suck her nipple in my mouth. I bit down on it, causing her body to twitch on the bed and her to cry out. "Did I hurt you?"

"No, more. I want it rough." I'd give it to her anyway she wanted.

I sucked her nipple and closed my teeth around it, trapping it like a prisoner. I pinched her other nipple and twisted it. Her legs moved, and her hips lifted off the bed. I played with her nipples until she was writhing underneath me almost unable to control the motions of her body.

"I need you in me, Kayden." She said in a whisper.

I ran my fingertips down her body as I held her nipple between my teeth and stroked it my tongue. I ran my fingers between her wetness. "How much?"

"I need you badly." She lifted her hips, "All of you."

I couldn't believe what she wanted. She liked it rough and big. Bigger than any man would be able to deliver with a cock. She wanted to be fisted and most men were turned off by the deed, but I'd never deny someone their kink. I worked in two fingers to start, getting the rest of my fingers wet on the juices running down her pussy. I kept my mouth on her tits while I worked my fingers, inserting a third and then a fourth. She could take it; it was more due to my hesitation that I worked them in slowly.

"More, more." She moaned. I've never been with a girl like Jennifer. The things she told me blew my mind, and I thought she was full of shit and playing a game, but in this moment, I knew that all her words were truth. I withdrew my finger and touched all my fingertips together, making my fist as small as possible. I placed the fingers at her opening and slowly worked them in and out until my entire hand disappeared inside of her. I didn't have the right angle, and my hand was cramped, so I removed it. I released her nipple from my lips and climbed off the bed.

"Why the fuck are you stopping?"

I laughed. "I'm not! I'm just getting a better angle. Quiet."

Her head dropped back on to the bed, and I stood between her legs and worked my hand back inside of her. I've always loved watching my cock disappear inside a pussy but seeing my hand do the same is something entirely different. My wrist was covered in her wetness as I worked my hand back and forth. I moved my fingers inside of her, hitting every

Kayden: The Past

crevice and spot she had. Her moans grew louder and louder as her body became covered in moisture, and her body twitched uncontrollably. I could feel my hand being squeezed by her walls, and my cock grew hard from the sounds, feeling, and sight of the scene before my eyes. It was like watching a porn movie but being the star instead of a watching it online.

"More?" I said as I stopped my hand inside of her.

"Oh, please. All of it. Give it to me. Nightstand." I looked towards the nightstand and saw a condom sitting out, waiting for me. I kept my left hand inside of her and leaned over grabbing the condom off of the nightstand.

I gave her everything she asked for. She wanted to be double stuffed but only by one man. I fucked her in the ass and fisted her pussy at the same time. It didn't last long though. Her body was so full and tight that I exploded inside of her within minutes, blow job or not.

It was the kinkiest moment, and I lived some wild shit. Would I ever do it again? Fuck, no. Once was enough. It was almost like watching a car accident that you try to look away from, but you keep peeking, unable to stop yourself. I'd never make someone feel perverted or gross for what they wanted in bed, but I knew that once was enough with Jennifer.

I called one of the guys to pick me up and bring me back to my car. I wasn't there to spend the night and share a bed with her. We both only had one thing in mind that night, and we each accomplished our mission. There was no love involved or a future for either of us. I wanted nothing to do with relationships or the complications they've brought into my life.

Jennifer and I continued to talk after that night, but we never had sex again. It was an experience, but not one I wanted to repeat. I could check it off my bucket list. She stuck true to her word and never asked for anything beyond that one night. She didn't let feelings get involved. We both got what we wanted out of the evening.

Chapter 14

A Piece of Home ~ Lisa

I'd been living with my mom for a month and Facebook became my link to my old friends and hometown. A beautiful blond caught my eye when scrolling through my suggestions one day. Lisa Jackson. She graduated a year after me, but I noticed she lived in the same town I did in Florida. We didn't date or hang out in the same circles in high school, but she was in some of my classes and had always seemed nice. I sent her a request and waited. I didn't have many friends besides the guys from work and the older ones at my parents' club. I could use a breath of fresh air.

I closed down the computer and headed to bed. I worked seven days a week lately, looking to make as much money as possible. I'd moved in to my own place and needed to make my bills each month along with extra cash for my evenings. I felt exhausted, but it gave me a purpose each day.

I checked Facebook the next morning before jumping in the shower. Lisa had accepted my request, and I had a message waiting.

Lisa: Hey Kayden. I see you live nearby; we should get together some night.

It was only five am, and I knew she wasn't on, but I wanted to respond to her.

Me: That would be great. I'm heading to work, but I'll be back on later tonight if you want to catch up.

We chatted well after midnight that night, talking about Ohio and what our friends were doing with their lives. I felt lost in Florida without a close group like I had in Cleveland. We talked online for days before we exchanged phone numbers and talked until we fell asleep. I can't recall any of the early conversations - maybe I've blocked as much out of my mind as I could. I'm not entirely sure why I have a hole in my memory when I think about my time with Lisa.

Lisa and I met a week later for a drink. Her mouth was dirty, and she had an aura about her. She was full of energy and spunk, and I wanted to wrap myself up in it - not as part of a relationship but a close friend in a foreign place. We started hanging out, watching football, shopping, and having dinner, but it changed along the way.

We shared our stories of lost love. We'd both lost people who we cared for due to cheating. We could understand each other and knew the pain the other felt. I felt comfortable with her, sharing my emotions with her without feeling like a total pussy. Being betrayed in that manner causes such extreme heartache; Lisa and I had a commonality that drew us together. She became part of my life, part of my world, and I was immersed in hers. I couldn't imagine not talking or seeing Lisa.

Kayden: The Past

Somewhere my hatred of relationships vanished, and we became an item.

I wish I could travel back in time and tell myself to run away. Don't look back... run - she's the devil in disguise, but knowing me, I wouldn't have listened. The breakup with Danielle was still fresh in my mind when I fell into Lisa. Maybe she was my rebound, but I jumped in head first and became infatuated with her. I should have slowed things down and got to know her more, but I never took the easy way and most certainly not the right way... I liked the bumpy path filled with debris.

We moved in together within months. Neither of us saw a reason to pay an extra rent, and we spent all of our free time together. She rented a house in an upscale neighborhood, and she wanted to share it with me. I was hesitant, but I felt that Lisa would never cross me the way the others had in the past.

You never really know someone until you live with them. You don't know about their bad days, their wicked ways, and their cruelty, but by then, you're so far lost that you need a wake-up call for you to comprehend it. Neither of us wanted to get married, just being in a relationship was a leap for me, but sometimes, your heart takes you somewhere your mind says do not wander.

Lisa and I had a wild sex life. We were like dynamite. Everything was explosive and violent at times. I was in such a dark place in my life, and the dynamic of our relationship fit me. She liked to be smacked in the face when fucked; she wanted bruises on her skin, and she clawed mine leaving her mark, warding off other women, although she claimed that wasn't the reason.

We fucked everywhere and anywhere. On an airplane – I earned my wings, at my class reunion – three times in the bathroom, on the side of the road – happened more than once. She liked the thrill of possibly being caught, and she made me feel alive again. I felt wanted when I was with her.

My cock did the thinking and led me astray. It betrayed me more than any woman ever had.

Every relationship has a honeymoon period, a time where everything is sunshine and fairytales, but eventually, the bottom drops out and reality smacks you in the face. Things began to change slowly – mainly she changed – her personality grew volatile, and her mood swings made my head spin. I was entrenched at this point; our worlds had become entwined.

Lisa became controlling and demanding. I didn't notice it at first. She did small things in the beginning: asking who was on the phone, checking my text messages, and logging in to my email. Alarm bells didn't sound; I just thought she was concerned, but every night, we'd fight over the crazy shit she made up in her mind. I turned to the bottle to deal with her crazy ass bullshit and unfounded accusations.

"Are you on Facebook again?" she asked me, standing over my shoulder at the desk.

"Yeah, I was just talking to Ron." I said pointing at the screen.

"I know you're talking to girls. Get the fuck off there!" I never had a girl be jealous to the extreme or suspicious of all my actions like Lisa.

"Okay, calm down." I said. That statement is the kiss of death, it starts half the arguments in the world. It doesn't help and is patronizing, but I didn't know what else to say. She was already in a shitty mood, and I didn't need a fight tonight.

I turned the computer off and started to put on my shoes. "Where the fuck do you think you're going?"

Kayden: The Past

"Out." I stood up, leaving the laces undone. I just wanted to get the fuck out.

"We need to talk."

"About what?" I stood there and jiggled my keys in my hand.

"You seeing other women."

I rolled my eyes. "Lisa, I'm not seeing anyone. I'm not a cheater. How many times do I need to tell you this?"

"Bullshit. I can smell a cheater."

I sighed not knowing what else to do or say. Her trust issues were starting to wear me down and make my pull to the bottle greater. I started drinking months ago. My daily beer turned into three then I graduated back to vodka. She made me miserable, but I felt she'd never cheat on me. Her jealousy and possessiveness were so fierce that I couldn't imagine her not being totally committed to our relationship.

"I'm not going to win this argument tonight, and I don't know how to prove it. I'm running to the store. I'll be back and give you some time to cool off."

She walked away, her footsteps heavy on the tile floor. Pissed off didn't even describe her anger level at the moment. I knew when I returned, the night would be filled with screaming, possibly her throwing some things at me, but it would end the same way it always did – I'd fuck her into oblivion.

At times, I think she picked a fight with me on purpose, wanting to yell and scream, maybe needing to. Her mood swings were vicious and came out of nowhere. I learned that she was bi-polar but often skipped her medication. That's the issue with a mental illness. When a person feels good, they don't think they need the medicine and then their other side comes out, and it's a struggle to get them to get back on it.

I allowed my drinking to grow out of control. It was the only way I could cope with her multiple personalities. It weighed heavy on our relationship at time but so did her disease. I found myself staying out after work a couple of months after moving in together, not wanting to face whichever Lisa I would get when I walked in the door.

I know it's no way to stay in a relationship, but I failed so many times I couldn't just leave. Why do people stay in a rotten situation? I wish I had an answer why I stayed with her. She became so overbearing, and I allowed it. Danielle and Bridget had ruined my view of a relationship, and as long as Lisa stuck by my side, I was in it for the long haul. Fucked up thinking I know, but I stayed and grew more miserable over time.

I became lost in the bottle, my only friend and savior. Lisa and I fed off each other, her anger and my drinking. We couldn't last forever in this fucked up state of being, but I didn't feel like I could walk out. Could I fail in love again?

Lisa had a rebellious side - one that reared its ugly head from time to time. She liked to steal, and it always made me nervous. I couldn't afford to get caught, but she didn't seem to have a care in the world. She said it gave her a high that she never experienced before. I understood the chase but not the risk of getting caught walking out with a pair of shoes on your feet you didn't pay for.

Lisa made new rules: no more drinking, no going out after work, no Facebook or other social media sites, and she needed access to my email account. She could read any of my mail or access any account I had; I didn't have anything to hide from her. The one thing I fought against in her demands was drinking. It became necessary to my sanity. I felt like a child with the rules

Kayden: The Past

she made, and like any normal teenager, I fought back and rebelled.

"Kayden, you big pussy! You going home to your broad or going to Greg's?" Mike asked after I called him to ask if he had a spare part. Mike and I shared a bond. Besides working together, we both had crazy bitches at home. We shared our misery and inability to leave, but Mike had an easier time putting her in her place than I did with bat shit crazy Lisa.

I didn't want to go home and listen to her bullshit tonight. Everything that could go wrong in my day already had, why not add to it? "Prick, I'll be there. She doesn't rule my life. I'm my own boss." I wanted that statement to be true. I wanted the spunky girl I met with the infectious laughter long ago, but that Lisa had vanished and was replaced by the controlling mad woman who was waiting at home for me. "I could use a night out with the guys."

"Sure, you say that now. You know she has you by the balls."

"Don't give me your shit! Your woman has your ass on a tight leash. Don't pretend she doesn't," I laughed.

"Who you fucking telling, but I have a free pass tonight. She's out of town visiting her mother." Why can't Lisa go visit her family back in Ohio and give me some breathing room. Maybe the absence would make her heart grow fonder and smash the invisible problem she has in her head.

"Lucky mother fucker! I'll be there after I'm done. I still have one more install and based on the beginning of my day, it'll be a couple of hours." I hung up the phone and decided to give Lisa a call. I needed to give her a reason I wouldn't be home in her expected time frame.

"Hey, baby. Just wanted to call and say hi." I twirled the keys in my hand feeling on edge.

"Hey. How's work? Almost done?" she asked.

She always wanted to know when I'd be home, so that she could watch me and make sure I didn't do anything to break a rule or betray her. "It's been shitty today; every install has had a problem, and I still have a huge job ahead of me. I'm going to be late tonight, babe, I'm thinking after nine." I held my breath listening carefully for her response.

"You need to quit that fucking job. Come straight home afterward, please." The please was bullshit. She added it to make it sound nicer, but it was a demand.

"I'll call you when I'm on my way. Some of the guys are going to Greg's. I may join them for an hour."

"What? Kayden, I told you this before. I don't want you hanging out with those guys. Your ass better be home right after work."

"Lisa, I'm not a child."

"You better not go there, that's all I'm saying." I could hear her breathing hard and fast in the phone. She was like a dog foaming over a squirrel.

"I'll call you later. I love you." There was no reply but a click. Fuck it! I'm a grown man, and I wanted a night out with the guys. Lisa did whatever and went wherever she wanted. A relationship should be about mutual respect, not ball busting and control. There'd be hell to pay when I walked through the door tonight, but I needed to grow a pair and take a stand.

Kayden: The Past

I walked through the door at Greg's two hours later ready for a cold beer. "Hey, he made it." Mike said as I entered the living room.

"Fuck you, Mike." I sat down on the couch needing to unwind.

"Beer?" Greg asked holding one out to me.

"Hell yeah, perfect way to end my day." I popped the bottle top and let the cool liquid ooze down my throat. I put Lisa out of my mind and laughed with the guys about work. That's the only issue with hanging out with people from work; they only want to talk about work. Tonight, it was fine with me, anything was better than talking about our relationships or personal lives. Mine was in disarray.

I lost track of time and the number of drinks I consumed while bullshitting with everyone. I finally decided to leave and head home to a hopefully calmer Lisa.

"Hey Lisa, baby, I'm on my way home," I said after she answered the phone sounding pissed off.

"I told you not to go out tonight. Have you been drinking?" Lisa asked in an accusatory tone. I didn't feel the need to lie to her; I wasn't a child and of legal age. Fuck her and her bossiness.

"I had a couple with the guys, no big deal," I replied assertively.

"I told you not to drink anymore, let alone hang out with those losers. Don't fucking come home tonight," Lisa yelled in my ear.

"Where the hell am I supposed to sleep tonight, Lisa?" I asked my heart starting to race and my temper beginning to rise.

"I don't give a shit. You're not welcome here. Don't come back here tonight or ever. I'm done with your bullshit and lies. You're an asshole and not worth the misery anymore. I'm through... we're through," Lisa screamed.

Click. Silence. I sat there for a moment almost in shock. This was the side of Lisa, the other personality that I hated. I said my goodbyes to the guys and walked out the door, hopped in my work truck, and drove erratically towards home.

The streets were empty, and I missed every red light. I drove like a bat out of hell, trying to get home and settle her down. We needed to talk about us, our future, and how a relationship should work as a team and not her as the Gestapo. I pulled into the gated community and was greeted by the guard.

"Evening, John. Can you open the gate for me, please?" I asked.

"Sorry, sir. Ms. Jackson said that you no longer live with her. I'm not to let you in the front gate."

You've got to be fucking kidding me. This has to be some cruel joke. "John, come on. You know I live here. I didn't move. She's just angry with me. Please," I begged.

"Sorry. Nothing I can do about it, sir, unless your name's on the lease, is it?" John asked with his eyebrows raised.

"No, it's not." I had a sinking feeling in my stomach – I wouldn't be going home unless I found my own way in. John didn't seem to feel the need to break any community rules; he took his job a little too seriously.

"Nothing I can do then. I can't let you into the community if you're no longer a resident," John stated to me in a matter-of-fact tone but with sadness in his eyes.

Kayden: The Past

I had nowhere to go. Even though my mother lived nearby, Lisa had made sure to sever that relationship with her craziness months ago. I should've known then to run for the hills. I had to be at work tomorrow, and I needed my work clothes from the house. I pulled out of the community and parked my car on the side of the road. *Where was I going to go? What was I going to do?*

The alcohol coursed through my veins and clouded my judgment. Lisa knew the consequences when she placed that call; she knew I'd be in a panic with no alternatives. I had to find a way into the community. She was vindictive and cruel. She never played fair. Fuck it, two can play at that game. It's my fucking house, too.

If I hadn't been drinking the following events would have never occurred. My relationship with Lisa would've ended either way. We were doomed from the beginning. We would've probably had a huge argument, and I would have moved out. The events that transpired were solely my fault, and the alcohol just helped make it seem like a great idea. I was a big fucking dummy and should have known the disaster I was about to bring down on myself.

I parked my truck in an empty parking lot hidden back in the woods. I walked through the darkened trees to the canal that surrounded the community. It was thirty yards to the other side, which I knew I could swim easily, at least when sober. The only problem could be the alligators that were hidden by the veil of night, but I put them out of my mind. I jumped in the canal with all my clothes on - there was no turning back now. I swam as quickly as I could and tried not to look around. Adrenaline and alcohol were giving me the stamina and strength beyond my natural abilities; they probably caused more stupidity than anything.

I climbed out of the water and collapsed on the bank. I could barely breathe, and my body was exhausted. I lay on my back staring at the stars, watching them twinkle in the sky. I thought about my love for Lisa and her ability to throw me out like a piece of garbage. It's one thing to end a relationship, make a clean break, but it's entirely different to lock someone out of their own home and toss them out onto the street. My blood began to boil with anger, and it propelled my body forward. I walked with a purpose... get my clothes and get the fuck out.

I walked through the streets with my clothes dripping and my shoes squishing. The house was dark and looked like no one was home as I walked up the driveway. I knocked on the door, but no one answered. I used my key in my pocket to unlock the front door and enter 'our' home.

I walked through the hallway and turned on the lights in various rooms, looking at all our things, things I bought or she stole. I started thinking about all of the money, sweat, and tears that I poured into our relationship and the home we made together. My anger increased, and my mind raced.

I should've grabbed my work clothes and left. I already looked like a crazy person walking down the street soaking wet. Would I have done any of this sober? I'd like to think not. I may have used my key to get in the house, but what I did next, I wouldn't have done without liquid courage.

Alcohol is a funny thing that way. It's like a little voice inside your head that tells you to do it – don't worry it'll be okay. It's the greatest traitor and my biggest seducer.

I wanted to break her things, make tears come to her eyes when she walked in. I started grabbing items off the bookcase, the coffee table, and the dining room hutch. I wanted to crush her the only way I knew how.

Kayden: The Past

At what point did I snap? Looking back, I'm not sure. I'd been so controlled and excluded from other people in my life... she'd played the last head game with me. There'd be no going back after this, and I didn't give a fuck.

I couldn't stop myself; she was throwing me away over hanging out with my friends and a drink, well maybe three or five. I came here to grab my shit for work and leave, but I got wrapped up in my anger. I wanted her to feel my pain.

I grabbed my work clothes out of the closet and saw hers hanging; the temptations was too great. I set my uniform on the bed with my keys and wallet and walked back in the closet. I grabbed as many clothes as I could handle and walked out to the pool. I thought about lighting them on fire in the grill, but I thought that would take too much time. I threw them in the pool, making the bitch have to work to get them back. I closed the sliding door behind me and walked out the front door.

I had become so consumed in my rage and revenge that I walked out of the house without my clothes, wallet and keys. I didn't think of it until later. It was my great epic fail, but I didn't realize it yet.

I walked the same path, tracing my wet footprints still on the street back. I swam across at a slower rate, no need to rush. I crawled out and reached for my keys, but they were missing. My heart started to beat quicker than it had from the physical exertion of the swim; panic began to rise in my throat.

Alcohol made me stupid. Let's not forget cruel and angry at times, but in this moment, I realized that the main reason I went there – my clothes, I'd left them behind with my keys and wallet. Why didn't I just leave a sign with my picture and name saying 'I did it'?

I walked back to my truck, hoping the doors were unlocked and maybe a spare key would be inside.

It was wishful thinking but no luck. I started walking with no destination in site. I needed to get to a phone; I left mine locked in the truck and called one of the guys to pick me up. A gas station was a couple miles away, but it seemed that I had all the time in the world. John had to call Lisa, and she made it home just as I left – it was the only way it could have happened so fast.

I started to walk, but I saw the police cars and their flashers moving up and down the street. I hid in the woods and evaded the police for a short time, but they caught up to me – they always do.

Maybe I moved slower than I remember or they were quicker than lightning, but it all happened in the blink of an eye. My world would be changed forever, and Lisa would be the one to deliver the final blow.

I sat in the back of the police car and watched as the houses passed by in a blur. I didn't say a word. What was there to say? I was immediately brought into the processing area of the police station. My fingerprints were taken; clothes removed and replaced, and I was brought into a holding area. I had flashbacks of St. Louis, and my brief stint in county jail. I knew I'd have longer to pay for this offense; this was a whopper, and Lisa would be out for blood.

I was brought into a little room for questioning. "Mr. Michaels, you're being charged with burglary. Remember, you have the right to an attorney."

"Burglary? I live there. It's my home." I sat there and stared at the guy across the table from me.

"You aren't a legal resident, and you didn't have permission to enter the property. You've destroyed thousands of dollars' worth of personal property during the break in."

"I live there. My mail is delivered there; my toothbrush is in the bathroom, and everything I own is in that house. How can you say I'm not a resident?" I tried to keep my body calm even though my voice was rising. "Go inside and look, try the key on my key ring."

"We'll look into it, Mr. Michaels. You'll see the judge in the morning."

"Yeah, yeah, sure you will." That was the end of the conversation. They were patronizing me by saying they'd look into it. I knew better. I was up a creek without a paddle in a river of bullshit.

The night crawled as I watched the minutes tick by on the small black and white clock outside my cell. I rested my body on the hard bed, but my mind raced... I needed to figure out a way to make her happy, and maybe she would take me back – I wanted her to drop the charges. It would be my only way out of this nightmare. *I must be fucking crazy too.*

The guard arrived outside my cell early in the morning to bring me to court. I was granted bond, and my mother had found someone to post it on my behalf. I didn't call my mom to even tell her what had happened, but in this sleepy town, I made the eleven o'clock news. My picture filled the screen along with all the gory details. Everyone I knew in this city had seen the story. I was embarrassed – no horrified – that my actions and alcohol had ruined my name and made my mom and Joe look bad.

I'd have a couple of weeks to meet with my public defender before my appearance in court. Public defenders aren't always interested in fighting your case, but more into helping you settle the matter in the best way they feel possible, whatever is quickest and least work. I shared all the details with him and made him aware that it was my home. He said he would work with the prosecution and see what could be done to throw out the case or reduce the charges. Burglary is a felony charge and required jail time.

It didn't really matter at this point. I knew I'd never be welcomed back at work, and it would take ages before I could show my face again without shame to the friends I made in town, especially my parents' friends who had taken me in as one of their own.

I made bail but had nowhere to go. My mom wasn't in court waiting to take me home; she may not have wanted her baby to sit in jail, but she wasn't ready to see me. I sat in the hallway of the courthouse trying to decide where to go while I waited for court, but nothing came to me.

"Why haven't you left?" I looked up from staring at my feet, like they had some magical answer, to the face of my asshole public defender.

"I don't know where to go. I don't have a home anymore."

"Salvation Army has a place around the corner you can stay. They have beds and programs to help you get back on your feet." He had a smile on his face like he just told me to go hang out at the Ritz in luxury while I waited to find out my future. "I'll be in touch about the case."

"Yeah, sure you will." I watched him as he walked away in the mass of people.

I followed his advice. I walked into the front doors of the shelter and tried to think of it as temporary. I'd only stay a night.

Kayden: The Past

The one good thing that came out of the Salvation Army was enrolling in their programs for alcoholics. I wasn't happy about it at the time, but it was a requirement if you wanted to live there. I sat through the meetings and listened to the stories people wanted to share, but I never shared my story. The only thing I had was my phone that the company returned to me after I made bail.

I worked in their store to help 'pay' for my room and board. Lisa contacted me shortly after my bail hearing. I didn't answer her first phone call or the second. I didn't have anything to say to her; she was the reason I lived in a shelter and worked in a thrift store, but eventually, my hard shell and fucking curiosity got the best of me.

"Hello."

"Kayden?"

"What do you want, Lisa? Not done torturing me enough?" I sighed as I stretched out on my uncomfortable mattress of metal springs and no padding.

"I'm sorry."

"That's all you have to say after all this bullshit?"

"I really am sorry. I want you back. Please, come back."

"How can I come back? I'm awaiting trial, Lisa, and you put me through hell for months."

"Come back to me, and I'll call and have the charges dropped, please."

I wanted to go back to my home and my record cleared more than anything in the world. "You get the charges dropped, and I'll come home; I'll come back to you."

"I've missed you, Kayden, more than the air that I breathe. I fucked up. I'm sorry! I don't know what else to say." I could hear her sniffle on the other end of the phone.

A woman in tears and I never mixed. I hated and loved her, why? I don't fucking know. She was the reason for my fucked up life being in shambles; well, not entirely, I played a pretty damn big role in my downfall too.

"I've missed you too, Lisa. I hate what's happened to us. Things need to change if I come back."

"They will," she said quickly. "I promise."

I wanted my life back.

I waited for the call from my attorney to tell me that the charges had been dropped, but it never came. My trial day arrived, and I walked into court feeling like a noose was firmly planted around my neck waiting for the floor to give way.

I stood in front of the judge and prayed that it was all just a cruel dream, but it was very much a nightmare that I lived, and nothing I did could make it go away.

I plead guilty and didn't contest the charges just as my lawyer told me to do. He said that the judge would go easy on me.

"The court accepts your plea, Mr. Michaels. I'm withholding adjudication until after your probationary period. Complete your probation and pay court ordered restitution, and your record will be cleared and no guilt will be placed upon your record," the judge said.

Kayden: The Past

My pulse increased, and my heart stammered with the news.

"Also, I'm placing a no-contact order on the property and Ms. Jackson. You are not allowed within fifty yards of said property or Ms. Jackson herself. Am I clear, Mr. Michaels?" the judge asked.

My heart sank, nausea overcame me, and I felt lightheaded. I couldn't go home and couldn't be with Lisa, or I'd break probation and be forced to serve jail time. My body felt numb.

"Mr. Michaels, do you understand?" the judge asked again.

"Yes, judge, I understand," I said.

Court dismissed, and my lawyer held out his hand to shake mine. I looked at it and then to his face, trying to grasp the orders of the judge. My lawyer smiled, but nothing about the verdict, or lack thereof, caused me happiness. I walked past him, without hesitation, into the hallway and collapsed on a bench. I had nothing and no one – my only salvation was in the shelter that I now called home.

Chapter 15

Saints & Sinners ~ New Orleans

I spent my days working in the store, my evenings in group meetings and my nights making phone calls trying to find work. I needed to make money and get the hell out of this place. Once I got my shit together after my trial, or lack thereof, I was issued a new ID card and went immediately to the bank. I had some money saved and could at least get out of the shelter for a night and go somewhere else to make a home, but there was a problem.

Lisa used the time I stayed in the shelter, without any way to get my money, to drain my account. She left about fifty dollars out of the kindness of her heart. She had all my passwords, and I should've known better than to think she wouldn't rip me off. I had no way to prove it was her because my account was used to pay bills, but it was her. I had enough money for a single bus ticket. I needed to make the right choice, one that would make my life take a different path.

Derek, the guy who brought me home after my release from jail in St. Louis, called me after weeks of waiting to hear back about possible work. I saw his name flash on my phone, and I hit the talk button as quickly as I could. "Hello."

Kayden: The Past

"Hey bud, how you been?"

"I've been better. Still haven't heard anything back on work. I'm starting to go out of my fucking mind."

"Well, I have some good news for you."

"What?"

"A company is hiring in New Orleans. They need workers ASAP, if you're looking to work. I hear they're even offering a signing bonus."

"Do they have company housing? I don't have a fucking thing to my name, Derek. The bitch stripped my bank account; I have just enough for a bus ticket."

"They do, and they'll supply the tools and the truck. Worth a shot. Better than sitting in that hell hole, are you still there?"

"Where else would I be? Text me the info, so I can jump on that shit and get things rolling."

"Will do, you okay?"

"I'll be better as soon as I get out of here. I need my life back."

"And Kayden?"

"What?"

"Stay away from women. You don't seem to have the best pussy picker."

"No fucking shit. I'm done, out, finished. Relationships aren't for me."

"Yeah, that's one way of putting it. Some of the guys from St. Louis went down to NOLA, so you'll be in good company." The thought of staying in the south for the winter gave me a sense of relief; I couldn't deal with another winter in the cold and snow.

Derek and I talked a few more minutes and then I waited for his text. I felt hopeful for the first time in weeks and slept through the night without the help of a beer. I called Human Resources the next morning and started the application process. It would take about two days for everything to process, and I could start immediately. I decided to get the fuck out of dodge as quickly as possible and bought my ticket that evening. I'd catch the nine p.m. bus to New Orleans and start over... again.

I wanted a fresh start away from the bullshit and chaos I always seemed to create and the waves of misfortune that followed me like an unending tide.

New Orleans is a place for new beginnings, a place one could go and get lost and leave old baggage behind, but not the right city for someone who craves alcohol. The party atmosphere's infectious and all consuming. It pulled me in and wrapped me in her southern Créole charm, making it feel like home to me more than anywhere else in the world. I could be anything I wanted here; I could live life on my own terms.

Déjà vu hit me as I walked through the door of the apartment. It wasn't the large home that eight of us shared in St. Louis but a small space with three bedrooms. It's common in the cable/satellite industry for the employees to live in company housing. The workers are transient and move with the work and money.

It was evening, and the apartment was buzzing with activity. I'd already stopped by HR and had all my paperwork cleared earlier than expected and got my housing key. I had to sign a million forms, signing away my life and most of my money for a while – I had to pay for the truck, tools, and rent out of each check.

Kayden: The Past

"Kayden," a voice yelled. Tom sat at the table in his work clothes, eating a sandwich with pieces falling on his plate. Tom and I worked together in St. Louis, and we'd kept in contact after I left. At least I knew one person walking through the door.

"Hey man, I didn't know you'd be here." I walked toward him and set my bags down on the floor. I held out my hand to him.

"I just got here a couple of weeks ago." He wiped his hands on his t-shirt; Tom wasn't always known for his class, but I still liked him. "That's Mark and John over there, and Tony's in the kitchen." He pointed to each one as he said their name. I looked at the guys and nodded my head, and they did the same. I was an outsider, but with such close living quarters, that wouldn't be the case for long.

"Where's my room? They said they had a single open." Most of the guys shared a room to cut down on the rent, but the last fucking thing in the world I wanted to do was share a room with strangers and definitely not another guy. It'd cost me a boat load, but after living in a shelter, I just wanted a room all to myself.

"Right there," he said, pointing to the first room in the hallway. "When ya start?" He turned his attention back to the sandwich.

"Tomorrow, I have to go stock my truck and pick up the keys; maybe they'll have me on the road in the afternoon."

"Go put your shit away and come have a drink."

It was inevitable. Liquor is part of the diet in this life, just like water when it's hot, alcohol filled the evenings for everyone. The bottles were already lined up on the counter waiting to be consumed. I'd have to learn how to control myself. The women in my life were what led me to overindulge; without them, would I be able to keep shit in check?

The bedroom had very little furniture, but that didn't matter. I'd be able to fill it up soon enough after I started working. We'd be paid weekly, and I didn't have any other bills or obligations, well, besides the restitution payments to Lisa, but I wasn't in a hurry to pay that off before I was required. I hung up my few pieces of clothing and sat on the bed and took stock in what I had and what I've lost.

I never had the chance to go back to get my things at Lisa's. The no-contact order meant I couldn't enter the property even with permission from her to get anything. I only had the clothes given to me at the shelter and a few small items. I had nothing for the first time in my life. Everything I owned fit into a duffel bag. I could hear the guys laughing, and loud music started to shake the walls, and I felt a happiness and inner peace that I hadn't felt in a long time. I felt like I had a home again.

Did I get drunk that night? No, I didn't. Did I drink? Yes. I didn't need to get drunk. I didn't need to show up for my first day of work with a hangover. I wanted to sit with the guys, find out about New Orleans and work, the hot topic of conversation. I listened to all their complaints and issues, but I knew I could work through anything. One thing I did well was work my ass off. I also fucked like a champ and could party like a rock star in my youth, but now was the time to put my head down and make cash.

I signed up for every type of online 'dating' website I could find during my first week in New Orleans. Facebook wasn't the only game in town. I made profiles on Match, Plenty of Fish, and even a site

Kayden: The Past

called Fuckbook. I didn't want a date – I was told these sites were strictly to hook up with chicks and get laid. I wanted to find someone looking for a little fun and a lot of cock. Each inbox filled up within days, and it was like a buffet of pussy sitting there waiting to be eaten.

I wrote and chatted with a few women, but they wanted relationships. My line to them always: I'm not looking for a relationship; I just want to fuck. Crude I know, but I laid it out for them. I only wanted one thing from a woman at this point. I didn't want the problems and complications that seemed to follow me around like a black rain cloud over my head. I found the promise land on Fuckbook and Facebook. Friends of friends on Facebook heard about me and wanted to chat and Fuckbook, I don't really need to explain.

I opened my FB messages, and Carrie had sent me a hello. She looked beautiful, but I knew pictures were usually bullshit. I used my picture, but most people try and scam with some random photo they find online. How do I know this? Because I kept seeing the same girl's photo popping up with different names all over the country. Her photo didn't send up any red flags, and her message was short and to the point: Hi ya, you're hot as fuck.

I loved a girl with a dirty mouth. I hit the chat button next to her name and took a shot.

Me: Hey. Like what you see? I know I do.

God, what do you say to someone you just want to bang and don't really give a fuck who they are or what they're doing. I wasn't going to be a dick about it. I wasn't entirely cold hearted at this point in my life, but I just didn't want to waste time or make false promises of a happily ever after.

Carrie: I'd rather see you without a shirt. Got something you can send me?

Her message gave me pause. Was I being played? I always thought I was the player, but I wasn't sure about Carrie. Too quick on wanting the skin photos, maybe.

Me: What are you going to show me?

Carrie: I have plenty to show. You live in New Orleans?

A photo filled the chat window – She wore a very low cut shirt and lots of cleavage. Her face was visible in the picture, and it matched her profile. All the little things you have to watch for when trolling online. So many ways to get duped.

Me: Yes and you?

Carrie: Just outside of NOLA but close enough to meet up.

Me: Nice rack. You looking for a relationship?

Carrie: LMFAO. Fuck no, why the hell do you think I'm on this site.

So far, she passed my test with flying colors. No relationship, check. Hot as hell, check. Dirty mouth, check. Doesn't live too close so clinginess wouldn't be a factor, check.

Me: I just want to be clear about it. I don't want a relationship; I'm done with the bullshit.

Carrie: Good. Listen, I want someone to scratch my itch, but I'd like to meet for a drink first – in public. I want to know you aren't some kind of weirdo or pervert, well at least not the bad kind.

So she wasn't a dummy. Things were looking up.

Me: Let's meet for a drink down in the quarter. I'm new to the area and would like to enjoy some of the city. You game?

Kayden: The Past

Carrie: Yes, can I bring some friends?

All the guys here were single, except one, and it sounded like a perfect idea.

Me: Sure and I'll bring some of the guys. We'll make it a group thing.

Carrie: Great! Saturday night good? Let's say around nine at the Hustler Club.

The girl liked strip clubs. Couldn't go wrong.

Me: We'll be there. I'll let you know if something changes.

It was Thursday, but I knew the guys would be game for a night out. We sat here every night and had drinks, but I knew they'd like to get out and be surrounded by ladies and naked strippers. I carried my tablet out into the living room and sat down on the couch; the guys were all watching television, busy with their own online entertainment. I looked around the room and felt sorry for the ladies we were about to meet. They weren't the best looking group of guys and gross in so many ways. They laid around the living room in their underwear with their bellies hanging out and their hand down their pants. It was more than a little disturbing; I needed to see a naked woman in person instead of these burping, snoring, belly scratching things I've become surrounded by.

"Guys, who's up for Hustler Club on Saturday night? Have a group of ladies we're meeting." They all looked at me; I had their full and undivided attention. Pussy always made everything else cease to exist. "You guys in?"

"What ladies?" Tom asked.

"I met a girl online, but she wants to meet in public first. She picked Hustler, and she's going to bring some friends."

"Really?" Tom seemed to be thinking about it, but I knew he hadn't been laid in ages just by looking at him.

"Yes, I told her I'd bring friends. Listen, even if her friends aren't your type, we'll be in a titty bar having drinks. How bad could it be?"

"I'm in," Tom said, and all the guys answered the same.

"Nine, Saturday night," I said as I walked in the kitchen and grabbed a beer.

"Finally, something interesting going on in this damn place," Mark said. "I don't want to spend another Saturday night looking at your ugly mugs. T & A it is."

Tomorrow was Friday and thankfully my first pay day. I needed the money to buy some fucking clothes and pay for a night out in New Orleans. The guys were nice enough to share their food with me all week. I cooked as much as possible since they went to the trouble of buying the food. Most guys can't cook worth shit, but my mom taught me how to fend for myself and cook a decent meal. Food and drinks were plentiful in this place but not always the best quality at least when it came to food. The liquor was always top shelf – Patron, Myers, and Grey Goose.

I had something to look forward to this weekend, something other than work. I'd hopefully meet someone looking for the same – a night of passion.

I bought a new pair of jeans, shoes, and a skin tight black t-shirt to wear to Hustler. I wanted to show off my body and all I had to offer. I didn't want to leave anything to the imagination. I shaved my head smooth

Kayden: The Past

as a baby's ass and trimmed my facial hair to perfection. I looked at myself in the mirror, and fuck it, I knew I looked good. If Carrie wasn't game or advertised herself incorrectly, I'd find some hot piece of ass in NOLA tonight. Everyone else had already showered; thankfully, we had two bathrooms, a necessity with this group.

I walked into the living room and stopped dead in my tracks. "What the fuck are you wearing, dude?" I asked Tom.

He looked down at his shirt. "What's wrong with it?"

"Where the fuck do I begin?" I laughed while shaking my head. He looked like a scene out of some cheesy porn. He had on baggy pants and an oversized t-shirt that had a print of the beach and palm trees. Not just a print, but the entire thing was a scene, a photo of the beach. He looked like a walking disaster, and he definitely wouldn't be getting any pussy in that outfit.

"Fucker, I just bought this shirt. I think I look damn good."

"First problem is you thought. Where the fuck did you buy it? Walmart?" I started to laugh so hard tears were forming in my eyes. The poor guy was dead serious. He honestly thought he looked good, and it made me laugh even harder.

"Fuck you, Kayden. I'm wearing it. You'll see; I'm going to be a pussy magnet tonight." The other guys in the room were all laughing and shaking their heads. No one else had the heart to tell Tom that he looked ridiculous; his outfit just made them look better. "And what the fuck is wrong with Walmart's clothes anyway, dick?" I had no words, just grabbed my keys and headed out the door with the guys in tow, and Tom pulling up the rear.

We rolled out of the apartment parking lot just after eight to catch the street car down to Bourbon. I'd already been through the city during my work day, but I hadn't experienced it at night. The street car stop buzzed with excitement. People were dressed in all types of outfits, corsets and miniskirts to casual shorts and tank tops. I heard anything goes down in the quarter, but I couldn't believe it until I saw it with my own eyes.

The streetcar was packed with people, standing room only, as we made our way down Canal Street. The streets were filled with people and cars, all looking to make their way down to the action, the place to be seen and party until you could hardly stand without help from another. Drinks weren't my goal tonight, finding Carrie and taking in the sights of NOLA were on the menu.

The streetcar stopped, and Mark nudged me, "This is our stop. Bourbon is right there." He pointed to the left, and I could see a street filled with lights and what looked like an endless sea of people. I'd never lived in a city that had been known for its nightlife and party atmosphere. Cleveland had a so-so night scene back in the nineties but had deteriorated over time, and Florida didn't have shit to offer but snow birds and Grand Marquis.

I followed the stream of people across the street and soaked in New Orleans. The smell of the city is unlike any other place I've ever known. There's a spiciness to it, an aroma of alcohol, sex, and Cajun flare. Men lined the streets with signs offering oversized beers and the most beautiful girls through the door behind them. Everyone fought for business and attention. Girls lined the doorways in just a few strips of clothing, grinding on the frame trying to tempt the passersby.

Kayden: The Past

I knew in that moment I would be fucking dead if I grew up in this city or moved here in a different time in my life. There's too much sin available on every corner; I would've overdosed or had gluttony tattooed on my ass. The lights from each bar, restaurant, and strip club caused a colorful haze to dance off the faces of the people and illuminate the entire street. There's an energy to this street that I can't describe in words because it has to be experienced to be believed.

"This place is fucking amazing," I said to Mark as he walked next to me, and the guys strolled further ahead.

"Yeah, it's NOLA. They may call Vegas Sin City, but it doesn't have nothing on NOLA." He pointed to a group of girls on the sidewalk. Their upper bodies were covered in paint, and they didn't have any clothing on except for shorts. "See those girls, they come here all the time, and guys pay to take pictures with them."

I couldn't believe people were so shocked by tits that it required a photo as proof of their wild time. They were here on vacation, but this was my new home. The possibilities are endless in a city like New Orleans. I checked my watch, "Hey, we should find the club and head in; it's close to nine."

"Yo," Marked yelled to the others as he pointed to the Hustler Club.

We walked through the crowd; our bodies touching as we bumped into other people trying to make our way to the other side of the street. The Hustler Club had a purple and red neon sign with the tagline 'Relax... It's Just Sex!' I couldn't have said it better myself. Pictures of women framed the doorway in various positions and levels of nudity. We each handed the barely dressed woman our money and were shown our way through a velvet drape and into the entrance. On the other side of the drape was a red room with tall backed couches made of red velvet that led the way to the main club area. Hustler is a multi-level club with various dance floors and seating areas. I had messaged Carrie earlier in the day, and she told me where they'd be. "They're gonna be at the bar. Let's go find them first."

The guys looked like kids in a candy store. There was so much going on around us, and these guys didn't look like the type who actually had the chance to bang a stripper; they could only stare at them and stuff dollar bills in their panties. I'd had my share of strippers and knew they weren't as glamorous as they looked on the stage. They were a fucking train wreck wrapped in a pretty package. Tom, Paul, and Mark could never land a stripper; it wasn't that they didn't have the looks, but they just didn't have the 'it' factor. They were frumpy, lacked any kind of skills when it came to women, and they lacked confidence. Fuck, they lacked everything that could draw a woman in besides a wallet full of money.

The bar was on the other side of the room, but I could see Carrie perfectly through the haze of pink lights and people. She sat on a bar stool with a short skirt and open back top. She sat sideways on the chair with her back clearly visible along with the side of her face. She had curly long brown hair and a bunch of it. I thought about putting my fingers in her hair and grabbing hold of her while I fucked her, bumping her ass and causing her body to move from the impact. Her top was white and almost sheer. Her legs were killer with black dagger heels that screamed to be held. I didn't know where I wanted to put my hands on this girl first. She laughed and tossed her head back, and my cock grew hard wanting to see her on top of me in the same position, her head tipped back, naked, and happy.

I shifted my shoulders and stood up straight – I wanted maximum impact when she laid eyes on me. I

Kayden: The Past

couldn't understand what a girl as hot as her would be doing on a site like Fuckbook, but then again, what the fuck was I doing on Fuckbook? We all have our reasons for the choices we make or the types of relationships we seek; I couldn't judge her on her choice or actions. I walked toward her slowly, trying to seem casual. I looked around the room like I hadn't spotted her yet until I was practically right in front of her.

"Kayden?" she said as she looked me up and down.

I smiled and gave her the same once over, although I already did that from across the room. "Yes, Carrie, I presume." I said as I held out my hand looking for hers in return. She slid her fingers into my palm, and I closed my fingers around them. Her fingernails were long and red and neatly manicured. I lifted her hand to my mouth and turned it at the last moment and kissed her wrist. It's such a sensual spot. I looked up at her, and she had a glimmer in her eye; I knew instantly she'd be perfect for the type of arrangement I wanted.

"These are my friends, Samantha and Kelly." Samantha was a brunette with thin straight hair, a plain face, and simple clothes. Kelly had a little more going on with blond hair, huge tits, big green eyes and clothes that looked like they were painted on. Samantha was more the type that would go for one of my friends, but I think she had more class than the guys had in their pinky fingers.

"This is Tom, Mark, and Paul." I pointed to them lined up at the bar all ordering drinks. "Want to get a table?" I asked.

"We'd love to." They grabbed their drinks and moved off their barstools. I never could understand how women walked in those fucking shoes, but they did crazy things to my cock. "Just so you know, Samantha doesn't like guys. She didn't want to give the wrong impression to your friends." Kind of made sense to me, but I'd think she would have gone the extra mile when getting ready in a room filled with opportunity for her.

"No problem. I'll pass on the word to the guys that she's not interested." I gestured with my hand for Carrie to walk ahead. I wanted her to pick the location, and I wanted to watch her ass jiggle as she walked. It had a bounce, and I fucking loved it. Not the bounce of extra pounds, but idea of some junk in the trunk, something to hold on to while my cock was buried inside her. "Do you and her...?" I whispered in her ear.

"Fuck no, I'm all about the cock, baby. Now Sam and Kelly... they're another story." She laughed. I wouldn't mind a front row seat at that show while Kelly sucked my cock, but I didn't feel like a group party, at least not tonight.

Carrie sat down, and I took the seat next to her while everyone else sat guys vs. girls at the table. I could see it wasn't a night for the group to co-mingle, but for everyone else to watch the ladies shake their shit on stage.

"Drink?" A waitress asked. They didn't waste any time; the more liquor in the system, the quicker the money flowed out of your pocket and into the hands of the girls at the club. I knew the game having been immersed in the scene back in the day.

"First rounds on me. I'll take a beer please, ladies?" I asked Sam and Kelly across the table. They both smiled and placed their drink order.

"Fuck, we already bought ours," Tom complained.

"Just order a damn drink. You'll finish those before she makes it back." I swear sometimes their brains didn't function. A room full of pussy and it all turned to mush.

I turned my attention back to Carrie. Her legs were crossed, and her body faced me slightly leaning forward. Her body language had a whole lot to say even though her mouth said nothing. She rubbed her legs together and nudged my knee a couple times, trying to find any reason to touch me.

"What's your story, Carrie?" My curiosity was peeked – what the fuck was her deal? Why was she here and not home with a boyfriend at her side?

"I'm in school and don't have the time nor want the hassle of a boyfriend." She ran her fingers down the middle of her breasts, and my eyes watched her nails leave goose bumps across her skin.

"So just not time? You want the pleasure without the bullshit?"

"Yes, I need time to study. I'm on a scholarship and can't fuck it up. I had a boyfriend freshman year and almost flunked out. No cock is going to ruin my future."

"Do you do this a lot? Troll Fuckbook looking for cock?" I rubbed my goatee and watched her face carefully. I looked for any telltale signs of lying.

"No, I hooked up with someone a year ago on that site. We met up a couple of times a month. Neither of us wanted a relationship, just sex. He moved away after he was done with school. I'm on the prowl for fresh meat, and you just happened to show up on my recommendations." Not a blink or fidget as she spoke. "Is it something you do often?"

"Fuckbook? Nope, you're the first person I've met off there. Have I met someone off the internet? Yes. I dated someone I found from high school on there. Total fucking disaster. I just need someone to blow off some steam with. I want to have fun without the heart and bullshit."

"Dance?" A girl tapped me on the shoulder, and I turned. Her tits were right in my face.

"That's up to the lady," I said looking towards Carrie.

"Sure, I'd like to watch." She leaned back in her seat and smiled.

I grabbed a fifty out of my wallet and handed it to the buxom blond. "You dance for her. I'll be the one watching."

Carrie didn't miss a beat or look shocked. "Gotcha buddy, whatever you want. I'm Angel by the way."

"Just grind on her honey, make her wet," I said. Angel moved Carrie's knees apart, putting her feet flat on the floor. Angel placed her knee between Carrie's legs, prying them apart just enough to fit her leg in between. She placed her knee in Carrie's crotch making contact. She rubbed her tits in her face and against Carrie's chest. She grinded and rubbed everything against her.

When a guy gets a lap dance, the contact is minimal and more about a good show. If they were naked right now, I'd swear to fucking God they were fucking. It was erotic, and Carrie, for all her cock talk, seemed to be interested and turned on. Angel turned around and bent over with her pussy practically in Carrie's face. She grabbed Angel's ass and smacked it. It was the best fully clothed porn I'd seen in ages. My cock grew hard and ached to be inside Carrie or any hot piece of ass at the moment. I'd fuck Angel in the bathroom right now if Carrie wasn't game. The lap dance was slow and sensual, not filled with fervor, but a slow lust-filled assault on the senses. Before Angel

Kayden: The Past

walked away, she leaned down and placed a very passionate kiss on Carrie's lips. I watched as Carrie leaned into her almost craving the touch and passion. I had her right where I wanted her.

I didn't want to wait a week to fuck her; I'd find a spot. Strip clubs are filled with nooks and crannies, all types of places for naughty things to happen. I'm sure Angel would help me. I watched as Angel touched Carrie's chin and winked at me before walking away. Carrie sat there still in a fog of lust. "Been a while?" I asked as I ran my hand up her leg to her inner thigh.

She shook her head yes. "Too fucking long. Damn that shit was hot."

I laughed. Some women would have been pissed off or embarrassed, but Carrie was a champ, maybe a pro, even. "Not pissed?"

"Fuck no, my panties are soaked. Wanna feel?" She grinned, parting her legs a bit further, and my cock pulsed in my jeans wanting to break free from its confinement.

I didn't answer but moved my hand into her skirt; she didn't have on any panties. I should have known; she didn't look like the type of girl who wore panties – too sexual to want the barrier. I ran my finger through her wetness feeling the smoothness of her skin against mine. She closed her eyes relishing the feel of the contact. Her legs spread a little wider, and her body leaned back in the chair, her hips tilting upward in invitation. I placed two fingers against her skin and raked the moisture pooling on my fingers. I didn't look around; I didn't give a fuck who watched. We were in a strip club not a fancy restaurant.

I pushed two fingers inside of her, her body already slick, and her head fell back from the sensation. I curved my fingers upward searching for her g-spot. I found it easily and rubbed it, moving my fingers in and out and curling them against her insides. Her legs closed trapping my fingers in their place. I leaned forward for more leverage to move inside of her. Her hands gripped the chair, and I started to rub my thumb against her clit. Her pussy clamped down on my fingers, sucking me in, holding them prisoner. I increased the pressure but kept my movement steady and unwavering. She raised her head and stared straight into my eyes as her pussy milked my finger, and she came apart with a silent 'oh' on her lips. Her eyes bore into me with a look of wonderment as her chest heaved, and her breath was ragged.

"Better?" I asked with a grin as I removed my fingers from her body and slid them down her legs leaving a trail of wetness in their wake.

"Fuck, your fingers are amazing." She licked her lips and couldn't take her eyes off me.

"Imagine what my cock could do." I picked up my drink and took a sip. No one seemed to notice what happened; if they did, they didn't let on. They were busy watching the girls dance on the stage and the action taking place in the room.

She raised her glass to her mouth with shaky hands before taking a couple gulps of the cold liquid. "Jesus, I don't know if I can handle you."

"You will. Just don't fall in love with me."

"Love won't be a problem," she said quickly.

"So sure, are you?" I asked with a cocky smirk on my face. "My cock might jumble your brain, cross a few wires, and bam, you'll love me hard."

She almost choked on her drink with the last words out of my mouth. I knew the double meaning of the words. "Why in the hell are you single? I know I just don't want the complication; school is too important to me, but you, I just don't get."

Kayden: The Past

I didn't feel like vomiting my whole life's fucked up history to this girl I barely knew. "I've been unlucky with women. I always seem to pick the wrong ones to commit myself to, so now, I want the physical without the hassle."

"Eh, we've all been unlucky. No one has the fairytale we read about as children, at least not easily. Have to walk through the shit to appreciate the good. At least that's what my mom used to tell me." She shrugged her shoulders and twirled the straw in her mouth. "Wanna get out of here and go somewhere else?"

"Some place more private? I thought this was supposed to just be a meeting and getting to know each other thing."

"No, big guy, you kind of ruined that when you stuck your fingers in me. I want to walk around and get a drink. I never like to stay in one place too long. Game? See where the night takes us."

Her plan sounded promising, and strip clubs weren't my scene anymore. They left a bad taste in my mouth. New Orleans had too much to see and experience to sit in a titty bar. "I'm game for anything, always have been. I'm kind of like Nike – just do it."

"I was hoping your motto is closer to Energizer – it keeps going. And going. And going." She winked at me.

"Just remember Timex took my phrase – Takes a lickin' and keeps on tickin'," I laughed. She was a smart girl; at least she had her head in the right spot, college before a relationship. A degree was something you could always depend on unlike a partner.

"I'll be the judge of that. Let's jet." She stood up and placed her drink on the table and ran her fingertips around the rim before sticking her fingers in her mouth and sucking on it. My cock twitched watching her suck on her finger with her eyes closed. "Kayden and I are heading outside. You all wanna come or you stayin' here?" she asked her friends.

The girls looked at each other and made a couple facial expressions that I didn't fucking understand. Women had more silent signals than a man could learn in a lifetime. "My feet are killing; we'll stay here and enjoy the ladies and the guys if they want to stay, too." The guys heard those words, and their faces were all smiles. They acted the entire night like they weren't interested in the girls and played it cool, but it was all a bullshit game. The guys didn't match the girls; they didn't hang on the same ladder rung of beauty, but I knew the guys would buy drinks, and possibly after enough, the guys would start to look better, but even then, it was a stretch.

"You guys staying here, too?" I asked looking at them not really needing their answer; they were as transparent as the condom in my pocket.

"Yeah, we'll meet up with you later," Mark said as he tipped his chin to me as if saying they got this shit. Hardly, but I guess a guy can dream.

"Come on doll. Let's hit the town. Where's the first stop?" I stood up and threw a fifty on the table. I knew it was way too much, but what the fuck, why not. Women didn't like cheap bastards.

"Pat O'Brien's. I want a Hurricane, and they have the most amazing courtyard." She grabbed her purse off the back of the chair, and I followed her towards the door.

"How old are you Carrie, if you don't mind asking?"

Kayden: The Past

"I don't mind. I'm twenty two and you?" she asked as we finally found our way through the club exit.

"I'm in my early thirties. Can we leave it at that? I feel kind of dirty now that I know you're so young."

"Oh fuck age, I'm legal." She had a point. I didn't want a relationship with her; I just wanted to bend her over a table and fuck her.

It became hard to talk with the music from the bars filling the streets and the mass of people chattering as we walked. I stayed by her side, and she grabbed my hand and led me towards Pat O'Brien's. The white and green sign hung above the door, and the exterior walls were decorated in a rusty red with green shutters. We walked through the space, and I let go of her hand; holding hands was just a little too much like being in a relationship for me to stomach.

The courtyard was a beauty with glowing fountains, twinkling lights, and softness. We found a spot at the bar and ordered Hurricanes. Funny that a city that was desecrated by a hurricane only a couple years earlier was known for it as a drink.

We talked mostly about New Orleans, a very neutral topic. I didn't want to know too much about her, and from what I could tell, she didn't want to know much about me. I needed to know that she wasn't a crazy whore who I'd have to deal with in the future. I wanted simple – I needed simple. I didn't give a fuck about what she was studying, where she came from, or who broke her heart. I didn't want to share my life with her; I wasn't looking to build a future. We listened to the music, and she told me about all the fun NOLA had to offer. She'd never leave New Orleans. "It becomes part of you. You'll see. It's a romance that never leaves your heart."

I've never felt that way about any place I've lived. It had always been just a place to plant my feet until the next great opportunity came, or my reckless choices caused me to leave.

Carrie touched me as she talked, small touches at first, my forearms with her fingertips to start and eventually clasping her hand around my arm and squeezing tightly. There was a chemistry between us and nothing said 'run the fuck away now', all lights were green - we were a go for liftoff.

We finished our drinks and walked around the city, taking in the sights of the city known for Mardi Gras. I felt almost overwhelmed by the energy in New Orleans, but maybe the drinks in my system had a little something to do with the over stimulation.

Carrie and I ended up having sex in the bathroom in some club that I can't even remember. They had a family bathroom, and families weren't on the street this late at night. It was a single small room with a lock on the door. We could be loud, and no one would hear us over the music. Carrie wasn't the type of girl you needed to take home and wine and dine. I fucked her long and hard and lived up to every motto I laid out while we were in Hustler.

I watched her as she rearranged her skirt and top; she looked like she just went through a war. I learned from Candy not to put a girl on the sink. As soon as she locked the door behind us, I grabbed her and smashed her against the wall. She wrapped her legs around me, and I undid my pants and used my hands to hold her by the ass. Her back looked a bit raw from hitting the tile over and over again, but I wasn't sorry for any of it. I tied off the condom and flushed it away.

"My back is going to be fucking killing me tomorrow." She looked in the mirror, studying the damage. "Worth every second of misery I'll feel

Kayden: The Past

tomorrow, though." She smiled at me with a devilish grin.

"I want to take it a bit slower next time... I want to make other things ache for days."

She laughed nervously, "I have no doubt you could, too."

"Shall we?" I asked as I unlocked the door. "I'll text the guys and see where they are and walk you to your friends."

"Such a gentleman." I opened the door and followed her out.

The group had never left Hustler, and we'd meet them there before parting ways. I knew Carrie would be back for more; I had no doubt. I could see the guys standing outside waiting for us as we approached, and the ladies came laughing out the doorway behind them. I didn't want to know what had happened while we were gone. Our two groups parted ways at Hustler; it was late, and we had to work the next day. We said our goodbyes and left the ladies on Bourbon to head home to our empty beds and uncomplicated lives. NOLA could work out perfectly; it's just what the doctor ordered.

Carrie and I had a standing appointment. It sounds boring and unromantic, but romance wasn't the name of the game - lust, passion and sex were. We met about every two weeks, sometimes sooner if we felt the need. We never shared too much or held deep conversations.

After some time away from the situation, I missed Lisa, maybe I was glutton for punishment and my curse was crazy ass bitches. Could I like a normal girl who didn't turn my world upside down? Did I crave the unknown and want to live on the edge of uncertainty? I sent my monthly payment to the probation officer, waiting until the last minute possible. I hated parting with my cash and sending it away to someone who had everything I owned while I slept in a used bed.

I had been lying in bed trying to fall asleep for what felt like hours, but it didn't come. I turned on the television and started watching ESPN, hoping that it would help drown out the thoughts of my failures in love and especially Lisa. I stared at my finger that held her name. My ring finger, she'd promised herself to me always and wanted me to put her name on my body to prove my devotion to her. I jumped as my phone started to ring and jump from the vibrations, dancing on my night stand. I answered it without looking at the caller ID; I figured it was Carrie wanting to plan our next night.

"Hello."

"Hey," said a small voice. My heart stopped with the sound of her voice. I didn't know what to say to her, what was there to say? "Kayden?" she asked in an unsure tone.

"Yeah, what do you want?" I asked not moving from my bed although I felt the need to pace around my room.

"I miss you," she said in a soft tone that I hadn't heard in a long time.

"That's hard to believe."

"Kayden, I do miss you. God, I've fucked everything up." Her voice cracked, and the sound became muffled.

Kayden: The Past

"The only person who got fucked in this is me, Lisa."

"I know. God, I was just so pissed at you. It just got all out of hand."

I know I got out of hand. If I wouldn't have destroyed our things, I wouldn't have been arrested and be on probation. "I'm sorry I broke in and fucked things up. I just couldn't believe you locked me out, and it didn't help that I'd been drinking either."

"I just wanted to piss you off. I was so fucking mad at you. I wanted you to feel a little of what I felt. I would've cooled off after a night without you, and it would've ended there." She sighed, "But you had to come in and destroy shit. You crossed the line, Kayden. I had to call the cops. I fucking saw red when I walked in the door."

"I know. Everything got out of hand between us, Lisa. Where did it all go wrong?" I asked putting my arms over my head getting more comfortable. This Lisa was the one who I thought I fell in love with, the calm and remorseful woman who I had known before she became possessed.

"Do you think we can start over? Can I come visit you, Kayden?" I didn't answer right away. So many thoughts went through my mind with the thought of seeing her again. "Please." She started to sob.

Fuck. I was a sucker for tears. "Yes, you can come for a weekend if you want."

"The house has been so empty without you. I'm lost without you."

"We're not getting back together, Lisa, but you can come spend some time with me." I couldn't commit to her. I couldn't give my heart to her; it was already raw and an open wound.

"I just need to sleep in your arms. Maybe someday we can be a couple again."

"I don't think so, Lisa. We're like oil and water. We just don't mix well together. I don't know if I can ever trust you again. What's to stop you from doing it again?"

"Let's handle it one trip at a time. I'll let you know when I book a ticket. Thank you, Kayden."

I must clearly be a fucking moron. "We'll talk then." I wasn't going to give her free reign to re-enter my life and rub salt in the wound. I should've told her no, to go fuck herself, but we had history, and I didn't want to cut the last string of possibility without knowing it was totally over between us. Her kindness on the phone made it impossible for me to say no; she did have a loving side, although I hadn't seen it for ages. The holidays were coming up; I'd use that as an excuse for my total lack of judgment.

Carrie was my easy lay, the one who came without complication, expectations, and rules. My life was easy, but I felt it was about to get a bit rocky. I didn't tell Carrie since we weren't an item. I didn't ask her if I was the only one in her life, and she never asked me. Lisa wouldn't be in my life; I needed the closure and maybe we'd put the hurt and anger behind us with this trip. I could get on with my life and move forward free of the anger.

Chapter 16

Auld Lang Syne ~ Lisa

Lisa booked her ticket and would be spending three days and two nights with me, including New Year's Eve. My stomach ached, my heart thundered in my chest, and my palms grew wet against the steering wheel as I drove to the airport. I hadn't seen her in months, and I didn't want to get sucked in and lose myself again. I finally felt like me again, the Kayden I used to be before the ladies in my life decided to use me as a rug.

I sat near the exit and waited for her to appear through the endless line of people. I checked my watch; her flight should have landed by now. Maybe she changed her mind and didn't get on the plane realizing what a cluster fuck this would turn out to be. I leaned forward in my chair as a sense of relief and calm overcame me as I stared at my feet. She wasn't coming - I could breathe again.

Furry boots stopped in front of me, and I slowly looked up. She made the flight and stood before me with a giant smile on her face. She looked relaxed and happy. She looked like the girl I first met to chat with over drinks so long ago. "Hey, stranger," she said her eyes crinkling into little slits from the large smile on her face.

I stood up, and she wrapped her arms around my waist. She melted into my body, a feeling I knew well and a comfort that I'd been used to and felt the loss of late at night. I wrapped my arms around her and inhaled the scent of her as I held her. She buried her face in my chest and squeezed me so tight that my chest hurt. "Hey," I said, grabbing her arms trying to pry her off me.

"Sorry about that," she said as she let go and wiped her eyes. "I'm happier than I've been in a long time." She looked me in the eyes, "I'm so sorry, Kayden."

"Ready?" I wouldn't say I felt happy as I stood with her in the airport. I felt more on edge than I had in months.

"Yes." I grabbed the bag out of her hand and started walking toward the exit. She walked quickly to catch up to me before reaching out to hold my hand. I didn't pull away from the contact; she'd be sharing my bed for two nights; I needed to get used to it even if it made me uncomfortable.

I still felt betrayed, but I knew I played a role. My drinking had been a cause as well as my inability to control my temper. I'd been just as big of an asshole as she had that night. The ride to my apartment was quiet; quieter than any time I could ever remember between us and tension filled the air. She stroked my arm as I drove, and I felt relieved as I parked the truck in the apartment lot.

"Come on," I said as I opened my door and climbed out of the truck. The air had grown cold after the sun set, and a gust of wind caused me to shiver as I pulled her bag out of the back of the truck.

"Shit, I'm freezing." She wrapped her sweater around her body a little tighter as she followed behind me through the courtyard.

"It's not bad, not like Florida, but nowhere near as shitty as Ohio." I unlocked the door, and only Mark sat in the living room.

"Mark, this is Lisa," I said as I kicked off my shoes, and Lisa walked into the apartment.

"Hey," Mark said looking at Lisa with suspicion. The guys knew all about Lisa. I had spilled my guts on what she'd put me through, and they thought I was fucking crazy letting her come here. Maybe they were right.

"Hi," she said as she looked around the apartment, judging the way we lived. I could almost see the wheels spinning in her head; she was so deep in thought.

"Want to stay out here or go in my room," I asked.

"Room, please." She smiled, but I could tell the joy on her face wasn't real.

Lisa followed me to my bedroom and set her purse on the dresser. "This is it?" she asked.

"It's all I have, remember?"

"I do. I just didn't think... I thought you had more."

"Lisa, I left with nothing. You have all my things. What you see is what I have to my name."

"I never thought of it that way. I'm sorry." She wrapped her arms around me. "Are you okay?" *Where did this tender caring Lisa come from?*

"I'm fine, Lisa. I've been happy and have all I need."

"Can't we try again?" I could feel her heartbeat against my chest.

"I don't think it's a good idea. We'd just end in disaster again."

She moved away from me and sat on the bed looking like she just lost her best friend. "I know… you're right. Can we just enjoy these few days? Like old times." My version of old times had to be different than hers. Enjoy isn't a term I'd use to describe our last few months together, more like torture. It went both ways, and we fed off each other.

"Can you at least send me my clothes or something?" I asked as I sat down next to her.

"I brought a couple things with me." She kneeled down on the floor and pulled out a couple sweaters. They weren't much, but in that moment, they felt like everything to me. She handed them to me, and I placed them on the bed. I reached out and helped her off the floor.

"Thank you, Lisa." I squeezed her hands and pulled her into me. She crawled on my lap and wrapped her arms around my neck. I didn't pull away or stop her. Lisa always made my cock hard.

We weren't only explosive in our fights, but our fucking usually reached radioactive levels. I grabbed her face and kissed her lips, drawing my tongue across her bottom lip. My cock twitched as she shifted on my lap and pressed her body weight against me, and I fell backwards into the mattress. I ran my fingers through

Kayden: The Past

her hair and grabbed it in my fist pulling her face to mine.

I didn't love Lisa anymore; she'd done more harm to me than any woman in my past. Danielle and Bridget left me, but Lisa, Lisa ripped my heart out and danced on it. The phrase 'there's a fine line between love and hate' fit the moment perfectly. I was so pissed and turned on at the same time. I needed to fuck her and use my cock to take my anger out on her. I've never hit a woman except when asked during sex, and I knew she'd ask for it; she always did. I'd think of this as therapy to rid myself of the Lisa problem forever and move forward with my life.

I increased my grip on her hair, pulling it away from her head. I thrust my tongue in her mouth and moved it across her smooth tongue, tangling them together. She tasted just as I'd remembered. I devoured her mouth, sucked the breath out of her and captured her moans. I deepened the kiss demanding everything she had to offer.

I reached down and grabbed her sweater, lifting it over her head. I unclasped her bra and removed the straps from her shoulder as I kissed her. My fingers danced across her skin, relishing in the softness and the curves I knew by heart. I gripped her ass, grinding my erection into her as a gasp escaped her lips. "I've missed your cock. I want you so bad."

She sat up putting pressure on my cock and helped me remove my shirt. I never thought I'd be in this spot again. She unbuttoned and unzipped my pants with quick fingers. I did the same to her before pushing them down her hips and waited for her to remove them. She had a pretty pink G-string underneath with her neatly trimmed blond hair peeking through the lace. I lifted my hips and let her pull my pants down as she moved with them down my legs. My cock sprang free and bounced hitting my stomach. She climbed off the bed and took both of our jeans with her, depositing them on the floor. She crawled up my legs like a tiger staring at me like a meal after a fast. The hair on my body stood up from the sensation or the déjà vu of seeing her on my body again.

She stopped at my cock and ran her nails up the length. It twitched calling for more attention preferably from her mouth. She knew I loved the feel of her lips wrapped around my cock. She ran her tongue around my balls and up the sensitive skin of my cock, latching on to the sensitive tip. She drew it in her mouth without the use of her hands. I watched her ass as her body moved up and down taking me fully, swallowing me whole. I laid there and took everything she gave for minutes – I was greedy and felt no remorse. It wasn't enough for me; I needed more and wanted to possess her. I needed the lust and passion, and my hands wrapped around her.

I grabbed her arms pulling her towards me, needing to be in control and wanting to bury myself deep. I reached down and grabbed her panties twisting them in my fist from the side. I pulled quickly, hearing the snap of the cloth as it ripped from her flesh. I lifted her by her hips setting her on the bed next to me and rolled on top of her, nestling between her legs. I held my cock in my hand as I poked her opening. I didn't give a fuck if she was ready for me or not; I was ready, and she wasn't protesting. I inserted the tip before withdrawing my hand and gripping her ass tilting her upwards. I jammed my cock in her, causing her body to move slightly across the bed. I moved my arm from her side to under her back and secured her in place.

I pumped and thrust, taking all my anger and frustration out on her pussy. She moaned and screamed not giving a fuck who heard in the next room. I knew she wouldn't last long as her pussy clamped down on my cock. I left my cock buried inside of her as I adjusted myself to a sitting position. I grabbed a pillow from the

Kayden: The Past

bed and placed it under her ass, giving me the angle and freeing my hands. I bent her legs placing them between her body and mine.

I leaned against her shins; my body hovering above her. I wrapped my hands around her neck as I increased my speed and depth. I pressed down on the veins in her neck, decreasing the blood flow to her brain. She wrapped her arms around my wrist and held my hands to her neck. Lisa loved to be choked when she came. It heightened the sensation and increased the intensity.

I became lost in the moment as I watched her face turn red while my hands were wrapped around her neck. Her eyes began to glisten, and my thrusting became angry and unrelenting. I squeezed and pumped until I felt her body tighten, and her pussy convulsed around me. The sight of her in my grip, vulnerable to me and my ability to end her life in a second made my spine tingle. It tipped me over the edge, sending shockwaves through my body.

I released my hands, and she began to gasp and cough, gulping air trying to catch her breath. I watched as the redness drained from her face, leaving a soft pink glow. "Just how you wanted it?"

"You scared me a little," she coughed. "I didn't think you were going to let go."

"I almost didn't. I could have ended you right there."

"I knew you wouldn't, Kayden. You love me too much to hurt me."

"Past tense."

"What?" She ran her hand across her face and settled it on her neck rubbing the now sensitive pink skin. "I almost blacked out."

"I *loved* you too much to hurt you before, but it was a temptation I had to fight." Her eyes grew huge as she stared at me. "You're lucky I have self-control, Lisa. I almost got lost in the moment."

Flopping on my back, I tried to steady my breath. She rolled over and snuggled into my side underneath my arm. "I know you love me. Deny it all you want. I'm part of you."

"Lie to yourself all you want, Lisa." The room became silent with only the sounds from the living room television filling the air. She rubbed her cheek against my chest before settling in and getting comfortable. I would have wrapped her up and enveloped her with my body if we were still a couple, but instead, I let her lay against me as I enjoyed the warmth and thought about my future.

My orgasm wasn't only a release of pent up sexual tension between us, but it was a release of the anger and hurt that she'd caused. I knew I could move forward, leave her behind and make a life that I wanted. Free of relationships and filled with sex.

We spent New Year's Eve day walking around the quarter. I showed Lisa as much of the city as I could since it was fairly new to me. The city buzzed as preparations for tonight's celebration were being completed. The Fleur de Lis sat atop a pole on Decatur Street, waiting for the clock to strike midnight. I made dinner reservations at a beautiful restaurant just outside Riverwalk for us to talk before heading into the hordes of people celebrating in Jackson Square.

We placed our dinner order, and there was an uncomfortable pause in the conversation. As we walked

Kayden: The Past

around, we talked about the city, but sitting here at the table with her, there was a tension between us. "Kayden," Lisa said.

"Yeah?" I sipped on my beer and waited for her to comment about my drinking. Why would today be any different than before?

"Since you've left, it's been hard for me to make the bills each month. I spent all the money I had on the plane ticket." She fidgeted with the napkin on the table, "Could you help me out?"

"You already get a couple hundred dollars from me each month," I stared at her. *Since I left? What the fuck?* She seemed to rewrite history. Maybe it made her feel better to think it was my choice instead of her forcing it on me.

"I know, but it's not enough. Christmas wiped me out this year, and I need some help," she begged. "Please."

One thing Lisa always liked was money. She liked to live above her means, and her five finger discounts helped her achieve that with her mediocre pay as a receptionist. "Fine, Lisa. I'll give you five hundred dollars and the cash for your ticket," I already owed her thousands, what was a couple hundred dollars more? "If you promise to send me my things, Lisa." I wasn't thrilled about the idea, but she said she'd send me some things from her home. I'd look at it as payment. If I didn't give her the cash, I'd likely see nothing. Everything had a price when it came to her.

"Thank you, baby," she said.

I held up my hand, "Lisa, I'm not your baby. We're through in that way, forever."

"Don't you feel what we have? Being with you reminded me how much I love you. How much I need you in my life."

"I know what we *had*. There's too much damage," I said.

She pouted in her chair, and I watched her as she flipped her phone over as if checking for something. Her phone hadn't beeped all day. Lisa always had text messages, and her phone was more like a musical instrument with all of the alerts, but since she'd arrived, it hadn't made a sound. "Expecting a call?" I asked as I watched her place it face down on the table.

"No, just wanted to make sure I hadn't missed one. So this is it? Once I leave… We're officially over?"

"Yes." I didn't have more to say to her. I never asked her here on the guise that we'd get back together and have our happily ever after.

"Okay, I'll wait for you. Maybe you'll change your mind once reality sets in."

Thankfully, our meal arrived. We could eat in silence, and I didn't feel the need to continue the conversation. She could wait for an eternity, but I wouldn't return to her. Reality? It had set in. I had no one in this world to depend on except me. Women freely offered themselves and asked for nothing in return. No funds exchanged hands. No expectations or rules to contend with – reality had been pretty fucking great since coming to New Orleans.

We joined the crowd on Decatur around eleven to enjoy the music and start the countdown. Lisa disappeared for a few minutes to use the ladies room, and I was thankful for the break. I saw an ATM nearby and grabbed her money that I'd promised her. I thought of it as a going away present. I couldn't wait for her to go home tomorrow. I should've told her no when she asked to come and see me. In twelve hours, I'd put her ass on a plane and fly her out of my life.

Kayden: The Past

Arms wrapped around my body as I stared at the Fleur de Lis and thought about all of the possibilities that lay ahead of me. I pulled her fingers apart and turned to face her, "Don't."

"God, you're such a kill joy at times," she said with her mouth in a hard line.

"Here's your cash you asked for," I handed her the money and watched her count it. Such an odd reaction, like I'd short her. "I'm going to grab a beer, want one?"

"You need a drink?"

Ah, there she is – the one who questions all my actions. "I want one. There's a difference." Carts were set up along the square, and I needed something besides her body to keep me warm.

"Still a drunk, I see."

She had her money and her attitude shifted suddenly. "Have I been drunk in the last twenty four hours? I've had one fucking drink."

"One turns into five, always does." Her arms were folded in front of her, and she looked like she was ready for a fight... One that I didn't feel like having.

"I wondered when the real you would show up."

"What the fuck does that mean?" She glared at me.

I shook my head, "I'm cold as fuck out here. It's New Year's Eve, and I want a drink. Immediately, you jump to the conclusion that I'm going to get shitfaced, Lisa. I hand you some money, and instantly, the claws come out."

"Okay, let's not fight. I want to enjoy my last couple hours here in New Orleans." She wrapped her scarf around her neck and rubbed her mittens together.

"Fine, I'm still getting my beer. Would you like one, yes or no?" I stood there waiting for her answer.

"I need something stronger."

"Stay here. I'll be right back." I walked away from her thankful for the freedom. She had always been so judgmental about my drinking, and it drove me further into the bottle. I watched her as I waited in line at a cart selling mixed drinks and beer. She typed on her phone and looked around unable to see me in the crowd. She looked nervous as I watched her eyes move and scan the crowd.

"What would you like, sugar?" a voice asked and pulled my attention away from her.

"I'll take a large beer and hmmm, a hand grenade, please." Lisa wasn't much of a drinker. A Hand Grenade would have her head spinning; I'd possibly fuck the shit out of her one more time before I sent her shitty ass on her way.

"Fifteen dollars, handsome." I handed the woman the cash with a nice holiday tip included and stood there watching Lisa for a minute. She feverishly typed something still looking around like a kid doing something quickly before possibly being caught by a parent.

I walked toward her with the drinks and watched her demeanor change as I approached. She placed her phone in her pocket and smiled at me. "What is this?" she asked as she grabbed the bright green plastic container from my hand.

"Hand grenade – don't worry it's not strong. Mostly fruit juices, you'll like it." I knew it would knock

Kayden: The Past

her on her ass. I lied to her and didn't feel bad about it at all.

She sipped the liquid through the straw and smiled, "This is great, thanks."

"Did I interrupt you?"

"Huh?" she had a look of surprise on her face.

"Your phone."

"Oh, no. I was just checking to see if I had any messages." She sipped again and fidgeted a little. I knew bullshit when I saw it.

"Looked like more than that." I eyed her, watching her reaction carefully.

"Nope," she turned around, so I couldn't read her face.

I wouldn't press her any further; I'd wait for the drink to work its magic. I checked my watch and thanked the Gods when I realized midnight was only ten minutes away. I felt like I was counting down the minutes until my release from prison. In a way, I was; Lisa's presence started to feel like a stint in solitary confinement.

Lisa finished her drink right before midnight. Her body swayed as she shouted out the last couple of seconds in the countdown, following the lead of the crowd. I stood there silently and watched the world celebrate the coming New Year.

"Happy New Year's, Kayden." She said as she hiccupped.

"You too, Lisa." I smiled at her. I had plans for this year, and they didn't include her. My year began with saying goodbye to my past and wiping the slate clean.

She leaned forward on her tippy toes to kiss me, but I turned my face and gave her my cheek. "Can I kiss your lips?" she asked in my ear.

"No, not tonight," I said. Lisa's eyes were dilated, and the look on her face told me that the alcohol had done the trick.

We stayed in the square for another hour and celebrated with the crowd. A band played, and people began to leave the square and filter into the French Quarter. I wanted to go home and crawl in bed. Sleep would help the hours pass quicker.

I knew by her actions that there was someone else in her life that evening. I knew I was being played and that she only wanted money. She enjoyed a free trip to New Orleans and left with a pocketful of cash. You don't go through two relationships ending in infidelity and not know the signs. She may have been honest when she said she wanted to get back together, but her devious actions and hiding her phone told me she had an ulterior motive. Lisa was a user and always would be. I may have been a drunk, but I never used her for anything, ever.

That night she passed out as soon as her head hit the pillow. I pushed her to the edge of the bed as far away from me as possible. I didn't want her sleeping against me. I set my phone alarm for eight o'clock since her flight would take off around eleven. That left only three hours for her to get ready and make it to the airport. No time for sex, fighting or anything. I just wanted to say goodbye.

I drove her to the airport and stopped the truck outside departures. "Aren't you going to walk me in?" she asked.

Kayden: The Past

"Why would I?" I leaned against the driver's door with my hand on the steering wheel and stared at her.

"Cause you're supposed to. How can we say goodbye in your beat up truck?"

"It's easy... Bye," I said curtly.

She rolled her eyes. "That's it, huh? No hug, kiss or I love you?"

"No, Lisa. I told you we weren't getting back together. We're over, and it's time for you to go before you miss your flight." I pushed the car lock button to make sure she could open her door without a problem and maybe to give her a hint that it was time to hit the road.

"I see you're still an asshole, Kayden."

"Goodbye, Lisa. I'll send the payments to the probation department each month but nothing extra. Don't call me again for money."

"I didn't call you for money. I wanted to see you. I wanted to try us again."

"There is no us, babe. You got what you came for and maybe something extra. Go back to your boyfriend."

She squinted at me, her eyes throwing daggers in my direction. "Just make sure that check is there on time. I'd hate for you to violate your probation and be arrested again."

"It'll be there; you can bet your ass I'm not spending another night in jail because of you. You're going to miss your flight." I looked at my watch not wanting to spend another minute trapped in a small space with her.

She opened the door, crawled out, and slammed it behind her. I pulled away and didn't look back. She was out of my life. I wouldn't be free of her until my debt was paid in full, but I'd take my sweet ass time doing it.

Lisa never shipped a thing to me as she'd promised. I knew her offer was too good to be true. She dangled a prize in front of my eyes, and like a fool, I reached for it and gave her the cash she asked for. I could've easily filled my closet with five hundred dollars in clothing, but I wanted my things - lesson learned - I always seemed to learn the hard way. Lisa was out of my life, and I could move on. The ladies of New Orleans needed me, wanted me, and I was in the mood to share.

Kayden: The Past

Chapter 17

Parade of Pussy ~ Carrie, April, and who's that brunette?

I partied my ass off feeling more alive than I had in years. I felt a weight had been lifted off my shoulders when Lisa left my life and boarded the plane that day. Life returned to my new normal. Carrie and I met only once a month after the holidays. She needed to study and make sure she graduated on time. She kept her promise and never fell in love with me or became clingy. She was a lady of her word, and for that, I respected her.

Women moved in and out of my life at a fast pace. With Carrie busy and my cock as hard as ever, I added to my list of conquests. I met April at a bar around the corner from my apartment. She was a regular, and we'd strike up a conversation when I ran into her. We flirted and ended up at her apartment one night. I put April on the sex rotation with Carrie, they both hand standing appointments, to help relieve the ache I felt.

I had two lovely and willing ladies to fill my evenings, filled my room with new furniture that was mine and not borrowed from the company, and bought myself a new flat-screen television and blu-ray player. I upgraded my tablet, getting rid of the out dated ultra-slow model I'd purchased from the company when I arrived.

I wanted to see my family and go back to Ohio for a visit. I hadn't had a day off since Lisa walked out of my life. Summer was fast approaching, and Ohio was beautiful in the spring. I made plans to meet up with some friends from high school on my way home. I had a convenient overnight layover on the east coast to catch up with an old friend before finally arriving in Cleveland.

I ended up fucking a friend of my friend during that 'lay' over. I can't remember her name, but I remember the look on her face when I didn't want her number. I wasn't looking for a relationship, and we wouldn't be a 'thing' after the one night of alcohol infused passion; I made that perfectly clear. I always did, but I guess sometimes women thought that after a taste of their magical pussy, I'd change my mind. It didn't happen. Pussy was plentiful, and I wouldn't settle for anything but freedom and options.

I happily departed the Carolinas and boarded the plane headed to my hometown. I had a grandmother and aunts and uncles to visit during the day and friends to fill the nights during my short trip. I sat at my Aunt Sarah's kitchen table, sipping some coffee and scrolled through my newsfeed.

Today was Freddie's birthday. I hadn't seen him in years; high school friends seemed to drift apart as we scattered across the country. I tapped his name to wish him a happy birthday. His page was like opening a yearbook but with photos of people who had grown older and changed through the years. Time's a motherfucker on the body.

A photo of a beautiful brunette caught my attention. She stood near the ocean with her hair

Kayden: The Past

blowing in the wind and her eyes covered with sunglasses. She made my cock twitch in my pants, who was she? The last name was familiar, the same last name as Kyle. I hadn't seen him since that night at the bar long ago when he gave us coke to party the night away. I wondered if they were related; they had to be. I wanted to know how he knew her, but I didn't. I pushed the add friend button and thought I'd talk to her someday to find out how I'd never met her before.

I posted my wishes to Freddie and shut down my tablet for the day. I had a busy schedule, and my aunt was dying to show me the Rock N' Roll Hall of Fame. I hadn't visited there when I lived in Cleveland, and my aunt felt the need to be a tour guide. Sometimes family members forget you lived there and knew the city; she wanted to show me how the city had changed and evolved while I continued my life elsewhere. I had an evening flight to catch and thought it was a great way to end my trip.

Cleveland was barren compared to New Orleans. Traffic didn't fill the streets. No one sat at the café tables outside the restaurants, and the Hall of Fame had only a trickle of people moving throughout the space. The city I'd once loved was now a shell of its former self and not the home I once loved.

I sat at the airport thankful to be heading back to a city as alive as New Orleans. I'd fallen in love with her in the last eight months. A love that didn't make me miserable or cause me stress, but one that embraced me with open arms and a good time. I said goodbye to Cleveland as I stepped into the tiny metal tube that would carry me back home to NOLA.

The flight was bumpy and uncomfortable. I hate flying and always have. There's nothing pleasurable about it, but it was a necessity that's unavoidable in life. I crawled in bed and stretched out, flipped on my television and turned on my tablet. Sophia DeLuca had accepted my friend request, and I had a message waiting. I clicked the messages, and Sophia's face filled my screen and a smile danced across my lips.

Sophia: Do I know you?

The statement was simple. Maybe she was a careful girl. I could be vague in my answer, maybe flirt a little.

Me: Not yet.

My statement could've scared her off, but it was too tempting not to type it in the little box. I quickly messaged her to let her know how I found her, not wanting to risk being blocked. She didn't block me, but it took her a minute to respond. Maybe she was thinking about blocking me, but I knew once she started talking about Freddie and the people we had in common, I had her.

We chatted online for hours, the conversation easy with her. She seemed like a genuine person and made it very clear that she didn't walk the same path as her brother, Kyle. She went to school and became educated unlike me or her brother.

She told me her life had been navy blue. The statement confused the fuck out of me. What the fuck did a color have to do with her life? I thought about the statement, and if I had to choose a color to describe my life, I couldn't pick just one. My life resembled a tie dyed shirt with various colors and shades mingled together in a massive heap twisted together.

Sophia intrigued me, drew me in with her words, and I looked forward to talking with her. Did I want to fuck her? More than anything in the world. As the days and weeks flew by, I wanted her more and more. She was a good girl, but I knew if I peeled back the layers, there was a girl dying for some fun

Kayden: The Past

underneath. She needed color in her life, and I could give that to her.

I stopped seeing Carrie and April, not wanting to miss a night talking to Sophia. She made me laugh every day. She found a way of putting everything in perspective and found a way to make me laugh when I became the most frustrated. I shared everything with her during the day; I sent her photos of the places I traveled to, told her about the people I met, and wanted to know everything she did in her day. I became obsessed and transfixed with her.

I had feelings for her, and I'd never even touched her. I didn't understand how that was even possible, but it happened. I felt connected with her. The idea of being with an independent woman who had an education was beyond sexy. I pictured her in her librarian work clothes, hair tied up, and glasses. I wanted her to be my naughty librarian.

I spent more weeks trying to get her to New Orleans than I had ever spent on any woman in my life. Women had always been easy for me to lure to my bed, but Sophia fought hard to resist me. I eventually wore her down; her need for fun and excitement outweighed her cautiousness.

"I told my brother that I'm coming to see you," she said.

"What did he say?"

"He said he had a call to make and immediately hung up on me." My heart stopped. Kyle must not remember me or maybe he wanted to see where life had taken me after all these years.

"Think he's calling some of my friends?" I closed my eyes and started silently praying that nothing would turn up; I wanted the approval.

"No doubt—knowing my brother, he's looking for any red flags."

Thankfully, he found nothing, or my friends didn't feel the need to share my past. Sophia had told me that Kyle was super protective of her, but I wasn't looking to use or hurt her. I wanted to spend time with her and see if the connection I felt with her on the phone and online were real.

Sophia is everything she portrayed herself to be. She's a genuinely nice person who is beautiful and quirky. I can't describe every way she's different than any woman I've come in to contact with, but she is. She's my soul mate who I had to walk through hell to find. Sophia's my kismet, the one worth everything I went through to be with in the end.

I often wonder how different my life would have been if I met her instead of Danielle. Bridget was inevitable, and Sophia was too young at the time to get more than a glance from me. What if she'd been with her brother that night in the bar and caught my eye? Would I have escaped the heartache of the loss of a child and the betrayal by my wife? I would've never been arrested and may not have the drinking issues that I still battle with on a daily basis.

Life's full of what ifs, but none more than the Sophia question. I felt like I wasted years of my life without her by my side. The other women were meaningless and unimportant, although they helped me to realize what true love is and should be, and with Sophia, I found it and held on tight.

She saved me from myself and my life of misery. She showed me what true love is and stuck with me through everything: job loss, drunken nights, and despair. She believed in me when I didn't believe in myself.

I often wonder why in the fuck she did, but then I remind myself that I would've for her. When you truly love someone, you stand by their side and help them through the darkest time in their life. I'm thankful that she's a special person and has the patience of a saint. She was meant to come into my life when she did; she saved me, and I'll be forever indebted to her. I live my life for her and to be the man she deserves.

I'll never forget the day she said to me-

"Kayden, I love you for everything you are now, not for what you were. I want to know all of you, what made you into the man you are today, the man who has consumed my every thought and captured my soul."

It changed my life and altered my path forever. I'd seek help and get counseling, never wanting to abandon her again or break her heart.

Chapter 18
The Sister I wish I had ~ Suzy

Sophia did save me, but Suzy had a major impact on my life and holding on to Sophia. Suzy helped rescue me that day long ago when I hit rock bottom and got lost in the bottom of a bottle. Suzy was Sophia's roommate and welcomed me in her home when I had no where else to go.

The girls lived together to help save money and neither one of them wanted to be alone. Suzy told Sophia to bring me home with her that day. Not many people would open their home and heart to someone the way Suzy did for me. We knew each other but hadn't spent tons of time together, but from the first day, she made me feel like I belonged there. She's one of the most genuine and caring people I know. She's pure and naïve and wants to find love more than anything in this world.

Kayden: The Past

She never had that great love and dated a few guys who never treated her right. She was always filled with questions. She wanted to know about my marriage and why it fell apart. She asked how my love for my wife was different than my love for Sophia. Suzy had a million questions. She talked a lot. I was used to living with men, and they have so little to say, but Suzy just rattled on for hours if I let her.

When I found out I wouldn't be getting my job back, Suzy asked me to stay. She liked having a guy in the house; I think she just liked that I could fix shit. I mowed the lawn, fixed the faucets, cleaned the house, and cooked dinners. We were like a fucked up dysfunctional family, the three of us.

I felt protective of Suzy – she was like a sister to me. She always wanted to believe that people were good; she never thought they were capable of bad things. I took it upon myself to explain to her that men are assholes. We're looking to get laid. I knew I'd have to keep an eye on her and keep her safe from shitheads like I used to be. I'd vet her dates and make sure they treated her right.

Suzy cried when we moved out. I love her for that, but I didn't shed a tear. I wanted to make a home with Sophia. We lived in a bedroom – it was a love nest. I was overjoyed the day we packed everything and got the keys to our new apartment. Suzy had tears streaming down her face as she carried boxes to Sophia's SUV. We were only moving a couple miles away, but to Suzy, it felt farther. She felt like we were abandoning her. We weren't. She gave us the chance to be together – to make it through the hard times.

Without Suzy opening her home to me, I don't know where I'd honestly be. I don't think I would have crawled out of my pit of despair. Sophia would have left me most likely, and my addiction to alcohol would have ruined my only chance at happiness. Suzy has just as much to do with my sobriety as Sophia.

She's the little sister I always wish I had – one who loved me.

Chapter 19

I Held My Breath ~ Sophia

It seems like yesterday when Sophia said, "I'm pregnant." My heart skipped a beat before pounding feverishly in my chest with the realization that I'd be a father. Joy doesn't even begin to describe how I felt, but a sense of panic consumed me when I thought about the child I'd lost years ago.

I was almost paralyzed by fear for months. I waited for a call telling me that I'd live the nightmare again. I doted on Sophia, not wanting to risk the health of our baby.

"Kayden, really, I'm more than capable of washing dishes and cleaning. I'm pregnant not dying." She sat in the chair and stared at me like a child with her arms crossed. She rested her arms on her giant belly, and the sight of her and my child growing inside brought me the most joy I've ever experienced in my life. "I'm due any day now, sweetheart. The baby can come out and survive. Stop stressing out."

"Sophia, just sit and relax. Kick your feet up, babe. You have a baby to take care of, and I want her safe." I sprayed the counters and started to scrub the surface. "Who's the boss?"

"So sure it's a girl, huh? And the answer to your second question, Tony Danza."

God, she was such a nerd at times, and I loved her for it. "Goofball with the throwback. I can feel it, baby doll. She'll be as beautiful as her momma, too. Big brown eyes with a thick head of hair. I can't wait to hold her in my arms." I could be a hard ass at times, but I'm a mush on the inside. Sophia is really the only person I've ever let see that side of me. I'd never been vulnerable in front of anyone, but with her, I knew I could be myself.

"Well, I deal with enough girls at work all day at the school library, trust me… we want a boy." She leaned back and rested her head and began to scratch her stomach. "Who knew I'd be so fucking miserable with this alien growing inside me and fat as fuck, too."

"You're beautiful, Sophia."

"Ohhh, mmm," she moaned.

"You're making my cock hard over here, Sophia. Stop with all the noises." I stopped and watched her. She almost looked like she did when I made her come.

"I can't help it. My skin is so damn itchy. It's almost orgasmic." Her eyes rolled back in her head, and I stood there unable to move. It was erotic to watch although she didn't mean it to be; I'd been so horny lately but too scared to fuck her and risk hurting the baby.

"Stop, you're fucking killing me," I said.

Kayden: The Past

"Why don't you make me?" She continued rubbing her belly and making sounds that made my cock twitch.

I started walking towards her with the intent to give her other reasons to moan when she shot straight up and screamed, "Fuck."

"What?" I yelled and rushed to her side.

"Contraction..." her breathing stopped.

"Remember Lamaze, Sophia. Breathe, don't hold it in." What the fuck did I know? I listened to every word they said in that class and read every book I could find on pregnancy, but I didn't have a human clawing its way out of my body.

"Fuck Lamaze, Kayden." Well at least she had to take a breath to put me in my place. "Should we go to the hospital now or wait?"

"I'm not waiting, fuck, I'm not taking a chance with you or my little girl. I'll grab the stuff. You wait here," I said as I hopped up and headed toward the bedroom.

I could hear her say, "Where the fuck would I go?" I could see this wasn't going to be an easy process. Sophia rarely had crabby days, but this was going to be a whopper.

"Come on, baby doll. I have everything." I helped her to her feet, locked up the house and headed to the hospital for the birth of our child.

"One more push, Sophia," the doctor between her legs said.

"I can't. I'm too tired."

"Come on, baby. We're so close. You're the strongest woman I know." I patted her forehead with a damp cool cloth.

"It hurts too much, Kayden." Her head tossed back and forth.

"You can do it." The doctor patted her legs. "Now, Sophia."

She squeezed my hand so tightly I thought she'd break my fingers. I didn't say anything though; I'm not stupid. She pushed, and I held her back with my thankfully free hand, helping to hold her up while she gave everything she had.

"Excellent, a little more." She crunched her body up, and the doctor started to move back. I held my breath as the baby came into view. "It's a boy."

Sophia began to cry, and I stood there in awe. She'd given me a boy, delivered him safely to me, and we were forever part of another human being. We'd be together forever somewhere on this planet passed along to the generations. "It's a boy. I knew it would be," Sophia said.

I couldn't stop the flood of tears as I looked at our baby. To create a life is the most amazing thing in the world. To watch the woman you love bring that life into the world is indescribable. I cried the day our baby was born – my heart finally felt complete; I was whole again.

"You were right, Sophia. I couldn't be any happier than I am right now." I watched as they carried our baby boy over to a small table and started checking him and cleaning off his tiny body. His screams filled the air, and I stood there and didn't move. I almost held my breath and was scared to blink, thinking the sight in front of my eyes would vanish and be a dream.

Kayden: The Past

"Hey," Sophia said as she squeezed my hand. I looked at her and smiled. "He'll be okay; it's normal he's crying. Don't worry, love."

I leaned over and placed a kiss on her lips, "You've given me everything I've ever wanted, Sophia. You're the world to me, and my life's complete. A boy, Sophia, a boy," I said in amazement.

"I love you, Kayden." She stared in my eyes as I backed away from her lips. "We need to pick a name."

"I didn't spend too much time on boy names. I was sure as shit the baby was going to be a girl," I said.

"Well I like Jett or Tristan," she said.

"Tristan brings too many images of Brad Pitt on a horse; Jett sounds badass. I like it." I kissed her forehead and watched as the doctor approached with a calmer baby in his arms.

"Who'd like to hold him first?" the doctor asked.

"Go ahead, Kayden," Sophia said as she pushed my arm away from her.

"You sure?" I asked.

"Yes."

I didn't ask her again. I held out my arms as the doctor placed Jett in my arms. Relief flooded my body as I stared at the small baby with pure white skin and dark brown hair. He had a head of hair like his Mom, but his eyes were closed. I touched his hand, and his fingers moved. I held them between my fingers and couldn't believe how tiny he was. I sat down next to Sophia with him in my arms.

"I love you, baby boy. I've waited a lifetime to meet you."

I thought my life changed forever when Sophia pulled into my apartment parking lot, but I was wrong, as usual.

Jett turned everything right-side up. Sophia had given me the greatest gift and brought joy into my life. I'd do anything for her. She asked me months before his birth to see a counselor, and I agreed.

I'd stopped drinking long before her pregnancy, not wanting to risk losing Sophia. No drink in the world was worth that risk; she deserved better than that. Counseling helped me identify my triggers – women and trust issues stemming from my father. Writing out my life story helped the counselor and I to reflect on the journey that's my life. It was all a choice – I chose to drink, do drugs, and wallow in my own self-pity. I wanted my life back.

Sophia gave it back to me and showed me the light. She made me find my way back to my true self, the one I always portrayed on the outside, but didn't believe I was during the dark times in my life.

I've been sober for well over a year. Does liquor call my name still? Yes... it's an addiction for a reason, but I fight every urge that comes my way. I don't crave a drink because things are fucked up in my life, but because my body craves it, but I don't need it. Liquor can fuck off and go ruin someone else's life. For once, I'm content and happy with Sophia and Jett in my future.

Epilogue

Dearest Kayden,

 I read your journal as you wrote each word and followed you on your journey of self-exploration. Let me begin by simply saying I love you. I love you more today than I did yesterday. I never knew I could love another human being as much as I do you. I didn't think it was possible for love to grow over time, but it has, and my heart is full.

 I'm sorry I invaded your privacy and read beyond what you told me yourself. I knew you filtered your story thinking I wouldn't be able to deal with the whole truth, but I'm a big girl and can absorb it all and still accept you for the man you are today. You've led a full life filled with heartache, addiction, and let's not forget the sex. I skipped over most of those stories in your journal.

 I'll never leave you. I'm yours entirely and forever. I still love you for the man you were, are and will be. You've evolved during our time together, and you're always surprising me and filling my days with the great unknown. You've wiped the navy blue out of my world. Each day, I'm greeted by a world filled with a kaleidoscope of colors.

You love me like no one else ever has and never will. You're it for me, the one I searched a lifetime for and finally found. We may have found each other later in life, and you may have suffered because of it, but it's molded you into the man I love. I know you question how life would've been different if we met earlier, but you can't look at it that way. I was a mousy school girl who had her nose stuck in a book... you would have scared the crap out of me. I would have been another notch on your bedpost and forgotten. We were meant to find each other when we did. I'm sorry you've walked such a tortured path at times, but I'm here to dust you off when needed and hold your hand along the way.

You're mine always, and I'm yours forever. Jett is ours, a little piece of us will always roam this earth, and we'll never be forgotten. I can never express my sorrow for the loss of your child so many years ago. I pray he is watching over Jett and keeping him safe from harm.

Thank you for loving me enough to overcome your addictions and to keep fighting the battle each day.

I only feel at home when I'm lying in your arms. I feel safe by your side and never question my worth. I feel beautiful when you look at me and know that I'm loved each day when I kiss you goodbye.

Love always and yours forever,
Sophia

P.S. I read how you ruined Danielle after she left, bad boy. That alone will make me stay and never walk away. Oh, you were a man whore; I knew I was right about you.

Throttle Me Sneak Peek
Love at Last #2
Coming 2014

Chapter 1 - The Darkness
Suzy's Story

The road was dark as I drove down the desolate street. The moonlight illuminated the empty grassy fields and trees dotted the roadway. My steering wheel began to shake, and the car started making a hideous noise.

"Damn it," I said, hitting the steering wheel with my palm. My piece of shit car had been acting weird for the last couple of weeks, but I didn't have the money to get it checked.

I pulled off the road, turning on my hazards, as the car sputtered before dying. I shook my head thinking about the bad luck that seemed to be following me for weeks. I exhaled loudly, flexing my grip on the steering wheel, trying to calm my frazzled nerves. Times like this made me regret living in the country, far from my family and most of my friends.

It was late, but I knew I could call Sophia. Kayden treated us to dinner and drinks tonight; it had been over a month since Sophia had met me for drinks. He wanted to give Sophia a girl's night out and wanted their little boy, Jett, all to himself. Sophia lived close to the martini lounge we spent the evening at, but maybe I could catch her or Kayden awake and willing to help me out.

I grabbed my cell phone off of the passenger seat and flipped it open. "Shit." The battery was dead, and the screen wouldn't even power on. I looked in my rearview mirror to see if anyone was coming in my direction, but nothing except darkness filled my view. My heart began to pound in my chest as scenes from every horror movie I've ever seen with a lonely woman broken down on the side of the road being murdered in a gruesome manner filled my mind.

I closed my eyes concentrating on my breathing, trying to think of what to do now. *Do I start walking to God knows where? Should I just sit here and wait for a stranger to offer me help?* I didn't like any of those options. I never liked feeling helpless; I was too smart to be helpless, but that was the only thing I felt in this moment. I couldn't just sit here and wait. It could be hours before someone found me in my car on this isolated road. Why did I always feel the need to avoid main roads, looking for a short cut to find my way home?

I climbed out of my car and closed the door locking it up tight. I don't know why I felt the need to make sure it was locked; no one was out here wandering around, let alone looking to steal my stuff. I leaned against my car thinking about which direction I'd walk. Neither of my options were ideal or close, and I was exhausted from working all day. Thank God I could sleep in tomorrow after the way this evening was ending. I remembered seeing a gas station a couple miles back, and I felt that would be my safest bet. I didn't know what was in the other direction besides my home, but that was over twenty miles away. I pressed the lock button one more time on my key chain, helping relieve my OCD need to double check everything before pushing my body from the car.

I only walked about five steps when a light came over a small hill in the distance and almost blinded me. The roar of the engine, growing louder as the distance closed, tipped me off that a motorcycle approached. I waved my arms as a figure came into view, but the biker drove right passed me as I screamed "Hey! Hey!" and waved my arms.

I turned around still screaming toward the bike, but I knew it was futile. There was no way in hell he'd heard me yelling above the roar of his engine. The red of his break lights lit up the road as he slowed and turned the bike around. He was coming straight at me. I swallowed hard unsure if this was my best idea of the night. I've already made too many mistakes to dwell. He was my only hope to getting home and crawling in my bed.

I stood on the side of the road like a deer in headlights, unable to move. My hands began to shake, and my breathing grew shallow as the figure on the bike came to a stop in front of me. The bike was loud, almost deafening, and covered in black and chrome. The man wore black boots, jeans, and a leather jacket. By the time my eyes reached his face, he'd removed the helmet. His hair was black and short on the sides and a bit longer on top. He ran his fingers through his hair, freeing it from the smashed down state caused by his helmet. He had on riding glasses with yellow lenses. I assumed to stop the onslaught of bugs from blurring his vision. His face was only visible in shadows caused by the moonlight.

"Need some help, lady?" he asked.

I swallowed hard, unsure of how to respond. He looked more dangerous than anything that could be lurking in the woods. "Do you have a cell phone I could use to call for a ride?" I asked.

"Sure," he said leaning back on his bike. I studied his body as he reclined digging in his pocket to retrieve the phone. His jeans were tight, and his muscles showed through the denim fabric. He held out the phone to me, but I was too busy staring at him to notice. "Lady, you wanted my phone."

I snapped back into reality with the sound of his deep voice. "Oh, sorry." My fingertips grazed his palm as I grabbed the phone. A tiny shock passed between us, his finger closing on my hands as I pulled away.

I stepped back a couple of feet and dialed the only person close enough to give me a ride home. The phone rang, but I never took my eyes off the stranger unsure of his intentions. With each ring, my stomach began to turn over. I didn't have anyone else to call. "There's no answer, thanks," I said.

"Let me take a look and see if there's anything else I can do. Is that okay?" he asked.

I didn't have any other choice at the moment. I could turn him down and sit here for possibly hours. "Sure," I replied as I hit unlock on my car key. I walked toward my car but kept an eye on the stranger. *No one will hear me scream if he tries to kill me.* I couldn't let my guard down.

He moved the bike, angling the headlights to shine on the hood of my car. I pulled the hood lever and watched him climb off his bike. He was large, more than a foot taller than me, and I caught my first full glimpse of his body. He removed his leather jacket to reveal a black t-shirt clinging to the muscles of his torso. I swallowed hard, staring at him like a piece of meat, momentarily forgetting he could be a murderer. Everything clung to this man, his t-shirt and jeans, I wanted to follow their lead and join in the party.

Kayden: The Past

I hadn't had sex in so long. Every man I'd met wasn't for me. They were nice guys, but they didn't have that spark I was searching for. People think I'm a good girl, and I am, but my mind is filled with dirty thoughts that I could never share with another soul. Well, maybe not a soul, I've shared them with Sophia, but she doesn't count. I've never shared a fantasy with a man, and no one had ever done anything fantasy worthy with me. I can barely speak the words that you'd need to use to describe the things I want done to me or that I'd want to do to another person in this world.

"Ma'am," he said, snapping me out of the evaluation of my sex life or lack thereof.

"Sorry, yes?" I asked.

"Can you try and start it for me, please," he replied.

I climbed in the car and watched him through the tiny gap between the hood and the car. "Now," he said, and I turned the key. The car churned and churned. "Stop," he said over the screeching noise. I turned the key and watched him. He moved methodically throughout the engine of the car. "Try it again." I turned the key and still nothing. I turned the key to the off position and watched him as he stood up. The only thing I could see was his crotch area. I didn't move, just stared. His t-shirt covered the belt loops and stopped just above the most vital area. He filled his jeans beautifully.

The last guy who I'd slept with was more the size of a party pickle. It was the most unsatisfying sexual experience of my life. He was a lawyer, and I wanted someone who was educated and self-sufficient. I thought I'd found that with Sam, but I was wrong. He was a wreck, filled with more mental issues than anyone I'd ever known. He was germ-a-phobic, which was problematic when having sex. He'd jump right out of bed immediately after sex to shower and wash the dirty off. I sighed to myself remembering his need to be clean.

The hood of my car made a loud thump. "Your car is a little tricky. Foreign cars can be complicated. I can't seem to get it to start," he said.

"It's okay. Thanks for trying," I said as I climbed out of the car, leaving the door open in my wake. *What the heck am I going to do now?* I looked at his face; he was smiling at me, not moving to leave.

"I was heading to the bar up the road. Want to join me? You can call a tow truck from there. It may take them a while to get out here."

I stood there, thinking about what I should do. I could wait out here and face uncertainty, or I could go with this sexy man for a drink while I waited for a tow. If he wanted to kill me, he could have already done it without anyone knowing. He didn't need to lure me away from my car to slash my throat. "Okay, but I've never been on a bike," I said looking him up and down, my mouth going dry at the thought of wrapping my arms around his muscular body.

"Never? How is that possible?" he asked with a look of disbelief on his face.

I looked down at the ground a little embarrassed by my inexperience. "I don't know. Never knew anyone who owned one, really, and I find them totally scary."

"It's not far from here, and there isn't much traffic. I'll keep you safe," he said, holding out his helmet to me. I stood there, my stomach fluttering, before closing the door behind me. I grabbed the helmet from his hand and stared at it. It was plain black with no sides, and I didn't know if there was a front or a back.

Kayden: The Past

"Here, let me help you," he said. I placed the helmet in his open hands. He set it gently on my head. He ran his fingers down the strap to adjust it to fit my face. I inhaled deeply; he smelled different than any other man I'd smelled before. He had a slightly sweet scent with a hint of spice, almost like licorice. His fingertips brushed my skin as he tightened the strap against my chin. I closed my eyes relishing the feel of his warm skin against mine, lost in the moment. "All done, are you ready?" he asked.

I opened my eyes quickly. I could feel my face turning red, praying my voice wouldn't betray me as I spoke, "Yes."

I watched him as he climbed on the bike, sliding forward making room for me behind him. "Lift your leg and climb on," he said. I followed his directions and climbed on the bike; I placed my hand on his shoulder to help balance myself. As I sat on the seat, my body slid forward, smashing against him. "Put your feet up on the pegs and wrap your arms around me." I lifted my feet off the ground, turning over complete control to the stranger I was entrusting with my life. I locked my hands together completely wrapped around him. "Ready?" he asked.

I swallowed hard and closed my eyes. "Wait. I don't even know your name?"

I could feel his body moving up and down slightly but couldn't hear the laugh I knew he was enjoying. "My friends call me City, doll," he said as he started the bike, making my heart almost stop out of fear.

My grip became almost vice like, fear overcoming any need to be cool or seem calm in front of him. He patted my hand, reassuring me that we'd survive this trip and that I was safe with him. The bike began to move slowly, but I couldn't look. I buried my face in his back, avoiding any chance of seeing the road. The wind caressed my skin, causing my exposed skin to feel like ice compared to the warmth my palms experienced from his body heat.

I'd never been so close to someone for an extended period of time like this without them being a boyfriend. The bike picked up speed, and my heart thundered in my chest. He had to feel it beating against his back as I gripped him harder, holding on for dear life. The sound of the engine drowned out everything else around me, including the wind. He leaned forward and into the bike, his ass moving backwards and more snuggly between my legs. I didn't dare move. He was warm, comfortable, and I enjoyed every minute my body touched his. I closed my eyes and tried not to think about the movement of the bike underneath us.

The noise of the engine changed as the bike slowed. I peeked to see why he was slowing down and realized we were pulling into a small little bar, The Neon Cowboy. I'd driven by it dozens of times but never thought about stopping. The parking lot was filled with all types and colors of Harleys. This wasn't the type of bar for kids on speedy foreign-made bikes, but a place where tough bikers hung out, drank beer, and picked up chicks.

"You can climb off, now. Enjoy your first ride?" City asked.

"It was the single most terrifying thing I've ever experienced," I said, thankful when my feet were firmly on the ground. I stood there trying to get my body to stop shaking and my heart to slow down.

"Good thing I took it slow with you." He grinned, and my stomach plummeted from his sinful smile. I could see him clearly for the first time by the lights dotting the parking lot. His hair was darker than I originally thought, almost jet black, and an inch long on

Kayden: The Past

the top with the back trimmed short. It was a mess from the wind with the front hanging over his forehead. I couldn't tell the color of his eyes; they were still hidden behind the riding glasses. He didn't look dangerous without the shadows, at least not to my life.

Coming Spring 2014

About The Author

I'm an avid reader: consuming contemporary romance, dark reads, young adult, and all things erotica. I want to create books filled with characters who readers can relate to dealing with real world problems and matching wallets.

I love to travel, and my two favorite cities are New Orleans and Paris. I currently live in Florida with my amazing boyfriend and two kittens, Nola and Peanut.

Untangle Me is the first book in the Love at Last series and Throttle Me will follow Kayden: The Past .5 sometime during 2014.

Stalk Me Here:

Chelle Bliss Newsletter Sign-Up: eepurl.com/K37db

Pinterest: www.pinterest.com/chellebliss10/boards/

Facebook: www.facebook.com/authorchellebliss1

Twitter: twitter.com/ChelleBliss1

Blog: authorchellebliss.com

Kayden: The Past

Turn to the next page to read the Prologue to
Untangle Me
(Available on Amazon, Barnes & Noble, and Smashwords)

Untangle Me

PROLOGUE

Sophia

My heart hammered against my chest so strong, I thought it would explode. I clutched the steering wheel and concentrated on navigating through the streets of New Orleans.

"Stay right in a half mile, Interstate 610 west. Take exit one, West Napoleon Avenue and turn right. Your destination is one mile ahead on the right," the GPS stated.

One mile?

Butterflies filled my stomach, sweat beaded on my face. I increased the air conditioning trying to cool myself off.

Get it together.

"Are you okay?" he asked.

"I'm just trying to figure out where I'm going. There are so many buildings." I looked around trying to see an address amongst the numerous apartment complexes.

"I'll guide you," he said in a calming voice as I looked for him amongst the throng of cars.

"Do you see my car?"

"You just passed up my building. Do a U-turn and turn by the black gate."

"Shit." Sweat trickled down my temple.

I stopped the car in the middle turning lane and wiped the sweat from my face. I studied my face in the rearview mirror. It was shiny but otherwise looked unfazed by the long drive.

"I'm coming now." I blotted my face with a napkin left on the passenger seat and applied powder to smooth my complexion. I sat for a moment and took a deep breathe.

Calm down. He's just a guy. I gripped the wheel and turned back towards him, the man I had thought about constantly for weeks.

"I see you," he said. I looked around quickly, trying to catch a glimpse of him. My eyes stopped dead when I spotted a gorgeous man sitting in a truck with the door open. He was smiling at me, and my heart skipped a beat. I had seen him in pictures, but they didn't do him justice.

"I see you now, too. Be there in a second." I hit the end button.

Yes, he's beautiful, but you're not a hag; he'll like you. He's told you a million times how beautiful you are. You can do this. Calm the fuck down.

I tapped the steering wheel with my index finger as the gate opened painfully slow. I stole a glimpse in his direction. He stood near an empty parking spot, waiting for me. I studied him as I drove towards the parking spot. His body was muscular and lean covered in a pair of white knee length shorts and a blue t-shirt. The only visible hair on his body at a distance was a goatee that framed his smile. As the space between us closed, I could see his sage eyes dancing in the sunlight.

His smile had been a mystery to me. He didn't like to show his teeth because of a gap that was never fixed. It finally filled my vision, and it mesmerized me. The display made my heart melt; his teeth were imperfectly beautiful.

He motioned to the open spot. I parked my car in a haphazard fashion and turned it off. My heart rate increased, and I felt an ache in my chest. I clenched my hands into a ball and closed my eyes before reaching for the handle.

I slowly climbed out, leaving the door open, and stood in front of him.

"Hi," he said in a longing voice as he reached for me. Before I could respond, he embraced me. His heart was pounding as rapid as mine, and our heartbeats were responding to one another.

Thank god I'm not the only one nervous.

I inhaled deep with my face buried in his neck. A sweet masculine scent filled my nostrils as I closed my eyes. His scent was like none I had smelled before. He was free of cologne, and the scent was purely unique, him.

His body withdrew from mine; my eyes remained closed. Soft moist lips glided across mine. His kiss turned more demanding as he sucked my lip into his mouth. I moaned as a tingle moved down my spine. The passion was palpable. I opened my lips, and his tongue swept inside, exploring, as the taste of mint

Kayden: The Past

saturated my tongue. He gripped the back of my neck, tilting my head up to give him deeper access. The kiss conveyed all the longing and passion we felt towards each other. My heartbeat slowed, and my legs felt like jelly.

Have I ever been kissed like this? His lips pulled away from mine, and I swayed a bit.

"Let's go inside," he said as he steadied my frame, "We'll get your stuff later."

He closed my door, snagged the keys from my grip, and locked the car. He reached for my hand and enclosed it in his before squeezing lightly. My fate was sealed.

I followed slightly behind him taking in my surrounds. The apartment complex was shaped in a U with an open courtyard filled with palm trees, foliage, and paths leading to the apartments. The units were stacked three high and lined with wooden porches connecting the doorways. Birds sang in the trees as the sun shone, casting shadows upon the ground.

He turned the handle, and I immediately froze. Three men sat in the cozy apartment, but clearly, it was a male-only dwelling based on the interior. Sparse non-matching furniture filled the space. No decorations, only white blank walls. It was frat like in appearance. My belly began to dance, but I tried to walk confidently. One man was lying on the couch watching television, and two others were sitting at the dining room table using their laptops.

"Guys, this is Sophia. Sophia, these are the guys," he said as we walked through the living room without stopping.

"Hey," they said as three sets of eyes looked at me almost in unison. I felt their eyes peeling off my clothing piece by piece.

"Hey," I said as Kayden pulled me down the hallway to avert their stares.

His bedroom was filled with modern black furniture, a flat screen television, and a couple simple decorations. His bed was covered in red and black bedding. It was simple but matched unlike the living room.

I turned around to face him, and his lips were upon mine in a flash. He guided me backwards until the back of my knees hit the bed.

How far will I let him go? Oh Jesus, how far was he willing to take me?

My heart began to race, and my mind flooded with images of him naked. The only sound filling the room was our labored breaths and lips moving rapidly.

He laid me gently on the bed and crawled on top of me. Our hands moved across each other's bodies quickly. The man could kiss, and it was intoxicating. We had spent so much time talking, teasing, the sexual tension was suffocating.

I lost all will power with his kiss. His hands moved along my body, touching my breasts through my shirt and bra. I reached down, feeling his cock through his pants. He was large, very large—larger than any man who I had experience with.

Fuckin' hell. My mind raced, worried how I would be able to handle a man of his size.

I whispered to him, "You're going to kill me."

He chuckled a slow, sweet laugh against my lips. I wanted to feel his skin on mine. He began to trail kisses down my neck, causing my body to break out in goose bumps. He yanked my navy blue tank top down with my bra, exposing my breast. He grazed it with his finger and pleasure shot through my body. His mouth found my nipple, his appetite ravenous. I moaned from the tingle that flowed down my body to my core. His smooth hands slid up my thigh and into my shorts, pushing my panties aside. A solid bond formed between his lips and my nipple, pain mixed with pleasure when his finger entered me. I rubbed his head and scratched his arms, unsure of how to react.

His head dipped down, and my stomach sank.

Was I ready for this?

He didn't attempt to unbutton my shorts as he kissed my stomach down to the top of my shorts. He moved the cloth sideways; his mouth engulfed me, covering my delicate flesh. He licked and sucked like a starved man, and I freely offered myself up as a meal. Pure ecstasy. He stopped abruptly and moved back up my body, kissing me on my lips, deep and passionate.

"We need to go, Sophia." His body moved away from mine. "Are you ready to hit the town?" he asked me with a hint of mischief in his eyes.

"What?"

I'm so confused. One minute he was licking me in the most forbidden places, the passion was almost suffocating, and now he wanted to leave?

My head was spinning, and I shook it to try and clear my thoughts.

"We have to get out of here. If we don't, I won't be able to stop myself. Let's go downtown and enjoy the French Quarter." He climbed off the bed and watched me intently.

He's right, don't argue. "Okay," I said as I rearranged my clothing and pulled my underwear back into place.

He reached for my hand and helped me off the bed, sliding my palm down the cloth to smooth the wrinkles.

My thoughts were racing, but I was at a loss for words as we walked out of the bedroom. I kept my eyes towards the ground unable to look at his roommates, but I couldn't stop a smile from dancing across my lips.

Kayden opened the front door for me before grabbing his keys. He was half way out the door when we heard, "Damn, who knew he fucked like a teenage boy?"

Kayden closed the door, stopped, and placed his hand over his face. "I'm sorry, Sophia. They're so fucking immature."

"It's okay, Kayden. I know how boys can be. Let's just go."

"Come on, beautiful," he said kissing my cheek. "I can't wait to show you the beauty of New Orleans in person."

Made in the USA
Lexington, KY
02 August 2014